RAVENOUS

V. K. FORREST

KENSINGTON BOOKS
www.kensingtonbooks.com

KENSINGTON BOOKS are published by

Kensington Publishing Corp.
119 West 40th Street
New York, NY 10018

All Kensington titles, imprints, and distributed lines are available at special quantity discounts for bulk purchases for sales promotion, premiums, fund-raising, educational, or institutional use.

Special book excerpts or customized printings can also be created to fit specific needs. For details, write or phone the office of the Kensington Special Sales Manager: Kensington Publishing Corp., 119 West 40th Street, New York, NY 10018. Attn. Special Sales Department. Phone: 1-800-221-2647.

Kensington and the K logo Reg. U.S. Pat. & TM Off.

ISBN-13: 978-0-7582-5569-3
ISBN-10: 0-7582-5569-1

First Kensington Trade Paperback Printing: April 2011
10 9 8 7 6 5 4 3 2 1

Printed in the United States of America

RAVENOUS

Chapter 1

Liam smelled the perversity on their hands even before he flew over the wall into the courtyard of the *palais* in the *Marais* district of Paris. He knew what the Gaudet brothers were, what they had done, what they had gotten away with for two decades, but he had not expected such a stench.

Liam landed on the stone wall and gazed down into the courtyard, slowly flapping the wings of the raven he had become. Black, beady eyes focused on the iron bars in the windows he would have to slip through. Even among shape-shifters, Liam was an oddity. Not only could he shift from his human form to an animal form of his choice, but he could shift from one animal to another, as easily as a human shrugged off a coat.

Night after night, Liam relived the nightmare and it always began here: the stink of the Gaudet brothers' sins, the soft beat of his own wings, the reflection of pale moonlight on the old glass.

What happened next in the nightmare varied. Sometimes Liam felt his body rise and glide into the night air, wings spread. Sometimes he relived slipping easily through the bars in the window, a quiet gray mouse. But always the blood came. Always black and putrid, oozing from the stone walls. From their eyes. And the screams of the children. It was always the cries of the children that brought him out of a dead sleep.

Liam started, his eyes flying open as he gripped the thin sheet with stiff, cold fingers, his body bathed in perspiration. Darkness enveloped him; the sheet had become a death shroud and he threw it off. Had he screamed out loud again? Or was it just the screams of the tortured children in his head?

Trembling, he pushed up and off the narrow cot and stumbled, nude, to the bathroom. With a shaky hand, he pulled the string on the light overhead and the single, bare bulb threw pale, ugly light on the mirror. He leaned forward on the stained porcelain sink and gazed at his face: the face of a killer.

Yesterday at the local diner while he'd stood in line for his tuna on wheat, no pickle, he'd heard one of the old bats talking about him. They gossiped as if he wasn't there, standing behind them at the cash register. She said he'd been sent home to Clare Point in shame. She said that she'd heard the General Council was going to pull him off the Kill Team for good this time.

A cooling-off period. That's what he'd been told it was when they'd come for him in the dingy walk-up in Montmartre. Then they'd had the nerve to *escort* him all the way home to Clare Point, as if he would have disobeyed orders and gone into hiding if they hadn't. Which, of course, he would have.

Liam brushed his fingertips over the crucifix he wore around his neck, then spun the antique faucet handle and splashed cold water on his face. Then he washed his hands. As if he could ever wash the blood off....

He had disobeyed a direct order the night he had flown into the Gaudet courtyard. He'd broken multiple rules in the ancient book.

...Even before he had broken their bones.

Liam shut off the faucet and ran his hand through his dark hair, glancing into the mirror again. Black, heartless eyes looked back at him, the raven's eyes. He turned away. What if they really did pull him off the Kill Team? A hundred years, the penalty for his disobedience if it came down to punishment, was a hell of a long *cooling-off* period. What would he do then? He couldn't imagine living here in this silly little town with its silly little problems. Not after lifetimes of travel. Not after the things he had seen. The things he had done. He had the highest kill count of any man or woman in the sept; he was good at what he did and they knew it. The Council wouldn't really pull him off the Kill Team, would they?

The sweat on his body had dried and suddenly he was cold. Shivering, he went back to the small, bare room, pulled on a pair of sweatpants, a T-shirt, and a hoodie, then slipped on his running shoes. Just as the sun rose over the lip of the ocean, he burst into the cold morning air and ran, ran for his life, for his salvation. It never worked, of course, but you couldn't blame a vampire for trying.

After a five-mile run along the beach, Liam showered, ate a piece of cold pizza from a box on the counter, and went down to the antiques shop below his apartment. He'd been a *purveyor of antiquities* for more than two hundred years, although nowadays he was an *antiques dealer*. When he wasn't stalking serial killers and pedophiles. It was easy enough work, a good cover when he was forced to return home, and it allowed him to pay his bills and travel at his own expense rather than the sept's.

Liam bought things all over the world—some new, some already antiques—and shipped them home. He acquired items that struck his fancy: clocks, paintings, sculptures. He'd bought three Model T trucks in 1925 for $281 each.

He had sold the last one only the previous year for so much money that he was almost too embarrassed to accept the cashier's check. Almost.

He sold the items out of the little antiques shop when he was in town; otherwise, he advertised them and had someone in Clare Point make the actual sale. Internet sales were his latest venture. It had been three years since the last time Liam had been home, but he continually sent items back to the States so the place was stacked tall with shipping boxes, most never opened.

When Liam had returned to the *loving bosom* of the vampire nest, he'd been warned by the General Council leader that he'd be in Clare Point for at least a few weeks. He was to be interviewed and his case investigated. While imprisoned in the sleepy seaside town, he thought he might as well make use of his time and dig through some of the mess. He had a warehouse, too, but right now, he couldn't imagine even walking into it.

Thinking he'd start small, this morning he'd just picked a pile of boxes and begun to open them. They were pretty old boxes. Inside, he found all sorts of kitchen gadgets, which he organized on shelves along one wall of the shop. It was dusty, boring work, but he didn't mind; he liked the solitude. His reward for his diligence throughout the morning was the box he'd just opened. Inside was a brand, spanking new 1936 KitchenAid stand-up mixer. Still in its original packing. If memory served, he had three more somewhere.

Pleased with his find, Liam was searching for an electric outlet behind the impossibly piled-up counter when he heard the little bell over the front door ring. Surprised by the melodic sound, he turned. He must have left it unlocked when he returned from his run this morning. "We're closed," he called. "Read the sign."

"Sign says open." A gorgeous Asian woman turned the dusty sign around so that it now read OPEN on the back of the door.

Liam frowned. It must have flipped when he slammed the door. "I'm still closed," he told her, trying not to stare.

Liam didn't like HFs. *Human females.* Well, actually, he liked them a lot. Which was exactly why he stayed away from them. This one was stunning: late twenties, early thirties, tiny, with long, dark hair, brown eyes, and a rich skin tone. Her face was oval with sensual lips. Cherry ChapStick. He could smell it from here. He loved the taste of cherry ChapStick on a woman. She looked delicate. Fragile. But there was a fire in her eyes, fire and a definite hint of amusement.

"You know, I've been coming here for the last five years hoping to catch you open."

"Too bad you caught me closed again," Liam deadpanned. He stood where he was, not trusting himself to walk toward her. If he did, he might reach out to touch the silky black hair that had pulled loose from her ponytail and fell to frame her exquisite face. There was an equal chance he'd bite her in the neck. Then he'd have to erase her memory, deposit her on the curb, and hope no one saw him. He was already in enough trouble as it was. They were a messy business, humans, which was, again, why he stayed away from them.

"That a '36 KitchenAid? Wow." She walked toward him with little or no sense of self-preservation. Of course, she didn't know he was a vampire; they rarely did. "Brand new? You've got to be kidding me. You know, this was the first year they downsized them, making them practical for homes." She drew her small fingers over the white enamel and Liam found himself wondering what it would be like to feel her fingertips caress his bare skin.

She was pretending to look at the mixer, but he knew she was looking at him. He had that effect on women. All vampires did, on some level, even the old guys and gals. There was something about vampires that tragically drew humans to them, even though they never recognized them for what they were. Vampires accepted this age-old truth but never quite understood it.

He blinked, clearing his head. "You an expert on the history of the KitchenAid mixer?"

"Not an expert. But I love kitchen appliances. Kitchen gadgets, too: glass fruit reamers, oyster servers, ice cream knives. I sell antiques in a shop in Lewes." She looked at the electric plug he still held in his hand. "So, does it work?"

"I...I don't know."

"You going to plug it in and see?"

He was just about to give a smart-ass reply when a car horn beeped loudly out in the street. Through the filmy storefront window, he spotted a minivan. It honked again. Louder.

"That you?"

"That's me." She glanced at the window, then back at him. "Actually, it's not me. It's my dad. We're late for lunch."

"It's eleven-thirty."

"Senior citizen. What can I say?"

She opened her arms and he imagined the feel of them around him. He didn't know what was going on here. He wasn't usually like this. He was *never* like this. Not with an HF. But she kept looking at him and he couldn't keep himself from looking back.

Again the horn.

"I better go," she said.

He hesitated, then pushed the plug into the outlet and switched the mixer on. The motor purred.

She turned back to him, smiling. Her face lit up the room in a way that made his black heart ache.

"It works!"

"It works," he said, stifling his own enthusiasm. There was no need to be too nice. Nice got you in trouble.

She glanced around as she walked toward the door. "You *sure* you're closed? You have some amazing things here. Oh, my God! Is that a Neuchâtel clock Le Castel?"

"Where?" He followed her to the door, trying not to get too close to her. It was the smell of HFs that he loved. Not just their blood, but their skin, their hair, their sweet body scents; it was everything about them. The smell of their shampoo, their hand cream, even nail polish. Liam knew right then he should walk away. Play it safe. He wasn't good at safe.

"There!" She pointed to a pile of junk. "Inside that nasty birdcage."

He glanced in the direction she pointed. The place was so stacked up with crap, furniture covered in canvas drapes, wooden crates of mysterious stuff from far-off places, and cardboard boxes turned over, spilling their contents, that it took him a second to make out the outline of the clock behind the bars of a birdcage. "I think so."

"You *think* so?" She arched a dark eyebrow. "You know how much that's worth? You don't even have bars on your windows." She glanced at the dirty, old-fashioned storefront window. "No alarm system. You're lucky no one has robbed you blind."

"We don't see a lot of robberies in Clare Point." He opened the door for her and the bell rang over their heads, strangely melodic to his ears. The truth was, they had *no* robberies. The vampires of the Kahill sept owned all the property in the town and patrolled their own streets. The occasional burglar who tried to break into a house or store was escorted out of town by one of its citizens, and though his memory was erased, he never lost the feeling that something had scared the crap out of him in Clare Point. Scared him badly enough that he didn't return.

"I wish you were open," the woman said longingly, looking back over her shoulder one last time at the piles of treasures.

The old man in the front passenger seat of the van laid on the horn again.

"Enough, *Babbo!*" she shouted.

"You're *Italian?*" It was his turn to lift an eyebrow incredulously. She didn't *look* Italian.

"Sicilian and Vietnamese. I look like my mom. You speak Italian?"

"A little," Liam answered.

Again the old man blew the car horn. And against all reason, Liam found himself being drawn in to their sweet, mortal humanity and actually chuckling. Even more surprising, he heard himself say, "Maybe another day. When things aren't such a mess. I just got back into the country."

"I don't mind coming another time. When you're open." She studied his face. "But you're not planning on opening, are you? You're just blowing me off."

"No. I'm not." And he meant it.

"So how about if I give you a few days and then I call you? You got a business card?"

"Somewhere in this mess, probably." He looked around, then back at her.

"How about just a number?" She pulled a pen out of the bag slung over her shoulder and dug deeper. "Why can I never find a piece of—"

Her father hit the horn, long and hard, drowning out her voice. "I'm going to kill him," she said when Liam could hear her again. "But I guess that's illegal in this state."

"Most states," he suggested.

She poised the pen over her hand. "Give me your number and I'll get that public nuisance off the street."

He gave her his cell number, already having second thoughts. But then he realized there was no harm in giving her the number. He didn't answer his phone half the time anyway.

"Thanks." She started to back out the door, then took a step toward him, offering her hand. "I never introduced myself. I'm Mai, Mai Ricci. My dad is Corrato. The old coot in the backseat"—she leaned so she could get a better look at the van—"*that's* his *older* brother, Donato."

Liam held her hand a second longer than he should have. Her handshake was firm, her touch warm. This close, he could smell the fragrance of her shampoo and he found himself breathing deeply. "Liam McCathal," he said.

"Nice to meet you, Liam." She pulled her hand from his and raised the other, showing him the number written in black marker. "I'll call. Maybe we can do some business. I'd at least like to have a look at that clock."

Liam closed the door behind her, making sure he locked it this time. *I'll never see her again,* he thought to himself. Just as well. She didn't smell just of herbal shampoo; she smelled of danger.

"So exactly *what* is the purpose of this stakeout?" Katy stirred her mug with a spoon until it was a whirlpool of creamy white marshmallow and chocolate.

Kaleigh glanced out the window of the coffee shop that was situated diagonally across the street from Alice's Antiques. The lights were out. The sign on the door said CLOSED but she knew Liam was in there. She could feel his presence. She looked back at her best friend and sipped her iced tea. It was early October; it would be cold soon enough. She wasn't ready to switch to wintertime drinks. "It's not a stakeout."

"Feels like a stakeout."

Kaleigh's gaze drifted to the storefront window again. She hadn't seen Liam since she'd been reborn. This was always awkward, seeing people again through this young girl's eyes.

"You know, I heard he had to come home because he ate some bad guys."

Kaleigh cut her eyes at Katy. "*Ate* them?"

"You know, cannibalized them. Killed them, put them on a spit, and roasted their juiciest parts. Then he ate them."

"You need to stop listening to the gossip gaggle at the diner, Katy. Your brain is turning into rice pudding."

"I'm just saying, that's what they said."

"That's gross. Liam did not eat anyone. Can you imagine how nasty a serial killer would taste?"

Katy made a face and sipped her hot chocolate. "It does sound kind of disgusting. Even for Liam. The weirdo. He's way too dark and gloomy for me." She licked her finger, wiped it on the empty plate to catch any stray cookie crumbs, and popped it in her mouth. "Oh, I brought the book for you."

"I told you, I'm not going to read it. It's stupid."

"It's not stupid." Katy dug into the backpack at her feet and pulled out a hardcover book. "It's the best series that's ever been written." She slid it across the table. "You're the only person I know who hasn't read it, or seen the movies."

"I don't understand how you can like it. You said they got a lot of things wrong about vampires. And Bella makes out with a werewolf?" Kaleigh made a face of disgust.

"I've met a werewolf, Katy. They slobber. They're disgusting. There's no way you'd give a werewolf tongue."

"Please? Just read it. You should know what everyone is talking about, at least."

Kaleigh reluctantly accepted the book and crammed it in her backpack.

"And then we can watch the movies together. I have all the DVDs!"

"I'm not watching the movies with you," Kaleigh warned.

Katy exhaled. "Change of subject. You taking the SATs tomorrow?"

"My mom paid the money, but I don't know." She started picking her schoolbooks up off the floor and sticking them into her backpack.

"You don't know *what?*"

"I don't know if I'm taking them."

"You don't know if you're taking your SATs? Kaleigh, this is our last chance! College applications have to be in soon. You can't go to college if you don't take your SATs."

Her books packed, Kaleigh worked the zipper of her backpack. The stupid thing stuck all the time.

Katy watched her. "You're not really considering not going to college, are you? We finally all get permission to leave town for college and you don't want to go? Are you out of your cotton-pickin' "—she glanced around the mostly empty shop to make sure she saw no humans—"bloodsucking mind? Me, I'm going. I'm going as far as I can get from here. Stanford's at the top of my list."

"Stanford isn't on the list. We can only go to colleges approved by the General Council. It has to be a place where they think we'll be safe, where there's one of them close enough to get there if we get into trouble."

Katy sat back in her chair, crossing her arms over her chest. "Guess they better add Stanford to the list, because

I just might get in. And if I do, I'm going, and those old farts on the Council aren't going to stop me."

"Weren't you one of those old farts a couple of years ago before you were reborn?"

"We're not talking about me. We're talking about you, Kaleigh." She leaned forward, elbows on the table. "Why wouldn't you go to college?" she asked, softening her tone.

"I have responsibilities here. The world's changing. It's getting harder and harder to keep our cover and the humans seem to be cranking out more psychos every year. It's more dangerous when we're spread thin, all over the world. I think my place is here."

"Bullshit, Miss Wisewoman. If you're going to help us keep our cover, you need to be a part of the world. You need to know what we're facing."

Kaleigh knew Katy made a good point; she just didn't know if it was good enough. "Mom already paid, so I guess maybe I'll go."

"Great. Can you drive? We have to be at Cape Henlopen High School by seven forty-five."

"You grounded *again?*" Kaleigh laughed, finishing her iced tea. "What'd you do now?"

"Total misunderstanding." Katy got up, taking her backpack off.

"I can borrow Arlan's truck. He and Fia went somewhere for the weekend."

"Cool. See you in the morning." She pulled a couple of wrinkled bills out of the pocket of her jeans and left them on the table. "My turn. You pay next time."

Kaleigh took her time getting her stuff together. As she pulled her sweatshirt over her head, she watched the window across the street. She could still feel Liam's presence. It was hard to miss. He wasn't a weirdo like Katy said, but he was one of the darkest souls she knew. She respected him a great deal. She even liked him, but he scared her sometimes.

She didn't believe the nonsense about him eating those guys in Paris. But she had questions. And sooner or later, whether either of them liked it or not, she was going to have to walk through the door of the antiques shop and he was going to have to start talking.

Chapter 2

It was almost two in the morning when Liam's cell phone rang, but he was still awake. Particularly vivid nightmares like the one the night before tended to cause insomnia in a man, or a beast.

Still, the phone startled him. He didn't get a lot of calls. He wasn't even sure where his phone was. He rarely answered it, to the frustration of both his fellow Kill Team members and his mother.

Who would call him at two in the morning while he was in the States?

He got out of bed and walked toward the sound. By the light of the moon coming in through the bare window, he saw a pair of jeans on the floor. The jeans were ringing.

He glanced at the lit screen on the phone. It didn't identify the caller. He wasn't generally a curious man; curiosity was dangerous, but he answered it anyway.

"Yeah?"

"Liam?" The voice was tiny and filled with emotion. It scratched the surface of his memory, but he couldn't quite put his finger on it.

"This is Liam," he said cautiously.

"Liam...it's Mai. I...Remember me? I came into the shop today. I'm sorry to call you in the middle of the night." She took a breath. She had the quiet calm in her voice of someone on the verge of losing it. "I didn't know who to call. Your number, it was on my hand. I...just dialed it without thinking."

He sat down, leaning against the wall; the floorboards were cool under his bare butt. "What's the matter, Mai?" He was good in an emergency. The best.

"The...the police are on their way. My uncle Donato. My dad's brother who's been living with us. He's dead. Murdered."

Liam felt his jaw tighten, though the rest of his body remained relaxed. "Who killed him?"

"I...I don't know. Oh, God, there's so much blood. You wouldn't think an old, skinny man like him would have this much blood." She seemed to be talking more to herself than to him now. "Who would do such a thing? Kill a harmless old man?"

Liam thought he heard the sound of police sirens in the background.

"Liam?" she whispered. "I'm scared. There's no one else I can call. Could...could you come?"

"Come?"

"Here. I...don't know if I can do this alone. I don't want to get my cousins involved. Oh, God," she muttered. "The police are coming and they're going to ask questions and..." She let the sentence trail off into silence.

Of course Liam couldn't go to the human's house in the middle of the night. He was sorry her uncle had been murdered, but that wasn't his problem, was it? He was in enough trouble with the sept as it was; he couldn't go running around in the middle of the night, running to the rescue of HFs. Not even pretty ones.

"They're here," she whispered. "Could you *please* come?"

It was on the tip of his tongue to say no. Surely there was someone she could call: a friend, a relative. But he could tell from her tone of voice that when they met, she had felt the same inexplicable connection he had. Had this been their fate from the moment she walked into his shop?

He got her address.

Liam didn't like cops, *policia, jingcha, gingchaat.* Which was okay, because they didn't like him either. He arrived on his motorcycle, a 1936 BMW R5 he'd taken off the hands of a serial killer in Berlin not long after the war. No need to waste such a great bike on a dead man.

He parked a good way down the street and entered the property from the back. Dogs usually got chased away from crime scenes, but no one seemed to pay any attention to common housecats. No one noticed the tabby that walked past the six state and town police cruisers, the ambulance, and the fire truck. What the hell the fire truck was doing there, he didn't know.

He smelled the blood before he walked through the open door of Mai's shop. She was right. It was *a lot* of blood. It was arterial blood, thick and sweet. He had to take a deep breath to keep from getting lost in the scent of it.

Inside the cute little antiques shop was human chaos at its worst: local and state police, EMTs, the firemen who had apparently gotten lost on the way to a fire and stopped at a murder scene, neighbors who had slipped in before the police had time to put up the familiar yellow tape, all talking, walking in circles. Expressing their disbelief.

Liam slipped under a nice pre-1900 Victorian rosewood sewing table to get a better look. Amid the mostly male voices, he heard Mai's. She was talking softly, but he refused to allow himself to focus on her voice. It was too distracting. He padded to the body, then around it, taking care not to get his kitty paws bloody.

In the end, they had killed the old man by simply slitting his throat. Once you cut the carotid artery, the victim has only minutes to live because the blood comes directly from the aorta, pumping hard from the heart. When you bleed out from your carotid, you don't just leave a nice, neat pool of blood. It spurts. It splatters. On the floor, on your bathrobe, on the Sheffield armoire you were held against *as* your throat was cut. Bastards. Mai was right. Why would someone kill a harmless old man in a ratty flannel bathrobe? In an antiques shop in the middle of the night in a sleepy town in southern Delaware?

Tail straight in the air, he leaned in to the body to get a better look at the only apparent wound on the body. The blood smelled heavenly.

Upon closer feline inspection, he saw that there were, barely visible, additional marks on the old man's neck, inflicted antemortem. Somebody had been trying to get him to talk....

Mai wrapped her arms around herself. Everyone was talking at once and she felt light-headed. They had her father seated behind the store's counter, his little rat terrier cradled in his arms; an EMT was taking his blood pressure.

"I want to see my brother." Her dad kept saying it over and over again. "Where's my brother? Where's Donato?"

"Ma'am?"

Mai looked up at the state trooper addressing her. She hadn't caught the question. "I'm sorry. What?" She wiped her snotty nose with the balled-up tissue in her hand. Her feet were cold. She was wearing her old terry scuffs, no socks.

"About what time was it when you got up to check on your uncle?"

"I...I didn't *get up* to check on him. I got up to pee, and then I was thirsty, so I was going downstairs to get a glass of water. His bedroom door was open. That was when I realized something was wrong and I went in to check on him." She didn't tell them that the old man usually locked his door when he went to bed.

"And what time was that?" He was taking notes, writing on a little pad of paper in itty-bitty handwriting.

"Um. About one-forty. Maybe one forty–five." She tucked a stray piece of hair behind her ear. A lot of hair from her ponytail had come down and it kept falling in her eyes.

"You searched the house for him first?" The guy was tall. Not bad looking.

"Sure. I checked the usual places first: the bathrooms, the kitchen. When I didn't find him, I checked the other rooms in the house."

"And you found your father, Mr. Ricci, but not your uncle?"

"My father was asleep in his bed. He woke up when he heard me walk into his room. I asked him if he knew where Uncle Donato was and he said he didn't. I told him to stay put and I would find him."

"And then you checked here? Why did you come into the store, Miss Ricci?"

Okay, so he was cute, but he was also obtuse. Mai looked up at him, knowing it wouldn't be a good idea to sound like a smart-ass, considering the circumstances. "Because he wasn't in the house. It was the next logical place to look. There's a breezeway between the house and the back door to the shop. I followed the breezeway and found the door unlocked."

"So you just walked in?"

"It's *my* shop. I just walked in."

"Were the lights on or off?" the other trooper asked.

She had to think for a minute. "Off. I walked in, called his name, and flipped on the light switch."

"You weren't concerned there was an intruder?"

"My uncle wasn't in his bed. The door to the shop was open and I keep a set of keys in the kitchen, which were missing. I assumed he'd used the keys to let himself in."

"Your uncle walk around in the middle of the night often?"

She thought for a second, then lifted her gaze to meet the trooper's. "Actually, he did. "

He waited for her to go on. She waited for his next question.

"And this is exactly how you found the body?" He glanced in the direction of Donato, still lying on the cement floor.

"Right there," she answered.

"You didn't move him, check for a pulse or anything?"

"No, I didn't touch him. It was pretty obvious he was dead."

"And how did you know he was dead?"

Really obtuse.

"That's obviously a lot of blood." Her arms still clasped around her, she motioned in that general direction with her elbow. "And his eyes were still open, only I could tell he wasn't seeing anything."

"Hey! Get that cat out of here!" a voice shouted from the direction of the body. Someone was taking pictures. The flash kept going off.

"Can you tell me what's missing here in your store?" the trooper continued.

"Not for sure, not without doing an inventory, but like I said when you first arrived, I'm sure that a chest of Italian silver plate is gone. It was there in the window." She indicated the window the burglar had broken. He must have reached through it to unlock the dead bolt on the front door.

"And your alarm system?"

She sighed. She'd answered this question before, too. "I guess my uncle shut it off when he let himself into the shop."

"You're trying to tell me your uncle was nutty enough to wander around in the dark in his bathrobe, but smart enough to shut the alarm off when he entered the building?"

"You know anyone in the early stages of dementia?" she asked, trying to keep her building anger in check.

"She's got a point, Dan," the other cop said. "My mother-in-law, she's got Alzheimer's. She knows exactly what day of the week and what time *Dancing with the Stars* is on, but she keeps eating cat food. The wet kind, out of the can."

Mai felt like she was going to scream. Uncle Donato was dead on the floor and she knew damned well they hadn't killed him for silverware. But she wasn't going to tell the cops that. Couldn't. She took a breath. "You think I could go to the bathroom?"

"Sure. I guess so." The trooper made eye contact with the other one and they both nodded.

Mai went to the little half bath in the back of the store. After she washed her hands, she splashed water on her face and glanced into the pretty little mirror over the sink. She looked scared. Maybe because she was.

Her dad had been pretty unresponsive when the police arrived. Which was okay with her. She really didn't want him talking to the cops before she had a chance to talk to him. But even if he hadn't been out of it, she doubted he would have given them any information about Donato. The Ricci boys might have had their differences over the years, but they were still brothers with an oath of loyalty she'd never quite been able to understand.

When she walked out of the bathroom, wiping her hands with a paper towel, she spotted Liam. The minute she saw him, she realized what an idiotic thing it had been to do, calling him. She didn't know what she had been thinking. She hadn't been thinking, of course. She had just wanted someone here, and she hadn't wanted to involve her cousins, for more reasons than she could list, the first and foremost being that they had all been against Uncle Donato moving in with her and her father. So she had called Liam's number. It was as simple and ridiculous as that. She rubbed at his phone number on her hand with the paper towel. It didn't even smudge. Good old Sharpie.

She wondered if she could just sneak by him and hope the cops sent him home. Which of course was silly. You don't invite a guy to a murder scene and then give him the slip. She was lacking in dating experience these days, but she was pretty certain that was a hard and fast rule. Even on a first date.

He didn't give her the chance to give him the slip. He turned and looked at her, making eye contact with those intense, black eyes. "Hey," he said quietly.

He was smokin' hot and she was embarrassed to have even noticed, given the circumstances. Narrow jeans, black sneakers, and a leather jacket. His hair was inky dark and a little long at the nape of his neck. Very European.

She remembered him saying something about having just gotten back to the United States.

"Hey," she managed, letting her gaze slide to the floor. She crumbled the paper towel in her hand and bit down on her lower lip. She hadn't cried yet. Not a tear, but suddenly she felt like the floodgates were about to open.

Having some weird sixth sense, he saw it, too, and before she could muddle over the propriety of it, he opened his arms and she walked right into them. He was tall and strong and warm, none of which she was.

"I...I'm sorry I called you." His leather coat was open and she rested her cheek on the soft T-shirt he wore under it. She could feel his heart beating; it was strangely slow, compared to the pounding in her own chest. "I don't know what I was thinking."

He didn't say anything. No "it's okay," or "I'm glad you called." He just stood there, his arms around her, giving her a minute to compose herself.

Snuggled against him, it occurred to her that she was wearing nothing but a pair of flannel pajama pants and a long-sleeve T-shirt advertising a 5K she'd run in about a hundred years ago. No bra. Not exactly the way she wanted a cute guy or half the town to see her. But what exactly did a girl wear to her uncle's murder?

"Mai, I think they've got more questions for you," Liam said finally. "You up to it?"

"The sooner I answer their questions, the sooner they'll leave?" she asked, reluctant to pull herself out of his warm arms and reenter the lion's den.

"Something like that." He hesitated. "You're best to just keep answering their questions straight up, but don't volunteer any information they don't ask for. That'll just lead to even more questions."

That had been her thought exactly.

"You'll stay until they're gone?" She backed out of his arms, looking up at him. He seemed like a confident guy. Trustworthy. Though just a little scary on some level; where she was getting that vibe, she wasn't sure.

"I'll stay until they go," he agreed. His black-eyed gaze met hers. "Then I have a couple of questions of my own."

Chapter 3

The cops tried to push Liam out the door, but at Mai's insistence, they finally agreed to let him stay. He stood off to the side and listened to them question Mai; they repeated the same questions in a different way or in a different order. It was pretty typical crime-scene questioning of witnesses or potential suspects. They seemed to be bright enough to realize she probably hadn't done it, but they still asked for the clothes she was wearing, as well as her father's.

It was after 6 a.m. by the time the coroner came and went, the ambulance left, carrying Donato Ricci to the morgue, and the cops, EMTs, and firemen cleared out. Mai would be expected at the state police troop later in the day.

Liam followed Mai back to the house and waited in the kitchen while she put her father to bed. He seemed a little confused, but it was hard to tell if the old man wasn't quite right upstairs, or if his daughter was just treating him that way. When the police had tried to question him, she'd gotten pretty defensive. Liam wondered if she was covering for him. The old guy didn't look like a murderer, but they never did.

Liam tried not to look around the cozy house while he

waited. He didn't need to check out her belongings, and he didn't need to know Mai. He couldn't risk getting to know her.

He could hear her talking softly to her father upstairs. She was good with him. Kind. Patient. He wondered if she had been the same way with the dead uncle. Or had she felt over-burdened by caring for not one, but two old men, and taken it out on him? As far as he was concerned, it was a blessing that the Kahill vampires died in their seventies. The fact that they were immediately reborn as teens was a bit of a bummer, but then so was everlasting life.

Liam spotted an English porcelain teapot on the counter and, on impulse, he filled the electric teakettle with water. He didn't drink tea, but his mother did and he knew how she liked it. When the water was hot, he put some in the teapot to warm it, poured it out,˙and added tea leaves from a canister. He poured fresh hot water over the tea and left it to steep. He thought about getting a mug out of a cabinet for Mai, but that seemed too personal, opening cabinet doors.

He wondered if he should just go. He didn't belong here. This wasn't any of his business.

She came downstairs before he could slip out.

"Liam. You're still here." She sounded surprised.

"Of course." He felt like a bit of a shit saying it like that. It was as if she had known what he was thinking. And she wasn't even a vampire.

"I made you some tea," he offered lamely.

"Sweet Jesus, thank you." She got a mug down. French Provincial, with a rooster on it; not at all what he was expecting from her. "You want some?"

"Nah. I should go." Earlier, he'd been full of questions for her. The cops seemed to accept the *my crazy old uncle was wandering around at night and came upon a burglar* story, but Liam wasn't buying it. Burglars didn't interrogate old guys, and they didn't torture them before they killed them. Either Mai was lying through her teeth, or at the very least, she wasn't giving the full story. Something interesting had gone down here tonight and there was more to it than stolen cutlery.

But it wasn't his problem. "I...I'm gonna go," he said, motioning toward the door.

"Okay."

Her response so surprised him that he glanced back at her. She was putting honey in her cup of tea. She didn't look up.

"Thank you for coming. I mean it. I...I apologize again for calling you, for dragging you into this." She licked her spoon. "I don't know what possessed me to do such a thing. Shock, I guess."

He moved toward the back door. "You going to be okay? Your dad. The police. The funeral home."

She held the mug with both hands and blew on the tea. She'd been pretty tough when the police had been trying to question her father, but she looked vulnerable right now. Scared. Liam remembered the feel of her in his arms and a part of him ached to feel her there again. He opened the back door. "Call me if you need anything else."

He waited for her to make eye contact with him. When she didn't, mentally, he beckoned her. When his gaze locked with hers, he said softly, "I mean it."

"Right." She gave a little laugh. "And I have the number." She showed him her hand.

He went out into the cool, dewy morning, telling himself to just walk away. *Walk away.*

Liam spent most of the day working in the shop. He opened boxes, stacked stuff in some semblance of order, and made a list of items to put up for sale on the Internet. He knew approximately what the antiques were worth, but he'd have to do some research on some of the items that had been sitting around for decades. What did a person charge for a brand-new 1956 Disney domed school bus lunchbox?

When he had left Mai's, he was determined to have no further contact with her, but then he'd had second thoughts. It was after one when he called her cell. She didn't pick up. He left a message for her to call him. He called again twenty minutes later. Again, she didn't answer. Why would she? She was clearly embarrassed about having called him, a stranger, in the middle of the night to come to her aid. She didn't want to talk to him. Not ever. He was good with that. He was only calling to see if she and her father were okay.

It was after four and the autumn shadows had lengthened in the shop when Kaleigh knocked at the front door. He unlocked it and let her in.

"You're back," she said.

She looked cute in jeans and a hoodie sweatshirt, her hair pulled back in pigtails. Liam had always liked Kaleigh, though she scared him sometimes. She had a way of seeing through the bullshit, seeing right to the heart of things, to *his* heart.

"Right. Like you didn't already know. I saw you sitting at the café yesterday, spying on me."

She walked in and he closed and locked the door behind her. "I wasn't *spying* on you. I was hanging out with Katy and trying to gird up my loins to take the SATs this morning."

"How'd they go?"

"Sucked." She shrugged. "Boring. Took all morning. But I did fine. Scores'll be back in a couple of weeks."

She looked around at the mess. It seemed worse since he had started opening and moving boxes. In some places there were just paths between shoulder-high walls of boxes, sort of like a creepy hamster trail, only for people.

"Time for a little housecleaning?" she asked.

"Something like that."

"Maybe if you came home more often." She turned to him, slinging her fringed purple bag over her shoulder. "I was kind of surprised you didn't come home when your dad...died."

He'd actually been murdered, which was pretty unusual in vampire circles. Three years before, his father, the town postmaster, had been killed by some crazy human teenagers. They had discovered the Kahills were vampires and appointed themselves vampire slayers. Liam's father had been beheaded, which prevented him from ever being reborn. Dying without a chance to save his soul left him in some kind of purgatory that Liam tried not to think about. Four of the sept members had died before Fia Kahill, an FBI agent and one of their own, had caught the little bastards. Kaleigh had been one of the kids involved with the human boys, but Liam didn't hold it against her. It was damned hard being a vampire teen, and every adult in the community was as responsible for their actions as they were. Maybe more so.

"I was undercover," he explained. "An ugly case in Dublin. When I finally got the chance to talk to Ma, she said I should stay put, so I did."

The explanation sounded lamer now than it had seemed at the time. He regretted not being here with his mother, but he knew he wouldn't have been much help to her anyway. He wasn't good with grieving mothers, with anyone grieving, for that matter. Anyway, she seemed to have bounced back pretty well. This past summer she'd been involved in one of the juiciest Clare Point scandals in years. She and the old geezer, Victor Simpson, after being denied permission to marry, had run away from home and were currently sipping umbrella drinks somewhere in southern Florida.

Kaleigh glanced up at him. Even though she looked like a typical American teenager, her eyes were those of an old soul. She was the sept's wisewoman and the smartest person he knew on earth. Or at least she *would* be, once she came into her own again.

Liam grabbed the nearest box and pulled a utility knife out of his back pocket. "So...how's the mind-reading going? I hear you're getting pretty good at it, sticking your nose in other people's business. Listening in on people's thoughts, uninvited."

She frowned. "Who have you been talking to? The ladies at the diner? Did they also tell you that you were escorted home, handcuffed and shackled in the hold of a ship because you ate some guys in Paris?"

He leaned over the box to cut the packing tape, grimacing. "That's gross."

"That's what I said." She hopped up on a flimsy wooden crate. "Okay if I sit here?"

He glanced up, then back at what he was doing. "Guess we'll see in a minute. Hopefully that's not those Qing Dynasty statues I misplaced."

She leaned back, looking around. "I graduate in May. My parents think I should go away to college. Connor wants me to go, too. So he can have my bedroom."

"I agree."

"That Connor should have my bedroom?"

"That you should go to college. Maybe even in another country. *Université de Paris?* You remember how much you love Paris?"

"I can barely remember the Rice Krispies I had for breakfast this morning. And I can't speak French."

"You do speak French. You just don't remember yet. And German, and Greek and Portuguese and—"

"Enough already, Liam." She held up her hand. "I'm not even eighteen yet. Give me some time. There are some days when I feel like my head is going to explode. Everyone has all these expectations. They keep telling me about how smart I am and how much everyone relies on me. I don't see how there's any way I can live up to that."

He sighed, pulling an ugly vase out of a box of Styrofoam peanuts. "I hear you on that one."

She tilted her head one way and then the other. "I hope you didn't pay much for that thing."

He glanced at the bottom; there was no potter's mark. It was South American, but he couldn't place the piece. It was either Mayan or roadside Tijuana. "I hope not, either." He threw a handful of the white peanuts at her.

"So...seriously. Why are you back?" She plucked a piece of Styrofoam off her knee.

"You've been in the diner. I know you heard all the gory details."

"Just the part about you making shish kebabs out of some French dude's liver. Hey, you want to go get something to eat? I think it's liver-and-onions night at the diner."

He returned the vase carefully to the box, wondering where its manifesto was. "And I was hoping it was muskrat night."

"Okay, so pizza."

"You're not supposed to be reading my mind, Kaleigh." He waggled his finger at her.

She made a face, jumping down off the box. "I wasn't reading your stupid, sick, dark-ass mind. I don't like liver and onions, either." She headed for the door. "So you coming or not? Arlan's paying. I found money in the glove box of his truck when I semi-borrowed it this morning." She plucked a twenty out of the back pocket of her jeans and waved it at him as she went.

"Semi-borrowed?"

"He's out of town. I know where he keeps his keys."

"You stole Arlan's truck?"

"Borrowed." She unlocked the front door and stepped into the dusky light of late afternoon, early evening. "It doesn't count as stealing if I put gas in the tank, does it?"

Liam locked the front door, glancing at the CLOSED sign. It made him think of Mai. "You put gas in Arlan's truck?"

"It was purely a hypothetical question."

Liam laughed. He wouldn't go so far as to say it was good to be home, but he felt a certain sense of relief at being among his own again.

Liam's cell phone rang as he walked alone in the dark. It had been nice to have dinner with Kaleigh, but it was hard for him to be with anyone for long. He was too much a loner. He answered the phone without checking the caller ID. Big mistake. It wasn't Mai.

"So finally you answer your phone."

"How are you, Ma?"

"Worried about you."

He followed the sidewalk down Main Street, the slight ocean breeze on his back. "So that makes us even. I'm worried about you. You didn't really run off to Miami with Victor Simpson, did you?"

"I think you've got bigger troubles than who I'm kanoodling with."

"Kanoodling? Ma, could you please not say things like that? I just ate." He lowered the phone for a moment, grimacing, then lifted it to his ear again. "You know I can't stand Victor Simpson. He was a cantankerous old bastard before Regan made him a vampire. Ma, you can't stand him."

"I'm not going to discuss my personal business with you."

But you're fine talking about mine? He thought it, but he didn't say it. He respected his mother and, more importantly, he loved her. Most of the time. It was just that she irritated the hell out of him.

"I called to talk about you," she went on. "Have you been interviewed yet? What does Peigi say? Does she think there're going to be sanctions?"

"I have not been interviewed. All Peigi said was that it would be a few weeks while they investigate and interrogate and then a decision will be made."

"They did not say interrogate," his mother corrected. "Peigi wouldn't say that. Even if it was true," she added.

Liam heard a male voice in the background. Someone was talking to her. It had to be Victor.

"No, I'm not going to ask him that," she said, her mouth farther from the phone. Now she sounded like she was speaking normally, rather than shouting. She always shouted when she talked to him on his cell. And the farther away he was, the louder she talked.

"No, I'm not going to," she repeated. "Oh, for Christ's sake." She got louder again. "Victor wants me to ask if you really ate them."

"Ma! I didn't eat anyone."

"Don't use that tone with me. I gave birth to you. Three days of hard labor—"

"Ma," he interrupted. "You can't still play the uterus card. You gave birth to me over twelve hundred years ago. It's time to get over it."

"It's time to get yourself straight. If your father was here—" Luckily, she stopped before she said anything she would regret. She sighed and started again. "I'm just worried about you, is all. You've been out there a long time. It gets to you and don't tell me it doesn't. All that pain, the sorrow, it has a way of getting into your bones."

"My bones are fine. I'm fine. This will all blow over.

The Council is just doing their job. It's a formality, bringing me home. I'll be out of here in a few weeks." He looked both ways and crossed the street. There were a few cars, a few pedestrians, but not many. The last of the human tourists would soon go home and Clare Point would have a respite. Until spring came again, along with the minivans of humans.

"Well, I certainly hope you haven't caused more trouble for yourself this time than you can get out of. Are you staying at the house? Mary Cahall says you're not staying at the house."

Liam squeezed his eyes shut for a second. "Ma. Why are you asking me if Mary Cahall already told you I'm not staying at the house?"

Her silence was worse than her nagging.

"I'm staying in the apartment over the shop," he finally said.

"You should stay at the house. I don't like it to sit empty. I left the house all ready for you when you came home. I had it ready before I left. I was expecting you to return after your last assignment."

"Ma, I never told you I was coming home. You said I was coming home. I like my apartment. That's where I'm staying. Maybe you should come back and then the house wouldn't be empty." He hesitated. "You could see me before I leave. I think I'm headed for Spain."

"I'm not coming home, not yet. Victor and I are having too good a time here."

"Where's that again?" he asked. He walked past The Hill, the local bar. Open only to locals. He thought about stopping, having a beer. Saying hi to some people. He kept walking.

"You're going to have to do better than that if you're going to trick me into telling you where I am. I haven't told anyone where I am because I don't want anyone coming after us."

"You know, you're considered AWOL, Ma. There'll be a hearing when you come home. You can't just take off and not tell anyone where you've gone. It's not safe."

"I'm safe enough." Her tone softened. "I have Victor."

So she really did have feelings for the old coot. Liam was glad. Losing a husband the way she had must have been awful. She deserved some happiness. "I gotta go, Ma."

"No, you don't. You just don't want to talk to me anymore. Call me in a couple of days. Otherwise, I'll call you. And I'll keep calling. And if you don't answer, I'll send Mary Cahall over to check on you."

"Bye, Ma."

"Check on the house," she shouted into the phone as he lowered it from his ear. "Better yet, stay there instead of the jail cell you call an apartment!"

He ended the call, vowing not to answer the phone again. He wasn't afraid of Mary Cahall coming over. Actually he was, but only because she could talk a vampire to death, which was pretty hard.

His phone didn't ring again for five days. When it did, he answered it.

Chapter 4

"I can't believe I'm doing this again, but you said I should call you if I needed anything else." Mai hesitated on the other end of the phone. "Can you come, Liam? Now?"

"I've called six times. I left messages. You never returned any of my calls." He put down the packing tape he was using to seal a mailing box with an Asian mahogany chess set inside. It had brought a pretty penny on eBay.

"I know," she said. "I'm sorry. I just thought it was better if... if we not talk. If we not see each other again."

He leaned against a wood-slatted crate. "You were the one who called me to begin with. I was just checking to be sure you and your dad were okay. That's all."

"I know. I'm sorry. It's just that... I'm a private person. And I felt stupid, calling you like that. And now I'm doing it again." She was quiet for a second. "We're not okay, Liam. Today's my uncle's funeral and... I just got a very disturbing phone call as I was going out the door. Someone..." Her voice trembled. "This guy, he threatened my dad."

"Threatened him how? Who was it?" As he spoke, he went up the back staircase to his apartment. He didn't have a suit, but he was pretty sure he had a shirt and tie. Somewhere.

"I don't know who it was. When I picked up the phone, he just said that if we didn't return what belonged to him, my father would be next. They're going to kill him, Liam," she said softly.

The obvious question might have been "Return what?" But not to Liam. "Why didn't you call the cops?"

She was silent for a second. He waited.

"No cops," she said finally.

He heard a dog bark and then Mai say, "Hush, Prince. *Babbo,* please, I'm on the phone." Then he seemed to have her attention again. "Sorry, Liam. My father didn't want to leave his dog at home. He's worried he won't be safe."

"So, back to the cops," Liam directed. "What you're saying is that there's more to the story than what you gave them the night your uncle was killed. It wasn't just a burglary gone bad and you knew it."

Again, she was silent. She reminded him of himself. He played the same game. Sometimes, when he didn't like the answer, he just didn't answer at all.

"You want my help or not?" he asked, digging through the closet he hadn't touched in three years. Possibly four.

"I want your help. That's why I called you. Because I . . . oh, God, I don't know why I called you. Because you said I should call you if I needed anything else." She took a breath. "No, it wasn't just that. I called because in my gut, I think you can help me. I think maybe you're the *only* person who can, Liam. Does that sound crazy?"

"Of course it does. You don't know me," he told her. "You have no idea what kind of person I am. I could be more dangerous than the guy who broke into your store and killed your uncle, for all you know."

"You're right, I don't know you," she answered calmly.

"But I do know what kind of person you are. You're the kind of person who comes in the middle of the night when a complete stranger asks you to."

Every fiber of his being told him not to do it. But her voice, *her voice* was killing him. She sounded so desperate. So scared. She didn't deserve that. No one did. And he had sworn to God to protect His fragile humans, hadn't he? "I've got to know what's going on, Mai. I can't help you if you can't be truthful with me."

"I understand that." Then she whispered, "I just don't want to talk on the phone. My dad's sitting right here. He's been through enough this week."

"Fair enough," Liam agreed. "I'll come, but I'm warning you, Mai. If you're not more forthright with me than you were with the cops, I won't be coming next time you call. You understand what I'm saying?"

"I'll tell you what I know. Everything. Dad and I are headed to the church. It's St. Clare's in Long Neck. The burial Mass is at one. Can you meet me there?"

He hesitated. He was making a mistake. A *huge* mistake. Whatever this girl was involved in, he didn't need to be a part of it. He could *not* get involved with an HF. Not one who made dates to murder scenes and funerals. All he had to do was say no and hang up. He'd never hear from her again. He was sure of it.

"I'll see you there," he said.

He found the tie, a white shirt, and black pants. He thought he looked like a waiter when he glanced at himself in the hearse's sideview mirror. The tiny church was nestled among tombstones and sturdy elm trees. The Kahill sept didn't get dressed up for funerals. They were wakes: a lot of drinking, some fighting, a little slap and tickle here and there, and buckets of tears. At Kahill vampire funerals, they gathered not to put the bodies of their loved ones in graves, but to greet them when the deceased arose from the dead, reborn, to live another life cycle on Earth. Each time a Kahill was reborn there was a deep sadness because rebirth meant the loved one's soul had not yet been saved by God and he or she was destined to live yet again. Immortality got pretty old after a few centuries.

He entered the front doors of the church. He had been to St. Clare's Basilica in Assisi, Italy. It was tiny and ordinary, but one of his favorites in the whole world. This St. Clare's reminded him of that great church in Italy. Humble. He walked through the narthex, into the nave. There were thirty or forty mourners, some seated in the front pews, others standing in a receiving line with Mai and her father at the head.

In front of the kneeling rail at the altar stood an open coffin. Liam had to fight not to recoil, his response almost physical. It wasn't the sight of the dead man that offended him; it was the stink of formaldehyde that came off the body. It was so strong and thick and revolting that it made Liam's stomach churn. Why the hell would anyone want to preserve a human body after it was placed in the ground? It seemed like sacrilege to him. He liked the idea of ashes to ashes, dust to dust. For him it was a dream. An ultimate, possibly unobtainable dream.

Liam dipped his fingers into the marble font, felt the sweet relief of the holy water, and went down on one knee. He crossed himself, whispering a prayer to God to give him the strength to keep walking. As bizarre as it seemed, he was a pretty religious guy. At least pretty religious for a vampire. Who murdered for a living.

When he came to his feet, he stood for a moment, watching Mai. The mourners offered condolences, then moved solemnly past the body. He wondered who these people were. What their relationship to Mai was. He was just about to take a seat in the back pew when she spotted him and left her father's side.

She looked damn hot in a simple navy dress and heels. Bare, shapely legs. In the dress, he could see that she was slender, but well built with curvy hips and small, pert breasts. Liam was a breast man. He loved them. All sizes, all shapes. Firm, droopy, big nipples, little nipples. He didn't care. He thought a woman's breasts might have been God's greatest creation.

"You came," she said. It sounded like a sigh of relief. She surprised him by wrapping her arms around him and hugging him tightly. Her father walked up behind her, a slightly confused smile on his face.

"Mr. Ricci." When Mai finally let go of him, he put out his hand to the older man. "I'm sorry for your loss."

Corrato shook Liam's hand. "Thank you. Thank you for coming. I know you?" He squinted behind his wire-rim glasses. He was dressed in a gray suit, his full head of white hair recently cut. His tie was neatly tied, by Mai, Liam guessed, and he looked sharp.

"We met the other night, sir."

"It's my friend, Liam, *Babbo*. Remember?"

"That's right. My Prince, he liked you. You remember him? My dog?"

Liam wasn't exactly sure what to say. "He seemed like a nice dog, sir, from what I saw."

"A fine dog. An excellent dog. He's in the car. We left the window down a little. I wanted to bring him in, but Father Renaldo doesn't care for rat terriers." He lowered his voice in a conspiratorial manner. "He has a poodle. I think he's prejudiced."

Mai looped her arm through her father's and steered him in the opposite direction. "Why don't you go sit next to Suzy? See her?" She pointed. "There, in front."

"I do want to get a good seat," he said, letting go of her and shuffling down the center aisle.

Mai turned back to Liam as soon as her father was out of earshot. "After the Mass, there's the burial and then we're going to my cousin Suzy's for a reception, or whatever the hell you call it." Her face was pale. He could see that she was upset, but to anyone else it probably just looked like she was mourning her uncle. Liam saw past that. She was genuinely afraid.

"We can talk there," she said, nervously applying cherry lip balm. "At this point, I'm scared to even go home."

An ancient organ in the front of the church began to moan. Mourners scattered to take their seats. "You should go sit with your father," he told her.

"Do you want to come sit up front with us?"

"No." He placed his hand on the small of her back. "I'll keep an eye on you from here. Go on, Mai. Your father needs you."

She walked reluctantly up the aisle, toward the front of the church. Liam took a seat in the last pew. The polished wood felt good beneath him. Solid. It offered a sense of familiar comfort. No matter where he was in the world, he got this feeling when he sat in a church.

The priest in white robes entered, signifying the start of Mass. Liam ignored protocol and pulled out the kneeling bench. He didn't care about Mass and he never went to confession, which meant he was a lousy Catholic. But he didn't need those things. What he needed was a one-on-one with God. He got on his knees, clasped his hands, and lowered his forehead until it rested on his knuckles. Considering the things he had done in the name of protecting God's humans, he always had a lot of praying to do.

* * *

Burial was in the small cemetery there at St. Clare's, and then Liam followed everyone back to Mai's cousin's house in a nearby neighborhood. Feeling awkward, even though Mai had invited him to join them, he didn't go inside with everyone else. Instead, he leaned against his motorcycle and enjoyed the fresh autumn air.

After a while, the front door opened and Corrato came out, followed by his little black rat terrier. The older man had shed his suit jacket and had a red plastic cup in each hand. Slowly, he made his way to Liam with that tottering gait that some elderly walked with. The dog stayed a foot behind him.

When he reached Liam, he pushed one cup into his hand. "Coke," he said. "Looked for rum. Couldn't find any. Usually under the sink at Suzy's. I think the young folks hid it."

Liam chuckled. "Thanks."

"Welcome."

They both sipped from their plastic cups. "You can come in, you know," Corrato said after a minute, using the cup to point in the direction of the house.

"I'm fine here."

The old man nodded. "I don't want to be in there, either."

He sounded pretty clear-headed, compared to the other night. Maybe he'd been in shock the night of his brother's murder. Humans weren't just physically fragile; they were emotionally fragile, as well.

"Talking about Donato, what a good man he was," Corrato explained. "Like they knew him."

Liam eyed the old man. He considered asking him outright what had happened to his brother; he had a feeling he might know more than Mai did. But this was between Liam and Mai. He didn't want to make this relationship any more complicated than it already was. He didn't want a relationship at all, with anyone. He didn't want to get to know this man. Relationships were just messy all the way around, and in the end, people got hurt.

So Liam and Corrato drank their Cokes and stood there in silence, both content. Liam found himself watching the dog. Animals often sensed there was something different about vampires, about the way they smelled, and this one was no different. Prince sat calmly at his master's feet watching Liam, probably trying to figure out exactly what he was.

After five minutes, Corrato looked over. "I think I'll sit on the step there. Sciatica." He rubbed the small of his back.

Liam noticed he wore a wedding ring.

"Care to join me?" Corrato asked.

Liam intended to say no thanks. Instead, he found himself seated beside the old guy on the concrete steps of Cousin Suzy's front porch. It was kind of serene, a situation Liam didn't find himself in very often. He spent most of his time hunting the streets of big, dirty, ugly cities at night, following, plotting...killing. He rarely had the opportunity to do something so human as have a cup of soda on a fall afternoon in a quiet neighborhood and watch the sun slip under the horizon.

The two of them sat there in comfortable silence for a good twenty minutes. The dog climbed up in Corrato's lap, and apparently seeing Liam as no immediate threat, went to sleep. The dog lifted its head when the door opened behind them. "There you are! *Babbo!* You scared me to death. I looked everywhere for you."

"No fuss," he grumbled over his shoulder. Then he looked to Liam. "She fusses."

Liam glanced in her direction, lifting an eyebrow.

She almost smiled. "Come inside, *Babbo*. Have some cake."

"We don't like cake," he said, handing his empty cup to Liam and lowering the dog from his lap. "Prince doesn't like it." He slowly got to his feet with the aid of the handrail.

"*Babbo*, you like cake and Prince would eat anything that didn't eat him first," she said patiently.

"Not Suzy's cake," Corrato muttered to Liam as he retreated. "Dry as sawdust. Ask Prince."

Mai brushed her hand across Liam's shoulder. "I'll be right back."

He heard the door open behind him, then close. A couple of minutes went by and Mai came out with two more plastic cups of Coke. She sat on the step, handed him the cups, and then took a pint of rum from under her arm and twisted off the cap.

"Your dad was looking for that."

"I bet he was." She poured a healthy portion into both and screwed the cap back on. "I hope Dad wasn't too big a pest."

"Not at all." When she set the bottle beside her, he handed her one of the cups.

"Cin-cin." She touched her cup to his and took a sip.

"Okay, so out with it," he said, drinking from his cup. The taste of the rum was sharp in the sweet cola. He wished she'd skipped the cola.

"Here?" She looked around. "I've got, like, a hundred cousins inside. They've already grilled me as to who you are. Someone might hear us."

"They're eating Suzy's dry cake," he said flatly. "Now tell me why someone killed seventy-something-year-old Donato Ricci and are now after your father."

"I don't know."

He cut his eyes at her.

"I swear I don't."

He took another sip of the foul concoction and set the cup between his feet on the ground. "Okay," he said with a sigh. "Let's start with the simple questions."

Chapter 5

"Tell me about you and your dad."

She took a minute. He could tell she was choosing her words carefully, which was smart on her part if she was hiding something, which she obviously was. Her approach might not help him get to the bottom of this any faster, but he liked her all the more for her caution.

"My dad raised me. He met my mom when he was in Vietnam. She was some sort of beauty queen. He was there at the fall of Saigon, and when the soldiers evacuated, he had to leave her. But eventually, he brought her to the States and married her. They had me and he tried to make her happy, but she missed her home and her family. She left when I was three. I don't even remember her."

"Your father remarried?"

She shook her head.

"But he still wears a wedding ring."

"I think he really loved her. He never quite got over the fact that she couldn't love him back." She smoothed the hem of her dress over her bare knees, took a drink, and went on in a soft voice. "When I was eight, my dad said the neighborhood in New Jersey where we lived was going downhill, that we needed a fresh start. So we moved here."

"Why Delaware?" Liam was always curious as to why humans went where they did. Vampires moved from place to place out of self-preservation, either to better feeding grounds or to escape danger. The Kahills had been running for their lives when they found Delaware the night their ship wrecked in a storm in the seventeenth century.

"He had a friend from the war here who offered him a job. Dad was an electrician. It was a way out of Jersey, and a way to get away from his family, gracefully."

"I hear a little tone there," Liam observed.

She half-smiled. "The Riccis are a very close-knit Italian family."

"Meaning, *controlling*."

Again, the little smile. "His parents and brother threw a fit. Threatened to disown him, never speak to him again. He packed up his little girl and came here anyway. After a while, I think his family forgave him. Sort of. Anyway, enough so that we still spent most holidays with them."

"You said these people here are your cousins."

"His mom's side. She had nieces and nephews who lived in the area. My dad still thought family was important, so even though he kept me at a distance from his dad's side of the family, he made sure I had cousins to play with growing up."

"And your dad had other siblings besides his brother?"

"Just a sister. Donato was the oldest. He ran the family business with their father and took over after his death. That was an issue between him and my dad for a long time, that Dad refused to work in the family business."

"And what was the *business di famiglia?*"

"Imports," she said into her cup. "I don't even know exactly what they imported. Dad never talked much about them and when I asked questions, he avoided answering, so after a while, I stopped asking."

"That how you got into selling antiques?"

"Not really. My dad liked old things and we used to go around to yard sales and antiques stores on weekends. Pretty soon he'd bought more than the house could hold, so he started selling things off the lawn. He'd buy a couple chairs, refinish them, and then sell them. When he retired, he opened the shop. I got a degree in nursing, was living in Dover, pretty happy with my job, and then about five years ago, Dad had a heart attack. I took time off to take care of him, ran the shop until he was on his feet again, and then just never went back to my old job."

"You never married?"

She glanced at him. "That's kind of personal."

"So is calling a guy you don't know to come to your uncle's murder scene, then his funeral."

She thought for a moment and then went on. "I came close once. He called it off the day before the wedding and married my best friend a couple of months later." She pointed to the cup at his feet. "You going to drink that?"

He handed it to her.

"So how did Donato, king of the family, end up here, sleeping in your spare room?"

She shrugged. "I don't know. He got old. His health really started declining. His wife was dead, no children. He and my dad didn't talk much, but about six months ago Uncle Donato started calling, talking to my dad. My dad felt bad for him and invited him to live with us."

Liam leaned back on the step. "Okay, back to this import business. I hate to rely on stereotypes, but an Italian family, in the import business. Was your uncle connected to the mob?"

"No." She exhaled, tucking a strand of hair behind her ear. "I don't know. There was talk over the years among my cousins. But families always talk about the guy who makes something of himself, don't they? It's jealousy."

Liam could tell she wasn't done, so he kept quiet.

"I'm not naive enough to think Uncle Donato was squeaky clean. He served some jail time when I was young, but that was for tax evasion or something like that." She shrugged. "He was a nice old man, Liam. A gentleman. He was never anything but kind to me. He used to send me birthday gifts when I was a kid. And once he moved in, he insisted on paying a share of the living expenses. He didn't want to be a burden to my father or me."

"So he had money?" Liam pressed.

"Not really." She thought for a minute. "I guess I don't really know. He cashed his Social Security check every month and insisted my dad take part of it to pay the household bills. My dad gave it to me. Beyond that, I don't know what he had. I guess we'll find out."

Liam sat in silence for a moment, then got up and walked down the steps.

Mai got to her feet. "Where are you going?"

"Home."

"Why?" She followed him down the sidewalk, the bottle of rum in her hand. "You said you would help me."

"You said you'd tell me the truth." He didn't stop until he reached his motorcycle. "The whole truth."

"But I *am* telling—" She broke off before finishing her sentence.

Liam mounted his bike, but he didn't start it. He waited.

She wasn't silent all that long. "A couple of weeks ago, the phone rang. Uncle Donato answered it. He argued with whoever it was. When he got off, I asked him who had called. First, he tried to tell me it was a wrong number. When I told him I heard him talking, he said it was some guy he used to know. The guy had just gotten out of prison and had tracked Uncle Donato down, looking for a favor. Uncle Donato said he told him no."

"This guy have a name?"

"He wouldn't tell me his name."

"And you didn't overhear anything that might help you figure out who it was?"

"No. Well..." She gave a humorless laugh. "I could have sworn Uncle Donato referred to him as the Weasel, but I was listening in on the conversation from another room. He could have just called him a weasel. Uncle Donato had a colorful vocabulary when he got angry."

Liam crossed his arms over his chest, thinking. "You ask your dad if he knew anything about who this guy was?"

"I asked. Dad said he didn't know a thing about it. When I asked him if he would ask Uncle Donato, he said he'd get information easier out of Prince." She rolled her eyes. Then she unscrewed the cap on the bottle of rum and took a drink.

"Hey, easy there." Liam grabbed the bottle from her and took a drink himself before putting the lid on and slipping it inside his coat.

"Please help me, Liam," she said, grasping his arm. "I need help. I need *your* help."

"Not me," he said. "I'm not your guy."

"You're *the* guy. I don't know why, but I'm sure of it." She looked into his eyes, her eyes pleading. She was so close, he couldn't smell just her shampoo, but the scent of her skin. She wore no perfume. It was her HF scent that made him light-headed.

The thing that made sense was to take off on his bike. The thing that did *not* make sense was to kiss her.

But he was already under her spell. There was no turning back, not if his soul had depended upon it. Which was a possibility. "This is a bad idea," he whispered.

She leaned closer, until her lips were almost on his. "I know."

"You've had a long day. A long week. A bad week."

She closed her eyes. "So make it a little better."

Liam slid his hand around her neck until his thumb was on her pulse. With his other hand, he stroked her cheek as he pressed his lips to hers. The first touch was gentle, cautious. She still had a chance to walk away. He still had the chance.

Then the kiss deepened. Liam's heart pounded as he tasted the rum on her lips. Her cherry ChapStick. She tasted sweet and forbidden. There was something about her mouth that was filled with promise, a promise of a brief moment of happiness, the kind that had been just out of his grasp for centuries.

Just one kiss, he told himself. Two. But by the third kiss, he didn't just want to kiss her. He wanted to make love to her. And not just make love to her, because for a vampire, it never stopped there. Liam wanted to possess her. To drink of her. He wanted to taste her blood.

Liam tightened his arms around Mai. Somehow she had ended up on the bike in front of him. It was definitely make-out by mutual consent. She slipped one hand under his jacket as their tongues met. Intertwined.

"Excuse me."

Somewhere in the back of his head, Liam heard a voice. The voice cleared its throat. "Excuse me. Sorry. Mai?"

Mai flew out of Liam's arms like she was on fire. "*Babbo.*" She was breathing hard. You wouldn't think an Asian girl could blush, but she was definitely blushing.

"I was wondering." Corrato held the rat terrier under his arm. If he noticed his daughter was making out with a man she barely knew, he didn't let on. He was wearing his suit jacket again, and a wool porkpie hat. He was obviously on the move. "I didn't mean to interrupt, but it's time for Prince's dinner. I need to go home."

Mai glanced at Liam, then back at her father. She wiped her mouth with her hand. As if she could take away the heat. The same heat he still felt on his own lips.

"I bet Suzy's got dog food," she suggested, her voice breathy. "Maybe you could borrow some of hers?"

Her father shook his head. "He eats special dog food. Other stuff, it gives him the runs. I need Prince's special dog food. I need to go home now." His voice quivered on the last word.

"*Babbo,* I'm not sure we're going home tonight. Suzy offered to let us stay the night and—"

"We can walk." With that, Corrato turned in his worn Italian leather loafers and headed down the sidewalk. It was almost dark, and he made a striking sight on the street, a distinguished old man in his suit and hat, carrying his dog.

"*Babbo,* no, wait." She went after him, looking back at Liam. "When he gets like this, there's no changing his mind. Maybe you could ride over with us? I don't know that we should go alone."

Liam rested his hands on the handlebars of the motorcycle. His heart was still pounding, though not quite as fast. He could still taste her human lips on his. The nectar of life. Turn the key, shift, hit the gas—that was all he had to do to be out of there. In the clear.

"I can ride over with you," Liam heard himself say. "You can get some things, the dog food, then you can come back here."

"You hear that, *Babbo?*" She hurried to catch up with him. "Liam will ride over with us." She looped her arm through his. "Come on, *Babbo.* You're not walking. It's ten miles." She steered him back toward Liam.

"I don't understand why I can't sleep in my own bed," he said, looking at Liam instead of his daughter.

"I told you," she said quietly. "I'm upset. Suzy offered and I took her up on it."

"You think they're coming?"

Mai halted, looking up at him, her arm still looped through his.

Liam watched carefully.

"Who, *Babbo?*"

"The men who offed Donato." Working his jaw, he held his dog tightly to his chest. "Men like that, they can't be trusted. They kill men. They kill dogs. It's probably better we don't sleep at home tonight. I'm worried about Prince."

Liam studied the old guy's face. He sounded not quite right in the head, but there was something in his eyes... something that made Liam think he might be just playing with them.

"I'll just run in and tell Suzy we're going," Mai said after a second.

Liam got off the bike. "I'll drive your car, leave my bike here." He wasn't sure how much she'd had to drink.

"I'll be right out," Mai called, going up the sidewalk to her cousin's house. "*Babbo,* get in the van."

"Shotgun," the old man hollered.

Liam knew something was wrong before Mai slipped her key into the lock of the back door. He laid his hand on hers. "Let me do that."

She froze and looked up at him. "What is it?"

"I'm not sure." He glanced over his shoulder at Corrato. The old man waited on the brick walk behind them while his dog nosed around in the grass, looking for a place to do his business. Liam never understood this thing humans had for pets. Maybe because as a shape-shifter, he could *technically* be one.

"Let me go in first." Liam turned the key in the lock, wishing he'd brought a gun with him. He rarely used one; he preferred his own hands, or teeth. In official assignments for the sept, a ceremonial knife was required. There were rules, as he was frequently reminded. But he would have felt better walking into this situation with a good old-fashioned 9mm Glock tucked into the waistband of his waiter pants.

The first thing he saw inside the back door were the clothes from the dryer lying on the floor. Then a puddle and a laundry detergent bottle, lying uncapped on the tile.

Mai flipped on the light. "What the hell?"

If he'd been suspicious in the laundry room, the kitchen left no doubt. Cabinet doors had been left open; dishes lay broken on the floor. Even the refrigerator and freezer had been emptied. Obviously someone was looking for something.

"Oh, God," Mai murmured, bringing her hands to her mouth.

"Shhh," Liam said, listening carefully. Like any vampire, his senses were more acute than those of humans. He didn't hear anyone in the house. He didn't smell anyone, but he wanted to be sure. After a second, he held his hand out to her. "Stay right here. I'll be back in a second."

Liam covered the first floor, then went up to the second; he didn't bother to turn on the lights. He didn't need them. His vision in the dark was as good as his vision in broad daylight, maybe better because he could see shades of heat or the absence of it. The entire house was strewn with Mai's and Corrato's possessions. Furniture had been tipped over, cushions pulled off the couch and chairs. They'd been relatively thorough.

The last room he entered was Mai's bedroom, upstairs. He didn't need to see the floral sheets on the bed or the perfume bottles knocked over on the bathroom sink to know it was her room. It *smelled* like her. Next to the bed, Liam paused and closed his eyes. Images of her naked, in his arms, in the bed, flashed in his head. He felt the weight of her bare breast in his hand, the taste of a taut nipple, the scent of the sweet, moist place between her thighs.

His eyes flew open. He really needed to get laid. He needed to find a nice, willing vampire girl and get this out of his system.

"Liam?"

He heard her call him from the bottom of the steps. "Are you okay? I think they're gone. They're gone, aren't they?" she asked.

He left her room, walking to the head of the stairs. The carved oak banister that ran down the length of the stairs was polished and smelled of linseed oil. "What are they looking for, Mai?"

"I don't know." She threw open her arms. "I swear I don't."

"I guess there's no way you would know if anything was missing."

She looked at him as if he was an idiot.

"All right. You should get your things. Some clothes, some toiletries," he suggested. "A few days' worth. Your father, too."

"*Babbo!*" she called over her shoulder. "Be careful. Don't trip over the seat cushions." She grabbed one off the floor at the foot of the stairs and flung it carelessly into the living room. They had all been ripped open, leaving tufts of stuffing all over the floor.

"Bastards," the old man muttered.

"*Babbo!*"

"They spilled Prince's dog food in the kitchen. You see what a mess they made? As if a man would hide anything in dog food." He passed Mai and slowly made his way up the stairs.

"Mr. Ricci," Liam said when he reached the top, "you have any idea what whoever did this might be looking for?"

"Nope." He brushed past Liam, going into his room.

"I'll be quick," Mai said, running up the steps. As she passed Liam, she drew her fingertips across his abdomen.

It was an innocent gesture, but it set his skin on fire. Slowly, he walked down the steps. He surveyed one room after the other and decided after a couple of minutes that whoever had been there hadn't really been all that thorough. No holes in the walls, no ceiling tiles removed, and no wooden floorboards jimmied up. So they weren't absolutely sure whatever they were looking for was even there....

Liam went out to Mai's shop next. The back door was standing open. The shop has been searched, too, but whoever did it hadn't made nearly the mess they had in the house. Liam locked the door and returned to the house.

As Liam entered the living room, Corrato came down the stairs carrying two plastic grocery bags, one in each hand, and a rattan dog bed under his arm.

"*Babbo,* I left a suitcase for you in the hall," Mai called from the top of the steps.

"Don't need a suitcase, got bags," he muttered.

"You have to leave the dog bed."

"Prince likes his bed," Corrato insisted stubbornly.

"Prince can sleep with you at Suzy's. We'll only be there a night or two. You have to leave the bed."

At the bottom of the steps, he reluctantly set down the dog bed. Then he headed for the kitchen. "Prince, come, boy. Prince, want a treat?"

Liam glanced over his shoulder, then took the steps two at a time. He found Mai in her bedroom, pulling a T-shirt over her head. She had taken off her bra and he caught a flash of breast as she spun around.

"Sorry," he said instantly. "I didn't mean to just walk in on you." But he didn't look away.

And Mai didn't turn away as she slipped the shirt over her nakedness. "I needed to get out of that dress. The underwire in my bra was killing me." She pulled two more T-shirts out of a drawer and left it open. "Can you grab that gray sweatshirt for me off the back of the door?"

Not trusting himself to get close to her just this second, he tossed it to her. Her bed was unmade and way too inviting.

She pulled the hoodie over her head and her gaze met his, as she pulled her long, dark hair free. She was thinking about the bed, too. About making love to him. Liam wasn't a mind reader like Kaleigh. He didn't have to be, in this case.

She took a step toward him, still gazing into his eyes. He knew that look. One kiss and she was his, right here, right now. It was the vampire thing; humans couldn't resist them.

"Mai!"

Corrato unintentionally saved Liam yet again. "Mai! Mai, he's gone. They took him."

Mai walked past Liam to stick her head out the doorway. "Who's gone?" she hollered back.

"Prince." The old man's voice cracked with emotion. "They kidnapped the Prince of Dogs."

Chapter 6

"*Babbo,* it's okay. We'll find him." Mai went down the steps.

Liam grabbed the duffle bag she had packed and followed her. "I'm sure he's around here somewhere," she assured her father.

"No. He wouldn't run away," Corrato insisted, his eyes tearing up.

Liam felt a tightness in his chest and glanced away in embarrassment. He was a vampire. He wasn't human. He had to remind himself sometimes that that meant he didn't have the same feelings as humans. He didn't really care if this man he didn't know was missing a dog. Liam didn't even particularly like the dog.

"Did you leave the back door open? Maybe he's just in the yard waiting for you. You leave it open sometimes." Mai rubbed Corrato's shoulder as she walked past him, headed for the kitchen.

"That was Donato. I told him not to leave the door open. I told him Prince would get out and get hit by a car."

Mai picked her way through the mess in the kitchen. In the laundry room, she stopped at the open back door. "Uncle Donato didn't leave the back door open this time, *Babbo,*" she said gently.

"He's not out there. I called him." Corrato shuffled after his daughter. The porch lamp cast a net of light over the grass.

No dog.

"Prince! Prince, come on, boy," Mai called, clapping her hands. Then she tried whistling. A dog down the street barked, but it was too big a bark to belong to the terrier.

Corrato clamped his hat on his head and headed down the brick sidewalk toward the driveway where the van was parked.

"*Babbo,* where are you going?"

"Where do you think?"

"No, you stay here. I'll find Prince."

Liam groaned inwardly. Exhaled. "No. Both of you go inside and lock the door." He pushed the duffle bag into Mai's hands, making no attempt to sound pleased. "*I'll* find the dog."

She looked up at him with those big, dark eyes and long lashes. "This isn't your problem. You don't have to—"

"Just get him inside. Finish packing what you need. The dog couldn't have gotten far. He's got short legs."

"Call him nicely," Corrato insisted as his daughter ushered him toward the back door. "He won't come if you're not nice to him. He'll think you're angry with him and he'll run. "

"I got it." Liam raised his hand.

It wasn't hard to catch the scent of the little runt. It had not been kidnapped by Donato's killer as feared but had merely wandered across the backyard in pursuit of fresh bunny. Liam picked up both scents right away and followed them down an alley, across a street, and into another yard.

The night air was chilly and it made Liam grumpy. It would be a wet ride home on his bike tonight. The smell of rain was in the air and it was damp. Thick, dark clouds hung low in the sky's canopy and there was no moonlight. He had half a mind to just head for home. He could probably call Kaleigh and get her to steal Arlan's truck and come get him. There were others in Clare Point he could call. There would be no questions asked. At least not until tomorrow.

After all, who was he kidding here? He was no rescuer of women in distress. He didn't even want to rescue the stupid dog. He didn't want to protect Mai or her father. He was just curious as to what had happened to the dead old man. Professional curiosity. That, and he wanted to screw the HF. That was all it was about.

"Prince," he murmured, feeling like an idiot. As if he had conjured up the storm clouds himself, rain began to fall. "Come on, boy." He was getting close. The rabbit had run in one direction at this point; the runaway dog had gone another.

At the corner of a six-foot-tall wooden privacy fence, he spotted a place where a board had been broken or kicked in. The hole was just big enough for a rat terrier to squeeze through. The dog had gone that way. He rolled his eyes. Of course it had....

Liam had the ability to morph into almost any animal he wanted. Reptiles were hard, but in a tight spot, he could even manage a crocodile or a Gila monster. He'd have no problem slipping under the fence if he was a cat or a small dog.

He used the gate instead.

The minute he entered the fenced-in yard, he heard the guttural growl of a big dog. The growl was followed by a small yip.

"*Puh-lease,*" Liam muttered. On the opposite side of the yard, he spotted a big-ass pit bull. It had the Prince of

Dogs cornered. The pit bull growled viciously and the terrier yipped back, the fence behind him, making his final stand.

As Liam crossed the bare dirt yard, he tried to avoid the piles of dog doo. A *pleasant* scent as it mixed with the falling rain. It smelled like it had been a long time since grass had grown here or someone had bothered to clean up the animal waste. It was a crime, people who kept their animals locked up like this. It turned them mean. He could hear the meanness, the deep sorrow, in the pit bull's growl.

As he walked, he scanned the ground for a weapon. Leaning against a rusted clothes pole was a three-foot-long piece of two-by-four. He picked it up. "Okay, back off, big boy. I take the Prince of Dogs, I get out of here, and you go back to...whatever a dog does in a forty-by-forty space," he said, using his best dog-negotiator's tone.

At the sound of his voice, the pit bull looked over its massive, muscular shoulder and growled at Liam.

"You don't want to go there," he muttered. "Trust me."

Realizing Liam was a true threat and the terrier was only a potential snack, the pit bull turned around, baring its teeth, staring with lifeless eyes.

"Just walk away," Liam suggested, motioning with the two-by-four. "And no one gets hurt. *You,* in particular, don't get hurt."

The dog, the size of a small Volkswagen, lunged without warning. That was the problem with caged animals. They were unpredictable. Liam considered giving the canine a little tap with the two-by-four, but midair, he realized he'd have to break the board over the canine's head to so much as get its attention.

So he morphed.

The Bengal tiger was an impulse. He could have just become a bigger pit bull than the VW and called it a day. But that seemed a dull option. The two-by-four went flying as Liam felt his body convulse. One minute he was leather jacket and waiter pants, the next, fur, stripes, and teeth.

He scared the hell out of the pit bull. They collided in midair and with a snarl, Liam brought one great paw across the dog's shoulder. His claws barely connected, but the dog howled with pain and terror. They both hit the ground at approximately the same time. Four paws to the ground, Liam prepared for the dog to come at him again, but instead, it took off, headed for a plastic igloo dog-house. It yipped all the way to the shelter and crawled inside.

Easy enough, Liam thought. Then, flicking his tail, he sauntered toward the rat terrier. To his surprise, the little dog didn't run and cower, but instead, threw his shoulders back and bared his needle teeth. Well, *of course,* the dog was afraid of a tiger. *How many tigers did he know?*

Liam morphed back to his human form. "Okay, Prince," he said, glancing in the direction of the lights in the house. Fortunately, they had the TV so loud, they hadn't heard their dog barking or the Bengal tiger kick its ass. "Let's hit the road, Prince," he said, trying to sound *nice.*

The terrier bared his teeth again and barked furiously.

Liam groaned. It wouldn't take long for the pit bull to realize the tiger was gone and he'd been replaced by a man. "Prince! Come on, damn it! It's raining out here and I'm standing in a pile of dog shit."

But he wouldn't come.

Liam glanced over his shoulder toward the gate. How did he get himself into these things? He knew the easiest way to get Prince home, but it was so . . . *emasculating.*

He gave the "nice dog" speech one last time. The dog took a step toward him, on the offensive now. If Liam wasn't careful, he was going to get bitten.

"Fine," Liam muttered. And morphed.

Prince took one look at him and lunged forward. Liam raced off. He hopped across the yard, through the hole in the fence, down the street, and into the alley that ran along Mai's property. In the corner of her yard, just out of the circle of light from the porch lamp, he let the rat terrier get almost close enough to catch a mouthful of rabbit dinner and then he morphed. One minute he was a brown bunny, the next, a vampire hit man, pretending to be an antiques dealer, scooping up a rat terrier.

Either Prince had figured out Liam was a shape-shifter and it was best to go along with the plan, or he was so confused that he didn't have time to react. At the back door, Liam knocked.

Corrato was there in an instant, pushing the yellow curtain aside, peering through the glass window. "Prince!" He unlocked the door.

Liam stepped in and pushed the dog into the old man's arms. "Mai," he called, "I've got him. Let's go."

"Thank you, thank you," Corrato said. "We'll never forget this, Prince and I. We got your back." He waggled a gnarled finger under Liam's nose. "You remember that."

Mai walked into the kitchen, shutting the lights off behind her. "Thank God. Thank you, Liam."

"So, you ready?" Standing in the doorway, Liam stuffed his hands into his pockets. He was cold now, wet from the rain. He just wanted to dump them off at Cousin Suzy's and get home. On his bike. In the rain. With dog shit on his boots.

"We're ready. *Babbo*, let's go. No, don't put Prince down. Just carry him to the car." Halfway across the floor, she stopped and wrinkled her nose, looking around the kitchen. "Does it smell like wet cat in here?"

* * *

Mai stood at the window of Suzy's living room, watching through the narrow opening in the drapes. Despite the pouring rain, Liam took his time walking to his bike. She felt bad that he was driving home in the rain. She'd offered to give him a ride to Clare Point, bring him back tomorrow to get his bike, but he seemed eager to just get out of Dodge.

Not that she blamed him. She'd be anywhere but here right now, if she had a choice.

The whole situation was crazy. It was crazy on every level imaginable. Uncle Donato murdered. The death threat. How could her life have turned upside down so quickly, just because she agreed to let an old man in failing health move into her home?

She watched Liam mount his motorcycle and pull the black helmet over his head. He was good-looking. More than good-looking—he was make-your-heart-thump-and-your-panties-damp hot. Those couple of kisses they had shared today were probably the best kisses she'd had in her life. She'd felt a connection with Liam from their first meeting, but when his lips touched hers, it was as if he was touching a part of her that no one had *ever* touched. As crazy as it sounded, even in her head, it was as if he could reach her soul.

Good kisser aside, what had possessed her to make him her knight in shining armor? Again? The first time, she had called him on impulse. But today, it hadn't been impulse. She'd hung up the phone after the death threat, thought about it, and decided not to call the police, but to call him.

What made her think she could trust him?

She just *knew*. It was something in his sad, dark eyes. She had seen right through his tough exterior the day she met him in his antiques shop. He played a good enough game, but not good enough to fool her. He had a good heart and somehow, from the moment she met him, she had known he was the kind of guy you could depend on. No matter what.

So if he was such a good guy, why would she put his life in danger?

Chapter 7

Liam stuffed his hands into his jeans pockets as he walked down the sidewalk midday on Friday. The rain had stopped around two in the morning. He'd awakened around then, breathing hard, covered in sweat. Despite the bright sun shining on his face, he felt chilled, even now, as he remembered the dream. Or maybe relived the moment. After a while, it was all the same.

That night in Paris, he'd fluttered on the wings of a raven between the bars, through the open window, into an outer hallway of the Gaudet *palais*. With no one in sight, he had returned to his human form. His mind worked at its best, at his quickest, when he was human. His human thought processes were still accessible when he was an animal, but he also had to deal with all the instincts, fears, and desires of that animal, which made situations more complicated. He needed no complications that night.

The tiled hall had been stacked with boxes, confirming his intelligence reports from spies, hired by the sept, to infiltrate the suspects' home, business, lives. The Gaudet brothers were *going out of town*, which was the reason he'd decided to pay a visit tonight, without sept final approval for the kill. He understood the need for bureaucracy, even among vampires, but sometimes the wheels of bureaucracy turned too damned slow, which was exactly how these men had avoided arrest and prosecution by the authorities all these years. If he let another day go by, Liam was afraid the murdering pedophiles would slip out of his hands and into hiding. The downside of going in without the sept's blessing, besides risking being tossed off the Kill Team, was the danger of having to go in alone. But he refused to put his fellow team members at risk of being punished alongside him. It was kind of the definition of going rogue, wasn't it?

But alone in the hall that night, he'd had second thoughts. What if something went wrong? What if he was able to capture only one brother and not the other? Surely they had a plan for a breach of security on the scale he was about to create; he had known these kinds of men long enough to know there were always backup plans.

The children would be slaughtered.

Witnesses were never a good idea. Especially victims of sexual abuse. Which meant Liam couldn't fail.

It was at that point, as he crept down the hall in the darkness, that his anger had begun to build. There was never room for anger in the workplace, but with his job, it was crucial that he remain emotionally removed. If Liam had any regrets about what he did that night—which he kept telling himself he didn't—but if he *did*, that's where they began.

He remembered tightening his jaw. His fists. He could feel his blood pumping, throbbing in his veins. Heat in his face. All those innocent kids, dead or damaged for the rest of their lives.

When he came around the corner and unexpectedly met a guard, Liam sprang without hesitation. The guy drew a pistol, equipped with a silencer, from his waistband. Apparently the Gaudet brothers were always respectful of their neighbors.

The guard, a big, burly guy with a ridiculous Hitler mustache, was quick enough. But there weren't many of

God's creatures quicker than an enraged vampire. The rule was self-defense, but no needless killing. When Liam flew into him, he'd fully intended to follow the rule. He knocked the pistol out of the brute's hand and sank his teeth into his fat neck.

The moment the blood rushed into his mouth, Liam tasted the foulness of it. *The children.* He tasted the children on his lips and it almost made him vomit. He'd have rather drunk sewer water. Apparently a perk of working for pedophiles was that you got your own opportunities.

Guilty. A sin punishable by death.

Too disgusted to drink enough blood to kill him, Liam pulled out his knife and cut the bastard's carotid artery. As he shoved him backward, he saw the fear in the guy's eyes and he was glad he had frightened him. He was glad his last earthly emotion would be terror. He was glad he was the one who had sent the Frenchman straight to the gates of hell.

Up to that point, the dream had been an accurate account of what had happened that night, but then he'd heard the screams and the blood had begun to ooze from the stone walls.

In truth, the screams hadn't come until later.

"Liam?"

He looked up, startled for a second. He didn't remember walking up her sidewalk or ringing the doorbell. "Peigi."

"I was around back raking leaves. Didn't you hear me? I hollered for you to come around." She pushed open the screen door. She lived in a pretty turn-of-the-century cottage painted a light turquoise, just one block off the beach. "You mind if I rake while we talk?"

"No. Not at all."

As they walked through the bright, cheerful house decorated in white wicker, yellow chintz, and Georgia O'Keeffe floral prints, he heard the distinctive sound of a video game coming from down the hall.

He glanced in the direction of the sounds of machine-gun fire and hand-grenade explosions. "You play a lot of 'Call of Duty,' Peigi?"

She wrinkled her nose. She was a small, stout woman with gray hair. Her haircut was a sensible short style, her clothing equally sensible. She had always looked to him as if she'd stepped off the pages of an L.L. Bean catalog. Apparently, an L.L. Bean gal who liked the blatant sexuality of Georgia O'Keeffe's work. "It's Brian."

Liam lifted his brow. Last time he had seen Brian, Brian had been a seventy-something male L.L. Bean model. Not exactly the PlayStation 3 "Call of Duty" sort of guy.

"You ever read your e-mail?"

He didn't answer.

"If you did, you'd know more of what was going on around here." She continued through the open, airy kitchen into a screened-in porch. "Brian was reborn last month." She pushed the door open, stepping down into the yard.

Liam followed. Peigi, the current leader of the General Council, always made him a little uneasy. She didn't seem to get that he was a killer by nature and that she ought to be afraid of him, or at the very least, cautious. Whenever he was around Peigi, she kind of made him feel like he was still an awkward fourteen-year-old.

"Sorry to hear that."

"So is he. He doesn't want to go to school. He wants to eat pizza, sleep half the day, and play video games." She grabbed a rake and tossed it to Liam. She was fast for an AARP card carrier with a bit of a beer belly.

Liam caught it.

"Into that pile," she instructed.

He did as he was told.

"Brian knows he has to go to school, but I may let it go until after winter break and then enroll him. My *nephew*." She rolled her eyes.

Sept members remained married to the partners they had at the time they were cursed by God in fifth-century Ireland. Any adult had the right to have sex with any other consenting vampire, but to keep life as simple as possible, one was expected to live with his or her spouse for eternity. Or until their situation on Earth changed. For couples like Kaleigh and Rob who were close in age, it wasn't really a problem. They died and were reborn within a couple of years of each other, but for Peigi and Brian, it was a little harder. Brian had been more than ten years her senior when they had been transformed into vampires, so while he had just been reborn as a teen, Peigi might not die and be reborn as a teen for years. It made for awkward situations, but like other couples, Peigi and Brian adjusted. That didn't mean they had to like it.

"He's got an attitude right now, that one." Peigi yanked her rake through loose leaves with a vengeance. "He won't listen to a thing I say. He leaves dishes in the sink. The toilet seat up. All he does is whine: It's not *fair*. It's not *right*." She frowned. "You know the drill."

He raked leaves into the massive pile she'd made in the center of the yard. "I seem to recall saying the same thing to my mother not too, too many years ago."

"You're another one." She pointed at him with her rake. "A handful." She smiled. "But you make good men when you grow up." She began to rake again, pulling leaves from a flower bed. "Oh, before I forget, can I borrow your Montclair?"

"Sure. Of course." Liam owned a 1957 light blue Mercury Montclair convertible. It was a sweet ride. He kept it in a storage unit in Lewes. "What for?"

"Halloween parade." She rolled her eyes as she raked. "My turn to be the Queen of the Crypt. I *won* the honor when I lost at poker the other night with the ladies."

He chuckled. "Fiona Hill?"

Peigi nodded tragically. "Damned fine poker player, that witch." She glanced up at him. "So how are you, Liam? Honestly."

"Is this an official interview?"

"Nope. Just the friendly neighborhood old lady asking the young man who's just returned home how he's doing."

He cut his eyes at her. "Right." He went back to raking. "I'm good. Fine. Terrific. Couldn't be better."

"Glad to be back in Clare Point?"

He chose his words carefully. "It's nice to see people."

"You need to visit. Reconnect. I know it's hard for those of you *on the road.*" She made it sound like he was a traveling salesman.

"I ran into Kaleigh. She's becoming quite the young woman."

"She always does." Peigi glanced at him. "But not just Kaleigh. Not just those you're close with. You need to reconnect with all of us, Liam. Otherwise, you forget who you are. Why you do what you do."

"I never forget," he said quietly, thankful for the rake in his hand and a job to do. He didn't want to look her in the eye. In some ways, Peigi was more like his mother than his mother was. For Mary McCathal, Liam could do no wrong. Peigi saw him as more... fallible. "You talk with your brother?" she asked.

"I was going to give him a call."

"He may be appointed to the state Supreme Court."

Liam's older brother, John, had made the decision to be put up for adoption in this life cycle so that he could separate himself from Clare Point. It wasn't something the sept allowed often, but it was done occasionally. John had been adopted by a clueless couple, with the help of sept lawyers in Maryland. He had become an attorney, and then a judge. Vampires in high places...

"I don't like to bother him. I know he needs to remain apart from us."

"That doesn't mean you can't have lunch with him. How about your mother? You speak with her?"

"I have."

"She come to her senses yet?"

He gave a shake of his head. "Not to my knowledge."

"Victor, of all people," she scoffed. "I never saw that one coming."

"Victor probably didn't either." He chuckled to himself. "So anyone go looking for them? She wouldn't say a word to me as to where she was, but everyone is saying they think they're somewhere in Florida."

"The Council talked about sending someone to retrieve them, but they decided to leave them a few months and let them get it out of their system. They'll come home. Our runaways always do."

Liam raked for a couple minutes in silence. "So, this investigation," he said, thinking it was time he got on with what he'd come for.

"Uh-huh?"

"The Council started it?"

"We're looking into the matter."

"That's not the same thing as launching an investigation," he observed. "And no one's called about interviewing me. No one's even asked me my side since the initial interrogation."

"Quit being so dramatic, Liam. You weren't *interrogated* and you know it." She set aside her rake, seeming pleased with the size of the pile of leaves she'd made. It was taller than she was. "You know the process is necessary."

"Yeah, I know." He leaned on the rake. "So when do we get started? I have no doubt that when the Council hears my explanation, I'll be exonerated."

"Meaning that you *didn't* kill the Gaudet brothers *without* High Council's say-so *after* you were given the order to *stand down?*"

He exhaled. "It was complicated, Peigi. In the field, situations change; decisions have to be made instantaneously. You know that. You've done what I do."

"Step back." Peigi waved him away from the leaf pile.

"What are you—" Before Liam could get the words out of his mouth, the enormous pile of leaves spontaneously combusted, exploding in a flash of bright light and intense heat.

"Damn, Peigi." He threw up his arms to shield himself from the blast as flames shot above the roofline of the porch. "You could have warned me."

Peigi was pyrokinetic. Apparently, she didn't get to use her gift as often as she liked. They were expected to take care with their gifts, always concealing them from humans, but no one would say anything to her about lighting a bonfire in the privacy of her own fenced-in backyard. Even a twenty-foot-high bonfire.

She stood back, hands on her hips, and watched with obvious satisfaction. "You want to put the rakes in the shed on your way out?" she said.

Meaning their chat was over. Meaning she wasn't going to tell him a thing about the investigation or how soon he could expect to get out of town.

"No problem. So, someone will contact me about my interview?"

"I'm sure they will." She smiled.

He didn't return the gesture.

*   *   *

On his way back to the shop, Liam's phone rang. "Fia," he said, genuinely glad to hear her voice. About once a century, they had a fling. It was always short-lived, but enjoyable for both of them. These days, though, she and Arlan were a permanent thing, apparently. As permanent as vampire love could be, at least. The guy had been in love with her for at least five hundred years, so Liam was happy for him. Jealous. But happy for him. "Thanks for calling me back."

"It's always good to talk to the local Jesse James," she quipped.

"Very funny."

As he walked down the sidewalk, he nodded to Mary Hall, who was in her yard, talking to her neighbor. He didn't care for the old biddy. She'd been having an affair with his father at the time of his death; permissible by sept law, but that didn't necessarily make for fun family dinners. He smiled sweetly and kept walking, even though she was hurrying toward him, obviously hoping to speak to him.

"I'm a funny gal," Fia said in his ear. "Better than being a cannibal. Please tell me you didn't strip the flesh off those creeps, dry it, and use it for jerky."

"Would it help if I *did* deny it?"

"Nah. Too good a story. So what's up?"

"I was wondering if you could do that magic thing you do with the criminal data banks and see if you can find anything about *a Weasel* in Jersey." It sounded silly when he said it.

"The animal?"

"Yes. Well, no. I know this girl—"

She groaned loudly. "Don't say it! Don't tell me she's human. You know better, Liam. God knows *I* do."

He smiled and went on. "I'm guessing the guy might be kind of old by now, so I need you to look at the mafia in north Jersey, possibly New York City area, twenty years back, maybe longer."

"Live next door to Tony Soprano?"

"Arlan know what a funny girl you are?" He looked both ways and jogged across the street, wanting to put plenty of distance between him and Mary.

She laughed. "Oh, he's well aware."

"So, anyway," Liam continued, "I've got no name."

"Just an animal," she offered.

"Just the Weasel. But something tells me you're going to find him pretty easily."

"You do know I'm an FBI agent, right? A federal government employee? I can't just go into FBI data banks and give random civilians information on other civilians."

"If you find anything, could you call me back?"

"If I find him, you going to eat him?"

"If I do, how about I save you some of the sweetbreads?" Liam hung up, smiling. Maybe it wasn't so bad being home. Today he almost felt relaxed.

A car went by and the muffler popped, and it was all Liam could do to keep from throwing himself on the ground.

Relaxation was highly overrated, anyway.

Chapter 8

Liam grabbed the milk carton and wandered to the curtainless window. He gave the milk a sniff and frowned. It wasn't the milk that soured him—the milk was still good—it was the teenager standing on the sidewalk below. She was wearing jeans and a sweatshirt with the hood pulled up so he couldn't see her face, but he knew it was her. He opened the window. "Don't we have a curfew for hooligans in this town?"

"It's only eight o'clock," Kaleigh called up, her tone of voice accusing him of being a moron.

"Were you planning on knocking on my door or just standing there all night?"

"Would you have answered the door if I had knocked?"

"Not if I'd known it was you." He flashed her a smart-ass grin. "So, you coming up or not?"

"Push the window up farther." She glanced up and down the street. It was dark and quiet.

Not sure what she was up to, but willing to play along, he opened the window.

"Get back." Kaleigh waved her hand. "Way back."

Liam stepped back. A second later, the teen was levitating outside his second-story window. She threw one leg over the ledge, then the other, sat down hard with a clunk, and then shot through the window, feet first.

"Nice," he said with a nod. "Not the most graceful I've seen, but not bad for a newbie."

She grabbed the milk from his hand, sniffed it, and took a drink from the carton. "Thanks. When I first learned how to do it, I was breaking glass, landing in trees. I even sprained my ankle on a landing once. It was ugly."

He leaned against the kitchen counter. He'd remodeled the whole room a few years back, but it looked unused, with bare walls and counters. Mostly because it was.

"Got any cereal to go with this?" She held up the milk.

He pointed to a cupboard.

She opened it and pulled out a box. "This is it? Rice Krispies?"

"I know I don't have to tell you that you shouldn't be doing that. The Flying Nun thing. One of those pesky humans might see you." He went to the window and closed it. It was cold outside and he was in only jeans and a T-shirt.

"You, know, that's the thing I don't get." She opened another cabinet door and got out a bowl. "You have dinner yet? You want some, too?"

"No. Yes."

"See, we're not supposed to practice any of our *gifts,* but we're supposed to *develop* them for the benefit of the sept. How the hell are we supposed to do that?" She poked around in the cupboard, then the sink, then took out a coffee mug from the cupboard. "What? You don't have two bowls?"

"It's just me. I can only eat from one bowl at a time."

"Fine. You get the mug." She managed to find two of the three spoons he owned and sat down at the dinette table.

He'd bought it in 1953, but it was in pristine condition: chrome, red vinyl, and red and gold sparkly Formica. It went with the 1950s kitchen design.

She set the mug and one of the spoons on the table, sat down, and started to make herself a bowl of cereal.

Liam took his appointed chair. "I guess you're supposed to practice them in the privacy of your own home."

"My mom yells at me every time I do it. She says I'm going to fall and get hurt." She pushed the box across the table.

He poured his cereal. "So what are you doing here on a Saturday night? You're seventeen. Aren't you supposed to be out on a date or something?"

"Aren't you?" She passed him the milk.

He studied the way the cereal washed up on the sides of the coffee mug as he added the milk.

Kaleigh's face lit up suddenly. "OMG!" She stuffed a spoonful of cereal into her mouth. "There's a girl! Really? I was just goofing with you. I didn't know you had a girl. Pie?" She scrunched up her freckled nose. "Her name is *Pie?*"

"Get the hell out of my head or you're going back out the window." He pointed at her with his spoon, using his best authoritarian voice. "You're not supposed to be levitating *or* reading people's minds, uninvited."

"So what's really her name?" She grinned, eating another mouthful of cereal.

"Kaleigh, I really don't want to discuss this with you. Frankly, it's none of your business."

She lifted a brow. She was a pretty girl, turning into a striking young woman with doe-like brown eyes and the most gorgeous red hair he'd ever seen. The little brown freckles that dotted her nose and cheeks were just icing on the cake.

"I'm your wisewoman. How can I be wise if I don't know what's going on in my people's lives?" She munched on her cereal. "She's human, isn't she?" When he didn't answer, she slapped her hand on the table. "I knew it! Oh, you're naughty, Liam. You're very naughty."

Liam took a second to put up a mental wall to block her from reading any more in his head. Most of the sept could converse easily without speaking. It was an ability they had cultivated over time to aid their survival. But Kaleigh, once she was fully of age again, at around twenty-five, would be one of the few who could read vampire minds, even with a mental road block carefully erected to keep her out. In her last lifetime, she had also begun to develop the ability to read human minds. It was a little scary, how she was growing stronger with each passing century.

"So...where'd you meet her?" Kaleigh asked in a sing-song voice.

He knew he shouldn't say anything. But he didn't have anyone to talk to. Loneliness was part of the job. And sometimes, not usually, but sometimes, it made him sad. He hadn't set out to be a loner. Not in the beginning. "She came here to the shop last week," he said into his cup of cereal.

Kaleigh smiled. "Her name's not Pie, is it?"

"It's Mai."

"That's pretty. She nice? She know you're a vampire? I don't think it's necessary in a relationship for them to know, but you have to be careful with the ol', you know." She drew back her lips and bared her fangs for just a second.

"It's not a *relationship*." He spooned cereal into his mouth. "It's nothing."

"If it's nothing, why can't you stop thinking about her? You think about her a lot. You're thinking about her right now."

"I said, stay out of my damned head," he barked.

She didn't seem the least bit offended by the anger in his voice. "I'm kinda surprised." She watched him from across the table, thoughtfully. "You usually try to stay away from humans. Shoot, you try to stay away from us."

He kept his gaze fixed on his cup of cereal. He didn't like the way she was scrutinizing him right now. Kaleigh could read not only minds, but emotions, too. He could handle the mind-reading, but he didn't want her to know how he felt about *anything*. Hell, *he* didn't want to know how he felt. "She needed my help."

"With what? Like a broken antique lamp? Gimme the box." She motioned for him to pass back the cereal.

"Kaleigh, I'm not going to talk about this with you. Now tell me why you're outside my window at eight o'clock on a Saturday night. Why aren't you out with your friends? On a date with Rob?"

She exhaled as she poured more cereal into her bowl. "Had a fight with Rob. Just didn't feel like hanging out with my friends. They're all so—" She put a spoonful of cereal into her mouth and slurped up the milk.

"What?" he asked.

"Teenagery."

"Teenagery?"

"You know, full of angst and woe. Flipping out over ridiculous things . Seeing slights when none were intended. Making bad choices. Just being genuinely stupid."

He laughed and finished his cereal. "I don't really think you can hold that against them, can you? I mean, they *are* teenagers. Actually, *technically,* Kaleigh, so are you."

"I know." She dropped her spoon into her bowl and pushed it aside. "I just feel so . . . so far removed from them sometimes. You know, the whole wisewoman thing." She folded her arms over her chest and stared at her bowl.

Liam let her sit quietly for a moment. "And Rob? What's going on there? He's a good guy, Kaleigh."

"I know." She groaned. "It's just that everything's so . . . complicated. Him, me, the sept. The friggin' world. I swear, it seems like it's worse every time I'm reborn. It just gets so...lame."

He wanted to laugh. Maybe cry. He understood *exactly* what she meant. There were times when it all got so *lame,* he might have ended his own life, if he could have. Of course, that was precisely the point of God's curse. They couldn't die until they got it right. Until their souls were redeemed.

"You need to cut yourself a break once in a while, Kaleigh. I think you've got it the hardest of any of us."

She frowned. "Right, and *you've* got it so easy." She leaned toward him, pressing her hands to the table. Her fingernails were painted a sparkly blue. "Having to kill people. I mean, even knowing they're evil, it's got to be hard. God still made them. They're still His children."

Liam absently touched, through his T-shirt, the crucifix he always wore around his neck. "It's not really that," he mused.

"No?" She met his gaze.

He exhaled, trying to find the right words. "No, it's—"

His cell phone rang and he pulled it out of his jeans pocket. Looking at the screen, he flipped it open, getting out of his chair. "Hey," he said, walking down the hall to put some distance between him and Kaleigh. He knew she'd eavesdrop one way or another if she wanted to, but he wasn't going to make it easy for her.

"Liam," Mai said.

He waited. He could tell she was debating whether to go on. He was debating whether he was strong enough to hang up. But he was a weakling. "What is it, Mai?"

"He just called again," she whispered. "Here. At Suzy's house. Liam, he asked for me. He gave Suzy some bogus name and acted like he was one of my customers." Her voice trembled. "He says he's coming after *Babbo* next if we don't give him *the package*. I don't know what to do. I can't stay here. I can't put Suzy's family at risk."

He thought for minute.

"Liam?"

"Yeah. I'm here." He walked back down the hall, toward the kitchen, his mind going a mile a minute. "Pack up your stuff. I'll be there shortly to get you and your dad." He hung up the phone. "Think you can borrow your parents' car?" he asked Kaleigh, who was rinsing off the dishes in the sink. "I need a ride to Lewes."

She turned around, grinning. "No *problemo*."

Forty-five minutes later, Liam was standing in Suzy's living room with Mai's duffle bag in one hand, Corrato's plastic bag in the other. He felt awkward and a little claustrophobic. The walls were covered with family photos, the upholstery with bright florals, and every flat surface with knickknacks. There were glass mushrooms and gnomes and fairies, ceramic owls and frogs, books, magazines, throw pillows, and hand-crocheted afghans. Liam liked his surroundings like his life, uncluttered and controlled. This room was definitely out of control.

"We'll get some more dog food at the store tomorrow, Mr. Ricci. I know a place that carries his brand," Liam smoothly lied.

"You should call me Corrato," the old man said. He was dressed, but, due to the hour, wearing corduroy slippers. The dog danced at his feet. "Prince and I have agreed, you should call me Corrato."

Mai walked back into the living room. "*Babbo*, don't carry your coat. Put it on. It's cold out."

"I don't understand why you're leaving like this." Suzy stood in the doorway between the kitchen and the living room, twisting a dish towel in her hands. "Have I done something wrong?" She seemed genuinely distressed.

"Not at all, Suzy." Mai patted her arm as she slipped into her coat. "We've already overstayed our welcome."

"But it's only been two nights."

"Your kids should sleep in their own beds. It's fine. Really. I'll call you tomorrow." Mai gave her a quick smile and glanced at Liam. "I think we're ready to go."

If Suzy wondered why Mai needed a guy she barely knew to take them home, she didn't say anything. Of course they weren't going home, but Suzy didn't know that. Liam hadn't had to say anything to Mai; she knew it was better for her cousin if Suzy just thought they'd gone home.

On the way to the car, Liam let Corrato get ahead of them so he could walk beside Mai.

"I'm not even going to say thank you because it's already beyond that," she said quietly, brushing his arm with her fingertips. When she looked up at him with those big, dark eyes of hers, the sexual tension between them crackled in the air like electricity. She'd been thinking about him. She wanted him as much as he wanted her. He wanted her lips, her breasts. Her blood.

Of course, it wouldn't happen. It couldn't happen. He was already hip-deep in hot water with the sept. To dally with an HF practically under their noses would only add insult to injury. He didn't do HFs. Not anymore. Not after Roxanne. Period.

"Not a problem," Liam muttered.

"Just the same, I want you to know I really do appreciate it. I don't know if I could handle this alone. Not right now." Again, the eyes. The touch.

Liam almost groaned out loud. He was in trouble. Big trouble. Fortunately, he'd thought this through on his way over. The easiest way to avoid having sex with women you weren't supposed to have sex with was to never be alone with them. Never have the opportunity. She had a father in his seventies and a dog practically glued to her hip. How hard could this be?

The plan was to take them to his mom's vacant house. They'd be safe there until he could figure out what was going on. No one would ever be able to track them there because no one knew who he was or where he'd come from. Not even Cousin Suzy. The plan was perfect.

Chapter 9

Okay, so the plan was *almost* perfect.

Liam stood in his mother's kitchen in the dark in half an inch of water.

"It's wet," Corrato announced. "Water all over the floor." He peeked into the half bath off the laundry room where they'd come in the back door. "Looks like your toilet overflowed."

"This is ridiculous." Liam stood there, baffled. "No one's been here in months." But the minute he flipped on the kitchen light, it became obvious that wasn't true. "Son-of-a-bitch," he muttered. "I'll kill them."

"Kill who?" Mai laid her hand on her father's shoulder. "*Babbo,* why don't you take Prince outside for a potty break? Keep him on his leash and don't go anywhere."

"Wet in here. Cold out there," Corrato grumbled as he went back out the door.

Mai walked into the kitchen, taking it all in. It looked something like her kitchen right now, only not to the same degree. Cupboards had been left open, dirty dishes in the sink, packages left open on the counters, but no one had been looking for anything. Except maybe snacks.

She wrinkled her nose. "You said this is your *mom's* house? I swear, I think I smell marijuana."

Liam grabbed his phone from the pocket of his leather jacket, flipped it open, and scanned his contacts for the right number. She answered on the third ring. "You know anything about your buddies hanging out in my mother's house?" Liam demanded.

"*My buddies?* What are you talking about?" Kaleigh asked, her hackles going up immediately.

Liam was so angry, he was gritting his teeth. Mai and her father couldn't stay here tonight. The water had run from the bathroom, through the laundry room, and all the way into the living room, soaking the carpet. There were thousands of dollars in damage here. It would take days, weeks to clean up this mess.

"You know who. The fucking teens. My house smells like reefer and someone apparently had the munchies!" He kicked an empty can that had once held peaches across the floor. It didn't go far; it only splashed water on the cabinets.

"I don't know anything about that, Liam, I swear I don't," Kaleigh said, taking on a placating tone. "But I'll see what I can find out."

He hung up without saying good-bye.

"You know who did this?" Mai asked.

He stuffed his phone back in his pocket. "I have an idea. Everyone in town knew the house was empty. It wasn't meant maliciously. The kids, they just get a little—" He didn't finish his sentence, thinking it better she just assume this was typical teenage mischief. Actually, young vampires, trapped by the pressure of what they were and how the process was played out again and again, were usually much more badly behaved than their human counterparts.

"Well, you obviously can't stay here." Liam gestured at the mess and let his hand fall to his side.

"It doesn't smell. It's just water. If we got a wet vac, maybe—"

"No. Those kids are going to have to come here and

clean this mess up." He walked around her, avoiding eye contact with Mai. In the car on the ride over, he'd become obsessed with her lips. He hadn't been able to stop stealing glances at them. He hadn't been able to stop thinking about how perfectly shaped they were. How full and kissable.

"Then just take us to a hotel," Mai said. "There's got to be a hotel in town."

Actually, there wasn't. Not one open. By this time of year, the seaside town of Clare Point was closing down for the winter, its inhabitants gently ousting the human tourists to give the vampires a break. Everything would be open again Halloween weekend for the big annual Pirate Parade, but the doors of the little hotels and bed-and-breakfasts were closed tighter than a drum this week.

Time alone in the winter allowed them to let their guard down a little and take a breather. It was hard keeping your life a secret from the outside world, especially when you depended on it for your livelihood, as a tourist town did. But over the years, the Kahills had pretty much figured it out. Part of the trick was never putting a house or a business up for sale, thus preventing any humans from moving into town. In Clare Point, not a single piece of property was owned by a human.

"Everything's closed." Liam flipped off the kitchen light, leaving her in the dark.

"So we'll go to a hotel somewhere else." She followed him. "No big deal. I'll drop you off at your place and we'll go to Dover for the night. I'll figure this out tomorrow."

He turned so fast in the doorway that he startled her and she took a step back. *Good.* If she had any sense, she *would* be afraid of him. "Use your head, Mai. Whoever this is who's calling you, he isn't screwing around. If you're not at home, he'll start checking hotels. What did the coroner say about your uncle's death?"

She looked up at him, her hands clasped and held to her

breasts. "What do you mean? He...he said they slit his throat. You saw him, Liam."

"I saw the wound, Mai. Exactly. And the first nick didn't kill him."

She looked away, but he saw moisture gather in her eyes. "How the hell do you know about mortal wounds?" she asked. "The coroner said they cut him a couple times superficially, but maybe because they didn't really want to do it, or weren't sure how."

"That's bullshit."

She let her hands fall and looked up at him stubbornly. "That's what he said."

"Then he's wrong." Liam glared. "They cut your uncle to try to scare him, to get information out of him. When he wouldn't or couldn't give them what they wanted, they got pissed and slit his throat. They wanted him to suffer. You want to go to a hotel and wake up to find your father lying in a pool of blood in the hallway in the morning?"

She opened her mouth to argue, then closed it. Even in the dark, he could see her face perfectly. She was scared. But she was angry, too. With herself. With him. But she still desired him. He saw that, too. Which made plan B all the more dangerous...for both of them.

He flexed his fingers, balled them into fists, and flexed them again, trying to release the energy coursing through his body. Part of it was his attraction to her, but part of it was his inherent resentment of anyone who preyed on others. It seriously pissed him off. It made him do things he shouldn't do. Like the night he had gone over the wall after the Gaudet brothers.

"You're coming to my place," he said, when he trusted his voice.

She didn't argue.

*   *   *

The short ride to the shop was filled with awkward silence. He parked Mai's van around back in the alley. Liam
knew he was taking a serious risk with the Council, bringing humans into the town to stay in his home in the winter
season. He didn't need to piss them off any further than he
already had, but he couldn't, in good conscience, send Mai
and her father to a hotel. Clare Point was the safest place
for them until he figured out who was after them and why.
Here, they not only had Liam to protect them, but an entire clan of naturally suspicious vampires. Nothing happened in Clare Point that wasn't seen or heard by a Kahill,
and strangers were immediately suspect, especially this
time of year. So not only would the sept be watching Mai
and Corrato, but they would know if the Italian mafia
came to town.

Liam got out and opened the back door of the van to let
Corrato and the dog out. Just as he slid the door open, he
felt two vampires approach in the darkness. He didn't
know who they were from this distance, but he shot out a
warning telepathically. *Back off, guys.*

Back off yourself, Mr. Hotpants.

Liam groaned. At the same instant, Mai, half out of the
van, gasped.

Jake and Elwood Hildegard walked down the alley,
straight toward the van, dressed in black suits, white
shirts, skinny ties, and dark sunglasses, their fangs bared.
The two were up to no good; Liam could smell it in the
night air.

"Liam?" Mai called from the other side of the van. Her
voice was higher pitched than usual. Even though she wasn't
aware of what the danger was, she seemed to sense they
were trouble.

The Prince of Dogs, trapped in his owner's arms, began
to bark ferociously. So, the dog had a good sixth sense,
too.

Liam ducked to look at Mai through the center of the van, over the front seat. "It's okay. I know these bozos." He helped Corrato out of the vehicle.

"It's okay, boy," Corrato soothed, stroking the dog. "Just silly boys in silly costumes. Let's make a wee-wee before we go to bed. Shall we?" He tottered off.

"Bozos?" Jake demanded. He was the older of the two brothers, but only by a year. Both of them were general pains in the ass, but Jake was a bigger one. He'd had a thing for Liam for centuries and no matter how many times Liam told him he wasn't interested, or threatened to cut his head off with an ax, Jake still came on to him. "*Avez-vous entendu cela, frère?* He calls us clowns."

Liam hurried around the back of the van, coming up behind Mai. She grabbed his arm. It was dark in the alley, but you couldn't miss the fangs. Hopefully, in the shadows, she wouldn't realize they were the real thing.

"Little early for Halloween costumes, boys? Parade's not until next weekend."

"Liam, *mon amour*. If you weren't so sweet"—Jake licked his upper lip suggestively, still not drawing in his fangs—"we'd be offended, wouldn't we, brother?"

"The pretty one is Jake. Elwood is the sidekick." Liam pointed, in introduction.

Mai surprised him by laughing. "As in the Blues Brothers?"

"Don't ask," Liam muttered. The guys had, in fact, named themselves Jake and Elwood after they saw the movie about ten years ago, right after their rebirth. Most vampires kept the same first names century after century, for simplicity's sake, but there were no rules saying you couldn't change your name. So they had. Everyone called them Jake and Elwood, mostly because they thought it was funny. Except the grandmother who raised them. She still called them by their given names, Peadar and Muirgeas. Equally funny.

Liam glanced over his shoulder, afraid of letting Corrato get too far out of his sight. The old man was ignoring the vampires; he walked the dog on his leash in a little section of grass that ran along the building.

Liam turned back to the brothers. "You two shouldn't be prowling."

Jake lifted a carefully drawn eyebrow, gesturing grandly, his other hand propped on his hip. His lips were blood-red, his eyes hidden behind dark sunglasses. He wore skin-tight black pants, a shirt, and jacket, his movements over-the-top exaggerated. Liam had no problem with his homosexuality; he disliked him because he was an idiot. And idiots were dangerous.

"*Oui*. And you, my bad-ass loverboy, *vous ne devriez pas jouer avec des humains*."

Corrato walked up behind Liam and Mai. He ignored the Blues Brothers. "It's cold. Are we going in?"

Mai glanced at Liam.

"We're going in," Liam said. He opened the back door of her van on the passenger side and grabbed the bags. "If you'll excuse us, gentlemen." He put himself between the vampires and the humans. "*Le retour ce soir et vous souhaiterez que vous n'ayez pas eu*," he warned under his breath as he passed them. *Back off or someone will be hosing your blood off the pavement.*

At the back door, he unlocked it and held it open for Mai and her father. Once inside the tiny hallway, he locked it behind him. "Straight up the steps. They're a little steep," he warned.

"Big stairs are hard on little dogs," Corrato announced to no one in particular.

Mai went up the staircase first. Corrato scooped up the dog and followed, and Liam brought up the rear. He could still feel the presence of the Blues Brothers outside, but sensed they were moving on. He didn't think they were any real threat to Mai and Corrato, but their sudden appearance reminded him that even though he was protecting Mai and Corrato from humans, he put them at risk from the vampires. It was a crazy cycle they all experienced century after century; a part of them desperately wanted to save the humans, from themselves, as it were. But a part of every Kahill wanted their blood.

"It's not much," Liam explained as they reached the upper landing, where a door led into the apartment and another set of stairs led down to the shop. "I'm not usually here."

All three of them stepped into the apartment and he closed the door behind them. For a moment, they just stood there.

"Liam, is there a light?" Mai said after a moment.

Feeling like an idiot, Liam flipped a switch. He spent so much time alone that he forgot that while he might not need artificial light to see, humans did. "This way. Down the hall. There's just two bedrooms, so you'll have to share. But at least there's two beds." He passed them in the narrow hallway, holding his breath as he walked by Mai so he wouldn't smell the sweetness of her skin. It was a tight fit, and his heart was beating hard by the time he got to the end of the spare bedroom. "Just the one bathroom," he said, pointing to the open door as they went by.

He stepped into the room at the end of the hall and flipped on the light, setting down the bags. There were two painted iron beds with bare mattresses, one dresser, and two nightstands. It was so stark it was almost embarrassing, now that he stood there showing it to his *guests*. No throw rugs on the hardwood floor, not a single picture or mirror hanging on the walls. The single window was covered by Roman blinds, but there weren't even curtains. "I...

I'll get some sheets and blankets. And, um...towels," he finished awkwardly.

Corrato entered first and put the dog down, unhooking his leash. The Prince of Dogs ran right to the bed near the window and hopped up on it. "Dibs," Mai's father called.

"Pillows." Liam gestured in the direction of the hall closet, thanking sweet Jesus his mother saved everything and had filled it years ago with linens he never would have used. "I think I have pillows, too."

"Liam." Mai stopped right in front of him, putting one hand on his chest. "It's fine."

She looked up at him with those big brown eyes of hers and he felt a familiar twinge in his jeans and in his mouth. It was almost as if his fangs vibrated when he became sexually aroused. He drew his lips tight to keep his fangs under control. There was nothing he could do about the woody.

"I really appreciate this," she said under her breath. She was looking at him as if she wanted to be kissed.

Rosy lips. Rosy, sweet, kissable lips. A long, beautiful neck. A throbbing pulse. He stopped himself there. "It's not that big a deal."

"Someone killed my uncle and is now threatening to kill my father," she whispered, her breath warm on his face. "You're putting yourself in danger by bringing us here. It *is* a big deal." She lifted up on her toes, wrapping her arms around his neck, and kissed him softly. "Thank you," she whispered.

Liam's pulse was pounding in his ears. Every sense in his body was quivering with desire for her. If she kissed him again, he didn't know if he could keep himself from responding. He took a stumbling step back. "I'll get those pillows."

Chapter 10

Liam had been prepared to face the Gaudet brothers. What he had not been prepared for was the children. Or his own subsequent rage.

His dreams tonight were shaky and slightly out of focus, like a black-and-white home movie, filmed with a sixteen-millimeter camera. He saw the guard he'd killed lying at his feet and the blood that pooled in a dark puddle on the floor. He seemed no less dead, even in sepia tones. Liam stepped over the dead man, wiping his blade on his pant leg before slipping the knife back into his waistband.

He didn't know where the brothers would be, but as he walked down the dark hallway with its ancient arched ceiling, he could have sworn he could smell their stench. Going on nothing but instinct, he sensed they were together, Anatolle and Donat, as he had hoped they might be. That would make things easier. For him. Unfortunately, his instinct was not taking him toward the center of the house, where there was a dining room, a library, parlors. His nose was leading him down another passageway, this one narrower and built at an incline. The air was cooler at the end of the hallway where he found a plank and iron arched door. Through the unlocked door was a staircase leading down. He was entering the bowels of the palace.

The closer he moved, step by step, to the Gaudet brothers, the more uneasy he grew. All of his senses were alive and hypersensitive. He could feel the hair rise on his arms and on the back of his neck. Somewhere, water dripped and he heard a faint human sound. For a moment he thought it might be one of the men's voices, but when he halted at the bottom of the steps and listened, he realized it was not a man he heard, but a child. A soft sob. The clink of a chain.

The journey from the dead guard to the bottom of the steps had taken less than a couple of minutes, but now, in his nightmare, each step was drawn out painfully long until he was trembling with fear of what the next step would bring.

But he knew. Even though he had relived this moment again and again, day and night, nothing prepared him for what he saw in the nightmare when he stepped around the corner.

Children. Chained to the stone wall. Shackled. Naked. A boy, asleep on a pile of rags. A girl with big, bloodshot blue eyes blinking up at him. That night, the girl did not speak; she didn't even move. But here, now, in his twisted dream, she cried out, putting out a hand, begging him to release her.

"I'll be back for you," he whispered in French, just as he had that night.

Instead of pulling away, she reached out to him. Her hands became claws and her blue eyes ran red with blood. Suddenly the dream went Technicolor. "*Trop tard*," she accused. *Too late.*

Liam tried to pull away, tried to hush her for fear the brothers would hear them. Her claws tore at his neck and face, sinking into his flesh.

"I'm trying to help you," he cried. "I'll come back for you. I swear I will."

But she didn't seem to hear. She tore at his body, ripping his clothes, his skin, her blood mixing with his. And then he was surrounded by the children, clawing, biting. "*Trop tard.* Too late. Too late," they cried.

"No! No! I'm sorry. I came as quickly as I could!"

The little one with the blue eyes sank her teeth into him and he cried out, as much in emotional pain as physical. "I'm sorry," he said with a sob.

"Liam. Liam."

He shook his head. They knew his name. They knew who he was. Even though he had set them free, they still came for him.

He felt her hand on his shoulder. "Liam!"

Liam's eyes flew open and suddenly he wasn't looking into the haunted eyes of little Marie Randulph any longer, but into Mai's warm brown eyes. His bedroom was dark. She was sitting on his bed, her hands on his shoulders.

"You were having a nightmare," she whispered, her face close to his.

Panting, he wiped his mouth with the back of his hand. He was cold and clammy and shaking all over. "A nightmare," he whispered, embarrassed to have her see him like this. Relieved to have someone there. Someone real to touch.

He was so fucking lonely.

"You okay?" she asked, her eyes filled with concern.

"I'm okay," he said with a sigh when he could find his voice. "I woke you. I'm sorry."

She stroked his bare arm, unembarrassed by his nakedness. "Don't be sorry."

She was leaning over him, so close he could feel her breath on his mouth. Liam wasn't sure what happened next. Did he lift his head from his pillow? Did she lower hers? But suddenly his mouth was on hers, hard and hungry. Desperate for life when all around him was death.

Maybe there was something inside her that felt the same way.

One second she was hovering over him, her soft lips on his. The next moment, he was on top of her, stretching out his legs, covering her with his naked body, pushing her into the thin mattress. She was wearing nothing but an old T-shirt and a pair of panties and he felt her bare thighs hot against his. He thrust his tongue into her mouth, needing to possess her, she needing to be possessed.

Their mouths twisted hungrily. She tasted clean, sweet, of summer berries and hope. He thrust his hand up under her T-shirt to cup one dainty, round breast. Her skin was soft and silky.

She moaned.

I shouldn't be doing this. I can't do this. It was forbidden. It was wrong for a hundred reasons.

But his groin was already throbbing, his need hard against her leg.

Liam caught both her hands and pinned them to the bed over her head. She struggled, but with him, not against him. He kissed her mouth, her chin, her throat, lingering over her beating pulse. Her blood was hot and pulsing, just under the surface of her skin.

He felt the vibration of his fangs...the need. But he resisted. Dragging his mouth along her hot flesh, he kissed her breast through the thin fabric of her shirt, wetting it as he teased her nipple with his tongue.

She struggled for a second, trying to pull one hand away, and he took a deep breath. If she said no, he could not do this. He would not.

He released her hand, shifting his weight, prepared to set her free. *Run,* he thought. *Run, while you have the chance.*

But to his surprise, she wasn't trying to get away from him. When he let go of her hand, all she did was grab the hem of her shirt and yank it, baring her sweet, small, round breasts to him. He needed no further invitation.

Liam grabbed the T-shirt and pulled it over her head. He covered her nipple with his mouth, licking, sucking. She moaned, moving her hips against his.

A part of him, the deepest part of him, wanted her blood, but another part of him wanted... needed this human act, to touch and be touched... more than the blood.

He slid his hand over her flat belly that had never known a child, to the waistband of her panties, and she parted her legs. He slipped his hand beneath the fabric and she was warm and wet and ready for him. "Liam," she whispered in his ear.

He shoved down the panties; she slipped out of them, kicking them to the floor, as eager as he was to feel flesh to flesh.

He raised his body over her and looked into her eyes. They were open, gazing into his. She looked lost. Found. "Mai," he whispered. And despite his urgent need, he kissed her tenderly on the lips, his trembling against hers.

He didn't deserve this. He had no right.

With one hand, he guided his way deep into her. She raised her hips, cried out, and for a moment he feared he was too big for her. She was so tiny, so delicate.... But she began to move against him, and he realized it was not a cry of pain, but surprise, then pleasure.

He thrust deeper.

She wrapped her arms around his neck, pulling him closer. He felt her heels dig into his calves as she cradled his body with hers. Heart pounding, pulse pumping, he thrust into her again and again.

Generally, he was a controlled lover. He prided himself

in the time he could take to please his partner. He could bring a woman to orgasm, human or otherwise, again and again. But he had no control left tonight. He moved faster, harder.

Mai's soft moans became louder, higher pitched. Another thrust and she cried out so loudly that she covered her mouth with her hand. That was his cue normally to slow down, give the woman a moment, but Liam was too far gone. He fell against her, only two...three more strokes and he felt the contraction of his muscles and the final, explosive release. He came with a groan and fell against her. She clung to him, both of them hot and sweaty and satiated.

He kissed her cheek, her earlobe. He had not drawn a single drop of her blood and was as shocked by that thought as she would have been if he had.

Liam shifted his weight, moving to her side, against the wall. He feared he was too heavy on her; his bed was so narrow that he had to lift her in his arms so that she lay partially on top of him. He let his head fall back on the pillow and he closed his eyes, still breathing hard.

"Wow," she panted after a second. "I didn't see that coming when I walked in here."

He smiled in the darkness. "Me neither."

She snuggled up against him, laying her cheek against his shoulder. "Now don't I feel like the perfect little hussy?"

He chuckled. "Actually, I think I saw it coming the second you walked into my shop that day. You did, too."

"Yeah, but I could have at least let *you* come to *me*. Then I wouldn't look like quite the brazen ho that I apparently am."

He stroked her bare buttocks, enjoying the feel of her skin beneath his fingertips. It was so soft. So...feminine. "I'm not saying I might not have tried it. I'm not sure there is room in there for me, you, your dad, and the Prince of Dogs."

She laughed with him, her voice soft, warm. She was all his life was not. "I still feel like a hussy."

"Don't." He kissed her temple.

She sighed and lay quiet for so long that he thought maybe she was drifting off to sleep. Then she spoke. "You have them often? Nightmares?"

"Too often," he answered, not entirely comfortable saying so. Assassins weren't supposed to have nightmares.

"After my mom left, my dad said mine were bad. Even in college, I still had them. I always dreamed of running after her in this vast, scary darkness, but never catching up."

She was quiet again, obviously giving him the opportunity to share what his nightmares were about. He didn't. Sharing a bed was one thing, but sharing his deepest thoughts, that was something entirely different.

They lay there for another twenty minutes in silence. Liam relaxed for the first time in months, maybe years, and began to drift off. He was almost asleep when she sat up. "I better get out of here before I fall asleep."

By the light of the moon coming through the curtainless window, she found her T-shirt and panties. She left his room carrying them, giving one glorious glance of her tight, round buttocks as she went through the door.

" 'Night," she murmured.

"Good night." And he slept a dreamless sleep at last.

As the sunlight coming through the window hit Mai's face, she couldn't decide if she felt gloriously alive or mortified by what had happened last night. She stretched beneath the blanket and yawned. Maybe a little of both? She smiled to herself.

That was the best orgasm she'd ever had in her life, with or without the assistance of a man.

She felt her cheeks grow warm just at the thought of it. Something else grew warm and she groaned, her thoughts heading back in the direction of mortification again. Was she out of her mind, crawling into a stranger's bed like that?

But she hadn't lied to Liam when she said she hadn't gone to his room to seduce him. She really hadn't. She'd never made the first move with a man in her life! She'd only gone because she couldn't stand the thought of someone else being so terrified. His cries had awakened her from a deep sleep and brought tears to her eyes. She had known he was suffering; she had seen it in his eyes even after she woke him.

Then he had kissed her. Or had she kissed him?

Slut. Ho. Hussy. She was obviously all those things.

But it had been so good.

Mai heard her father stir and glanced over at the other bed. He lay on his stomach with his dog tucked under his arm, only Prince's little head sticking out from beneath the blanket. Corrato's hair was so white and thin on his pillow. When had he gotten so old? And what was she going to do about this mess they were in? How was any of this even possible? This kind of thing didn't happen to ordinary people like her. How was she going to protect him when she didn't even know who or what she was protecting him from or why?

God, why hadn't she pushed Uncle Donato harder? Why hadn't she demanded answers when she had the chance? She had known. She had known on some level that Donato Ricci was not the man he wanted her to think he was. A part of her had known, even as a child, that he was dangerous.

Then she had let him into her home. She had allowed him to put her life and her father's at risk. She wished she had the skinny old man here right now, with his breath smelling of *limoncello*. She would demand the truth or she would put his skinny ass on the curb and let the Weasel have him. Again.

No, she wouldn't. She wouldn't because she always felt sorry for the old, the weak, the infirm. Whatever Uncle Donato had done as a young man, he had still been a feeble old man by the time he came to live with them. His memory had been hazy, the simple task of tying his shoes sometimes confusing, and he had begun repeating himself a lot. He had not been healthy physically or mentally.

Her father rolled over, opened his eyes, blinked, and gazed around the room. He focused on the slender crucifix on the wall, the room's only ornamentation. "We in a monastery?"

"Nope." She smiled. "Liam's apartment. We left Suzy's and came here last night." She slipped out of bed and pulled on a pair of sweatpants over her underwear. She needed a shower; she could still smell Liam on her skin. But that would have to wait. "Remember driving here last night?"

"Yes, I remember," he snapped. "It was a joke." He opened his arms and Prince wiggled free and hopped to the floor.

"I'll take him out." She stepped into sneakers, grabbed a sweatshirt off the top of her suitcase, and went to the door. "Come on, Prince. Outside."

"I want coffee," Corrato announced, slowly swinging his spindly legs over the edge of the bed. He was wearing a pair of blue flannel pajamas that were so old they were thin at the knees and elbows. Every time she ran them through the wash, she contemplated tossing them in the trash. But he loved those pajamas as much as she hated them, so she kept washing them and he kept wearing them. "And my newspaper. You think they've got coffee and a paper in this monastery?"

She grabbed her wallet out of her bag, slung over the single chair in the room. "I'll get coffee, *Babbo*. Just don't insult Liam by calling his house a monastery."

"What?" Corrato called after her as she went down the hall. "You think he hasn't noticed?"

Liam woke feeling heavy with guilt. The room was bright and he dressed quickly in the same jeans and T-shirt he'd worn the day before. He'd overslept. He found Mai, Corrato, and the rat dog in the kitchen. Corrato was doing a crossword puzzle in the morning paper.

"A small European fish, five-letter word, ending in T," Corrato read aloud.

"Hey," Mai called when Liam walked into the kitchen. "We helped ourselves to breakfast. Dad likes Rice Krispies. I hope that's okay." She was wearing a sweatshirt, sweatpants, and sneakers. Her cheeks were rosy, as if she'd been outside. Or was embarrassed.

He debated whether he should kiss her good morning. Some women expected that after you slept with them.

"*Sprat,*" Corrato announced.

Liam decided *no* on the good-morning kiss. Maybe she didn't want her father to know about last night. Liam sure as hell didn't. "Not much here to eat. Sorry. I haven't gotten around to getting to the store. Busy, you know, sorting things in the shop." It sounded lame. *He* sounded lame. What could a pretty, smart human woman see in a loser vampire like him? It was a good thing he'd enjoyed last night, because he knew it wasn't going to happen again. If she had any brains, she'd go now.

"I went across the street and got bagels and coffee.

There's a cup there for you." She wrinkled her nose. He thought it was the cutest nose he'd ever seen.

"Not very friendly over there, are they?" she asked.

He shrugged and got a carton of OJ out of the fridge. He didn't do caffeine. He was jumpy enough without it. "They're okay. We, um, just don't have a lot of visitors this time of year. Things kind of shut down."

"Royal fur, six letters, ending in E," Corrato read aloud.

The dog seemed to be the only one listening.

Corrato hesitated. *"Ermine."* He scribbled the word.

"I thought I'd run to the store later, get a few things my dad likes. I thought I could make dinner for us tonight. If that's okay." She looked at Liam hesitantly.

So, apparently she *was* staying, at least until dinner. He took a drink of juice from the carton, then thought better of it and went to the cupboard. All he could find in the way of a glass was a plastic cup from the local minimart. He poured half a cup. "Sure. Dinner would be nice."

She leaned against the counter and sipped coffee from a paper cup. "Your kitchen is beautiful. A little sparse, but beautiful."

"Guess I just haven't gotten around to getting dishes, silverware . . . stuff."

She laughed. "Liam, you've got boxes of dishes and silverware and pots and pans downstairs. How can you not have any dishes in your kitchen?" She met his gaze. "I know, you're not here that much." She took another sip of coffee. "So what do you *really* do for a living?"

"I told you, I buy and sell antiquities. For myself sometimes. I also act as a broker for other buyers. I'm gone for months at a time. All over the world, really."

She narrowed her gaze. "You really deal in antiques. Hmm. And I thought maybe this was just a cover-up. I thought maybe you worked for the State Department. You know, CIA or something."

He frowned and took a drink of juice. "Nah. What makes you say that?"

She was still watching him. Making him feel uncomfortable. "I don't know." She pointed her finger. She still didn't quite believe him. "Something. In your eyes. In the way you move. The way you observe everything going on around you. You're not the kind of man I would want to meet in a dark alley."

"Five-letter word meaning 'friendship,' " Corrato interjected. "Fourth letter, a T."

It was on the tip of Liam's tongue to ask Mai why if she would be afraid of him in a dark alley that she was willing to meet him in a dark bedroom, but he didn't. Instead, he finished his orange juice and headed for the door leading downstairs. He had a lot of work to do in the shop. A lot of thinking to do. "I'm going downstairs to get to work. Make yourself at home. Let me know when you're ready to go. Maybe I'll tag along with you, get a few things." The truth was, he wasn't exactly comfortable sending them to the grocery store alone. The owner, Hannah, could be . . . unwelcoming, this time of year.

"Five-letter word meaning 'friendship,' " Corrato repeated. "Fourth letter, T."

"Sure. And maybe I can come down and join you. Help you out."

Liam rested his hand on the doorknob. He really liked her. He really had to get her out of here. "You don't need to do that. It's my own fault I let it get away from me."

"Liam, I'm not offering for altruistic reasons."

She smiled at him mischievously and he remembered the taste of her mouth on his.

"It's my polite way of saying I want to pick through your stuff."

He shrugged, opening the door. "Suit yourself."

"Five-letter word meaning friendship," Corrato said again, louder this time. "Fourth letter, T."

"*Amity,*" Liam and Mai said in unison.

Liam closed the door behind him.

Chapter 11

That evening, when Liam's cell phone rang, it was a welcome escape from the tension in the kitchen. He'd been helping Mai wash the dishes, dishes she'd found in the shop, washed, and set the table with. They'd kept busy all day, treating each other nicely enough, but he could feel an apprehension building between them. It was the big question. Would she come to him again tonight? He wanted to tell her not to. That she couldn't. In the same breath, he was afraid he might shrivel and die if she didn't.

If only he could be so lucky.

"Excuse me," Liam said as he flipped open his phone. It was Fia. "Hey," he said quietly.

"Hey. Got some intel for you. Can you talk?"

"It's Sunday night. Haven't you got anything better to do than work at the office on a Sunday night?"

"Football is on in every bar in the city. Eagles are playing at home. I hate the fucking Eagles. You want the information or not?"

"Hang on a second." He glanced at Mai, covering the mouthpiece. "I'm going to take this outside."

"Okay." She smiled, drying a plate. It was 1920s Noritake dinnerware. Simple. Beautiful. Of course, when the plate was produced in 1921, the company was still called

Nippon Toki Kabushiki Kaisha, Limited. He'd bought the dishes in Nagasaki in the late '20s, thinking his mother might like them. He'd never gotten around to giving them to her.

"Do you mind taking Prince out?" Mai asked. "I'm not crazy about my dad going out alone after dark."

"Right. Sure. Good call." He backed out of the kitchen awkwardly. He hated that damned dog. "Prince."

The dog trotted out of the living room and down the hall to where Liam waited.

"Leash is on the door handle," Mai called.

Liam scooped up the mutt. "You run, I'm sending the pit bull after you, you got it?" he whispered in its pointy ear.

The dog looked into his eyes and Liam could have sworn it telepathed, *Not a problem, buddy.*

Headed down the stairs, dog under his arm, Liam spoke into the phone again. "Okay, sorry. I'm back. Hey, are dogs telepathic?"

"How the hell should I know?" Fia asked. "What's going on there? Someone there? I thought I heard a woman's voice." Her tone turned sweetly mocking. "Liam! Have you got a lady friend at your place?"

So . . . word might be getting around Clare Point by now, but it hadn't reached Philadelphia yet.

"It's just Kaleigh. She's been hanging out here a lot. I don't know what's up with her." He didn't know why he lied. Fia would find out. Everyone was going to find out. He just didn't want to deal with it tonight. "So what'd you find?" At the door at the bottom of the steps, he set the dog down, and together they went out into the dark.

"The Weasel, aka Salvador Machhione. Born in Brooklyn, 1939, a distant relation to the Gambino family," she read. "Apparently hung out with his Gambino cousins, learned some of the tricks of the trade from them. In his early twenties, he started working for a guy named Carlo DeCava, who had a legal front selling antiques and junk in Brooklyn. In the '60s, DeCava played the usual games: loansharking, racketeering. The young Machhione was a go-getter and had a thing for import/exports. A little stolen merchandise here and there—electronics, high-end clothing—but then he started moving stolen artwork and such. He was very good at what he did, apparently so good that he got too big for his britches. In '77, three guys who worked for DeCava were found dead in a coffee shop. Nice, neat single nine-millimeter round through each of their foreheads. Machhione was supposed to be with them, but *weaseled* away."

"Ah," Liam said. "Thus *the Weasel*." He snapped his fingers, leading the rat terrier to the end of the building where there was still grass growing.

"A month later, DeCava was headed to a baptism at Our Lady of Lourdes. Never showed up, him or his driver. Car was found abandoned. Never heard from them again. Machhione divorced his wife and married DeCava's only daughter, the old lady DeCava retired to Palm Beach, and lo and behold, the Weasel was suddenly the owner of the antiques store and all the business that went with it." Fia exhaled and then went on. "His name was tossed around once in a while among the Feds for a number of years, but no one could charge him with anything. Then in '86 he was charged with masterminding a diamond heist in South Africa."

"Diamonds? Damn."

"Big international fiasco," Fia continued. "Charges were eventually dropped due to a lack of evidence. He was alleged to have gotten away with stealing about six million dollars' worth of some kind of rare pink diamonds I've never even heard of. But the diamonds never show up, as far as anyone can tell. He finally slipped up in '89 and went to federal prison for tax evasion and racketeering. He was released in 2010 due to health reasons. I guess they figured he was too old to cause much trouble. Let's see, that made him—"

"Seventy-one when he was released. Okay." The wheels in Liam's head were turning. "You come across the name Donato Ricci anywhere? R-I-C-C-I. D-O-N-A-T-O." Liam snapped his fingers. The dog was digging in the grass. Eating something.

The dog ignored him.

Fia gave a snort of disgust. "I came across, like, a thousand names. You asked me about the Weasel."

"I know, I know. Cut that out!" He pushed the dog's head away with his toe. He was eating something disgusting in the grass.

"What?" Fia said. "Cut what out?"

"Prince, knock it off." Then into the phone, "Dog-sitting. Don't ask."

"I have no intention of doing so," Fia answered dryly. "So you want me to check out this Donato Ricci?"

He hesitated. The dog was still gnawing on the unknown substance. It smelled like crap. Literally. He scooped up the dog. "Yeah, if you don't mind."

"You're going to have to give me a few days. Might even be next week before I can get to it. I've got a field assignment."

"As soon as you can get to it." He thought for a second. "And see if you can find anything on a Corrato Ricci, while you're at it. C-O-R-R-A-T-O. They're brothers."

Liam hung up with Fia, made an instantaneous decision, and called Kaleigh. He had to get out of here. He had to get away from Mai. He needed time to think. Time to get ahold of his emotions. It was the perfect night for a road trip.

"I haven't gotten to the bottom of it, but I swear it's going to get cleaned up," Kaleigh said into the phone.

Liam walked to the door. "You're damn straight they're going to clean it up, but that's not why I'm calling. I need you to do me a favor."

"Sure. Hang on a sec. Connor's listening in on private conversations again," she said in her best nasty-teenager voice.

"Am not!" Liam heard.

It was Kaleigh's little brother. At fifteen, he was a pain in the ass. He would become a bigger pain in the ass as time passed.

"Okay," Kaleigh said after a few seconds. "What's up?"

"I need to go out of town for a day or two and Mai and her dad are staying at my place."

"So I heard."

He didn't respond. It was the vampire network at work. "I'm not sure when I'll be back. Can you just check in on them?"

"I've got school. Mom caught me skipping last week, so I've got to go. She's threatening to go to classes with me."

"I was thinking about after dark. Elwood and Jake were poking their fangs around here last night. I think I'll pay them a little visit on my way out of town, but if you could just drop by and check on her? Make sure they don't need anything."

"No *problemo*."

Upstairs, Liam deposited the dog in the living room. Mai had found a TV for her dad somewhere in the shop and had hooked it up. Liam had no cable and the antenna on the house was old, but Corrato seemed to be content watching *60 Minutes*.

Liam stuck his head through the doorway in the kitchen. "Something came up," he said, stuffing his hands in his pockets. He kept his gaze at her feet. "I gotta take off. Might be gone a day or two, but you'll be fine here."

She turned to face him, a wet dishcloth in her hand. She was a good cook. The shrimp scampi she'd made was amazing. "Okay." No questions. No anxiety. She didn't look like she even cared.

"Um, you'll be fine here, but you should probably stick close to the shop. Not...go anywhere. Stores or whatever."

She watched him carefully but said nothing.

"I've got a friend. She's a teenager, but she's cool. You can trust her. Her name's Kaleigh. She'll stop by, see if you need anything."

"Okay. Have a good trip." She turned back to the sink of dirty pots and pans. Just like that. No questions. No whining about him leaving her alone at the mercy of the mafia. Nothing about sleeping with her and dumping her. Not a word.

Liam headed down the steps, totally relieved that Mai hadn't given him a hard time about taking off. And oddly disappointed at the same time.

Late in the afternoon on Monday, Mai was still busy opening boxes and sorting through the contents. Liam had an incredible inventory, from what she could tell. She couldn't even guess at the value, but everything was so disorganized that she didn't see how he could sell much of anything. Right now, customers couldn't have gotten in the door if they wanted to.

It had occurred to her midmorning as she was making an area to put lamps that Liam might not want her picking through his stuff, or organizing it. But she had to do something; otherwise, she was going to go crazy. And since she obviously couldn't go to her own shop and work, Liam's was the next best thing.

Besides, he had *way* too much baggage to be worried about something this trivial. She could just tell: the nightmares, the sad-beyond-his-years look in his eyes, the way he moved like a caged animal. He said he wasn't CIA, but she didn't believe him. She'd dated a CIA agent just after college and she knew the look, the way they moved. Liam was *so* a spy. Or something equally crazy. She just felt it in her bones.

Which was yet another reason to get out of here while she had the chance. The relationship with the other CIA agent hadn't gone well. She arranged books she'd unearthed on a bookshelf on the back wall of the shop. She couldn't believe how many first editions Liam had.

Things with Robert had definitely not ended well. She'd broken up with him when she discovered he slept with a semiautomatic under his pillow. Loaded. There was also one in the linen closet and one taped to the back of the toilet tank. Also one in each of his cars.

She hadn't checked Liam's toilet tank. Not to say it hadn't occurred to her.

But who was she kidding? If she found an Uzi taped to the back of the toilet tank, where was she going to go? With her seventy-five-year-old, headed-for-senility father and a five-pound rat terrier? The truth was that whether she liked it or not, the only thing she could do was hope that Liam would be able to help her figure this out. If she could just talk to this crazy Weasel, find out what he wanted, if she had it, God knew she'd give it to him.

A tap at the door of the shop caught her attention. She saw a red-haired teenager with a backpack on her back standing on the sidewalk. Liam had said he was sending a friend by to check on her. This had to be Kaleigh.

Mai walked to the bottom of the staircase. "*Babbo? You okay?*"

"Why wouldn't I be?" he shouted from the living room upstairs. "We're watching our stories."

Thank God for soap operas.

Mai went to the door but didn't open it immediately. Better safe than sorry. "We're closed. Sorry."

"It's okay, Mai. I'm Kaleigh. A friend of Liam's. He asked me to come by. Can I come in?"

Mai hesitated, thinking she should just tell her they were fine and send her on her way.

"It's safe, really," the teen said from the other side of the door. "I'm, like, the safest girl in town."

Mai smiled and unlocked the door, even though a part of her didn't want to meet this Kaleigh. She didn't want to get to know Liam's friends or in any way make herself a part of his life. She was just sticking around because she had nowhere else to go right now. She wasn't going to make whatever this was between her and Liam a *thing*. He'd been amazing in bed; they'd been amazing together, but she wasn't naive enough to think that meant anything. He obviously wasn't interested in a *thing,* and she had bigger problems right now than her lack of bedsheet action.

"Thanks for stopping by." Mai stepped back to let her in and locked the door behind her. "You really didn't have to. I'm fine. We're fine. I imagine Liam will be back tonight."

"I don't know about that. He gets antsy sometimes, takes off. Could be days before he's back." She glanced around the shop. "Wow. You do all of this? Is that a wall over there?"

Mai chuckled. "That's a wall. I think there are four of them."

"Liam's been working for almost three weeks and I think you made more headway in a day."

"I'm good at organizing." Mai opened and closed her arms. "What can I say?"

"So, you need anything? Groceries or anything?" Kaleigh wound her way through the stacks of boxes toward the back wall where Mai had been arranging the books.

"Nope. We're good. We went to the grocery store yesterday. Liam and I."

"Cool." She stopped at the bookshelf and dropped her backpack to the floor. "Now I'm doubly impressed. He never has any food in the house except for Rice Krispies. Not that I don't like Rice Krispies, you understand." She gave Mai a look and grabbed a book. "Is this a first-edition Kipling? You've got to be kidding me." She glanced back. "But Liam's, like, thirty-five years old. It's really time he got past the college-boy thing and had some dishes and some food in his refrigerator."

"He's got an autographed Samuel Clemens, and a first-edition Henry James." Mai pointed. "Well, he's got food now. And dishes. I took a box upstairs yesterday. He's got the coolest stuff lying around here. I don't think he knows half of what's here."

"Sounds like Liam." Kaleigh flipped through the pages of *The Jungle Book*. "So, he tells me you're in a little trouble?"

Mai wasn't sure what to say. Surely Liam hadn't told this kid what was going on with her and her father.

"That why you're here?" Kaleigh asked.

"I don't think it's a good idea that we talk about this. Frankly, it could be...dangerous."

"Hey, that's cool. I wasn't trying to get in your business or anything." She returned the book to the shelf and reached for another. "I was just kind of surprised when Liam told me you were staying here." She flipped pages again. "It's just not like him." She glanced over the book cover. "He must really like you."

Mai felt her cheeks burn. "He's a good guy."

"A super-good guy," Kaleigh agreed. "Always coming to people's rescue and such."

"You mean he's done this before?"

"I really can't say." Kaleigh returned the book to the shelf. "I don't suppose there are any Rice Krispies left? I'm starving and if I go home, my mom's going to make me clean my bedroom."

Mai hesitated. The smart thing to do was to show Kaleigh the door. She didn't need to be making friends in Clare Point. Not friends with Liam's friends, for sure. But she already liked Kaleigh. There was something about her that made her seem wise beyond her years. "I can do better than Rice Krispies. Come on." She waved her toward the steps.

"No such thing as better than Rice Krispies," Kaleigh argued, grabbing her backpack off the floor.

"No?" Mai asked, leading the teen up the stairs to Liam's apartment. "How about Rice Krispie treats?"

The Weasel's old stomping grounds in Brooklyn had been fairly quiet Sunday night. Monday, Liam spent the day poking around, first at the courthouse, then the best place for info in town, the post office, where he talked to an old woman who had known DeCava and Machhione. She'd gone on a blind date to the homecoming dance freshman year with Machhione. Said he was a lying, sly bastard back then.

Mrs. Ditonio, pretty lively for her age, had then invited Liam back to her house for dinner. And something else, he suspected. He passed on both.

Liam gleaned a few tidbits at a diner at lunch and then hit pay dirt that night at an Italian restaurant two blocks from where DeCava and later Machhione had operated their antiques store and other assorted businesses.

What he learned wasn't good news for Mai and her father. Apparently, Uncle Donato knew Machhione from high school and had been the Weasel's consigliere for years. He had been demoted when he made a business deal in Machhione's name, without Machhione's knowledge. The only reason the Weasel hadn't offed Ricci was that the deal was successful and made a bucket of money. There had been serious trouble between Machhione and Ricci just before the boss went to jail. Liam's informant, a seventy-odd-years-old bookie named Anthony Pallota, didn't know what the rift was about, but he said word on the street had been that Ricci had taken something from Machhione.

Bingo. Had the Weasel gotten out of jail and decided to collect on old debts?

Liam was pouring the old man his fourth glass of Chianti when the door to the street opened. Liam's danger radar immediately went off. He and Anthony were the only patrons left in the little trattoria. A bartender was putting glasses away behind the bar. Liam hadn't seen the waiter in at least half an hour.

"Nope. Nope. Never heard what it was he was supposed to have stolen." Anthony sipped his wine. "Some said he never took nuthin'. It just pissed off the Weasel that Ricci was a better businessman than he was." He gave a snort. "That and the fact that the missus had an ongoing thing with Ricci for years."

Liam watched over Anthony's right shoulder as two men in their thirties wearing leather jackets walked into the restaurant. They looked like they were trying out to be extras on *The Sopranos*. One had a tattoo on his neck. Something idiotic like a panther, its claws bared.

They walked up to the bar and muttered something. They weren't from around here. Sounded like New Orleans to Liam's ear.

Liam flexed his hands beneath the checkered tablecloth. Panther Neck glanced around. He spotted Anthony's hunched back. Maybe recognized that the old man was drunk.

Liam ducked his head, blocking the thugs' direct line of vision with Anthony's torso. The bartender served the guys each a shot of Jägermeister, with a beer chaser.

Anthony rambled on. He didn't know where Liam could find the Weasel, but he was around, all right. Retired. Out of the business. Enjoying his freedom.

The two at the bar flew off their barstools straight at Liam without any warning. Vampires were like that.

Chapter 12

*B*old bastards, Liam thought as he leaped onto the bench in the booth he'd been sitting at and reached across the cannoli to shove Anthony under the table. The bigger of the two, the one with the panther tattoo, was temporarily taken-aback, midair, when Liam stepped onto the table, fangs bared.

"I'm calling the police!" the bartender yelled from where he had taken refuge on the floor behind the bar.

"*Mon dieu!*" the vampire exclaimed, coming to light on the back of Anthony's bench seat.

Fortunately, the old Italian had the sense to stay under the table. From there, he couldn't see anything. With any luck, he had no idea he'd almost been bitten by a vampire.

Liam half-smiled. He *knew* he knew these bastards! "Levi Rousseau," he muttered. The Rousseau brothers were a nasty nest of Cajun vampires out of New Orleans. They dealt in drug trafficking, which was probably why they were in Brooklyn. "Nice tattoo."

Levi ran his hand over his neck. "*Merci beaucoup.* It's new." He remained perched two feet from Liam. "You know my brother, Dan."

Liam leaned right to meet the other vampire's gaze. "Didn't recognize you, Dan, without your cape."

Dan didn't smile. He had no sense of humor. He and his brothers ran around New Orleans at night wearing black capes and scaring the crap out of tourists on Bourbon Street and feeding on the idiots passed out in the alleys. Still, they weren't vampires to mess around with; Liam wouldn't trust one of the Rousseau brothers any farther than he could throw him.

Levi retracted his fangs and jumped down off the back of the bench. In the distance, they could hear the wail of a police siren. There was no sign of the bartender or anyone from the kitchen.

Liam stepped onto the bench, then down to the tiled floor. He was slower to retract his fangs. He'd need to feed sometime in the next couple of days. The sept's rule was no feeding except on other willing vampires, or the wildlife they cared for and protected on the game preserve in Clare Point. When members of the sept were out of town, the rules were a little less strict. Of course, neither Rousseau would be *willing*, but Liam wasn't above bending the rules. He was in a crappy mood tonight and had half a mind to pick a fight with these jerks just so he could get a taste of their nasty-ass bayou blood.

"So, what are you boys up to?" Liam asked, glancing toward the street. The sound of the siren was getting louder. If they were going to do this, it would have to be elsewhere. Vampires, the good guys or the bad ones, didn't like tangling with human law enforcement. The cover-up afterward was always complicated.

"You know, in town on business," Levi said. "You?"

Liam crossed his arms over his chest. "The same."

"We only came at you because we wanted the scrawny one. He yours?" Levi pointed under the table.

"Afraid so."

"Up to sharing?"

Liam stared at him with a cool, dangerous gaze. Vampires were very territorial, with land and victims. "Afraid not."

Levi put up both hands and took a step back. "No offense intended."

"None taken." Liam glanced in the direction of the street again. "We should probably take the back door."

"Probably."

Liam drew his hand back grandly. "After you, gentlemen."

"Thank you." Levi walked past Liam, followed by his brother.

"You going to leave him here?" Levi asked as they ducked behind a curtain leading to the rear of the restaurant.

"I don't need any trouble with cops," Liam muttered. He had the bookie's number. If he had more questions for Anthony about the Weasel, he could probably call him. With any luck, Anthony hadn't really seen anything but a pair of showboating thugs in leather jackets.

They found the rear door and stepped out into the chilly night air. The two brothers turned one way, Liam the other. The cops were arriving out front.

"So, you in the States long?" Levi asked, walking backward behind his brother as if he had all the time in the world before Brooklyn's finest crashed into the alley.

Liam made the decision he wasn't up for a fight tonight. He could probably take these boys, but it would be messy. Bloody. He had more important matters to attend to. "A few weeks."

"Maybe we'll stop by Clare Point on our way home, after we've got things squared away here. Let you buy me a beer at The Hill."

"You bet." Liam turned away and jogged down the alley, into the darkness.

* * *

Liam killed Tuesday reading newspaper articles on mob activity in the area in the sixties, seventies, and eighties on a computer at the public library. It beat the hell out of the microfiche years. He learned enough about the Weasel to guess that even in his old age, he might be a formidable enemy, not physically, but strategically. There wasn't much about Donato; he'd apparently been smart enough to keep his name out of the paper for all those years.

Liam called Anthony that afternoon. The old man had been so drunk the night before that he barely remembered the incident at the bar with the Rousseaus, only the police driving him home. He promised to look into where the Weasel was living these days, and Liam said he'd get back to him. Before Liam hung up, he wagered a hundred dollars on the next Eagles game, in Fia's honor.

Back in Clare Point on Wednesday, he went for a long walk on the beach and stepped into his apartment at dinnertime. He could smell marinara all the way up the staircase. The Prince of Dogs barked wildly as Liam unlocked the door and walked in.

"It's okay, boy," he said, soothing the dog.

Corrato looked up from his dinner plate. A pristine white napkin was tucked into the collar of his shirt. "About time you got back," he muttered and returned to his plate of linguine. "I got enough to worry about without having to worry if you're all right. There's killers out there. You ought to know that better than any of us," he chastised gruffly.

Liam glanced questioningly at Mai. She just shrugged, suggesting she didn't have any idea what he was talking about either.

"Hungry?" Mai asked. She got up from the dinette table and pulled a Noritake plate from the cupboard. In the time Liam had been gone, an Italian espresso machine and a stainless-steel KitchenAid toaster had been added to his countertop. And an olive wood cutting board. Between the new appliances, the dishes, the cloth napkins, and the smell of tomato sauce, the place almost seemed homey.

"If you have enough. Sure."

"Prince is almost out of dog food," Corrato announced. He looked straight at Liam, fork poised over his plate. "I have to go get dog food. And I need clothes. I need my brown corduroy shirt. This apartment is drafty."

"*Babbo*," Mai admonished softly, "Liam's been kind enough to welcome us into his home. You shouldn't speak to him that way." She slid a plate of pasta in front of Liam.

"It's okay. I...had to go out of town, Corrato," Liam explained, almost feeling guilty he had left them. It had never occurred to him that Corrato might be afraid. Or worried about him. "But I'm back now. We can go to your place tomorrow and find your brown shirt and we'll get Prince some dog food."

Mai smiled down at Liam. *Thank you,* she mouthed, handing him a fork, a knife, and a neatly folded napkin. She slipped back into her chair.

Liam expected her to ask him where he'd been. She didn't. Instead, she sliced a piece of baguette and handed it to him.

Liam took a bite of pasta, coated in marinara. It was heavenly. "Can I ask you a question, Corrato? About your brother?"

"You can *ask*." The old man continued to eat, but he would no longer make eye contact with Liam.

"What kind of work did Donato do?"

"I don't know. This and that."

Liam eyed Mai across the table. "Was he involved in anything illegal?"

The old man harrumphed. "Think I'd tell you if he was?"

"*Babbo!*"

Liam smiled. "He worked for Salvador Machhione, didn't he? He worked for the Weasel?"

Corrato slurped noisily.

"*Babbo,* did Uncle Donato work for a man named Machhione?"

"What four-letter word beginning with D means 'to pound'?" Corrato asked.

Mai cut her eyes at Liam, with concern, then back at her father. "*Babbo,* can you answer Liam's question? Do you know anything about the Weasel?" She said it as if it was a ridiculous name. Which, of course, it was.

"It's okay. Your father doesn't want to talk about it now. Maybe later." Liam took another bite. "*Drub.* The four-letter word meaning 'to pound' is *drub.*"

They finished the meal, mostly in silence, but the whole time, Liam could feel Corrato watching him. Something told him that the old man wasn't as confused or disjointed as he wanted people to think. The term *crazy like a fox* came to mind. Corrato knew his brother had worked for the Weasel, all right. What Liam wanted to know was if Corrato knew anything about missing pink diamonds.

That night, Mai came to him in his dreams. Liam was in the dungeon, leaving the children behind, moving deeper into the shadows, when she appeared before him.

"You shouldn't be here," he told her, half-awake, but still half-asleep. "It's not safe."

She pressed her lips to his, tearing him from that terrible place, back to the present and the warmth of his bed.

"Right now, this is the only place I feel safe," she whispered against his mouth, slipping naked beneath his blanket.

Liam opened his eyes to gaze into hers. Cold air had seeped in under the blanket when she climbed into his bed, but her body was warm and yielding.

He wrapped his arm around her hip and pulled her close. "I was afraid you wouldn't come," he whispered with more emotion in his voice than he would have liked.

There was a silly half-smile on her face. "I had to wait until he was asleep."

"Who? Your dad or the dog?"

She giggled, snuggling closer. "Both."

He bit down lightly on her earlobe. "If you hadn't come..."

"What?" she whispered. "What would you have done? You would have come into the bedroom for me, would you? You wouldn't dare."

"I don't know," he admitted honestly. "I just know that I missed you while I was gone. I thought about you."

"Shhhh," she soothed, pressing her finger to his lips. "Let's not do this. You and I both know this is only... temporary. Let's not talk about it. Let's not... make it uncomfortable."

For a moment they were quiet and still, left alone with their private thoughts. With Mai wrapped in his arms against his chest, he could feel her heart beating, feel her rhythmic pulse. Despite what some believed, vampires had a heart, but it was somehow different from a human heart. Not so vital, not so... *alive*.

Wanting to feel as alive as Mai, Liam rolled over and pushed her into the mattress, covering her body with his. He took her mouth hard, thrusting his tongue, squeezing her breasts. Their movements were quick and purposeful. There was very little foreplay; she seemed to want that even less than he did tonight. At once, she was parting her legs, lifting her hips up to meet his.

As he pushed into her, his lips found the pulse of her throat and, for a second, he had to cease his rhythmic thrusts.

"What is it?" she panted, digging her nails into the flesh of his back. "Did you hear something?"

Her pulse beat so hard beneath Liam's lips that he felt that familiar vibration in his fangs. He groaned aloud, tensing every muscle in his body, fighting the urge that came from so deep inside him that for an instant, he feared he could not stop himself.

He would have her blood. He had to have it. It was the way of the world. Of his world.

"Liam?" Mai whispered. Her voice was so soft, so gentle.

She didn't deserve this.

She drew her hand over his bare buttocks. "Are you okay?"

He took a deep breath. He had the blood of more men on his hands than he could count. He would never be okay. Never, ever again.

But he was stronger than this. Stronger than God's curse, at least at this moment. So he fought the urge and after a few beats of his heart, he felt his fangs retract. He kissed her gently on the neck and pushed into her again.

She sighed. She moaned. And in seconds, they were moving together as one. Nothing mattered but the pleasure they shared in the darkness. She came and then she came again before Liam allowed his own release.

Afterward, she lay on her back beside him, breathing hard. "That was too good. I don't deserve you."

He smiled in the darkness. His heart was still pounding. He wiped the sweat from his brow with the back of his hand. "You deserve far better."

She rolled onto her side to look into his eyes. "I don't buy it, you know. The whole tough-guy thing. I'm not afraid of you. Of whatever it is you're not telling me."

He felt as if he was drowning in the depths of her dark eyes. She had captivated him. Captivated his heart. How had that happened? How had he let it happen? "What makes you think there's something about me I'm not telling you?"

"I just know."

"You know, you should be afraid of me," he breathed, reaching up to stroke her cheek. "Of men like me who will break your heart." He could still smell the scent of her on his hand.

She smiled at him again. "You can only break my heart if I give it to you and I have no intention of doing that." She was quiet for a second. "You went to find him, didn't you? The Weasel."

He didn't answer.

"My father might know something. It's hard to tell with him anymore. But I don't know if he'll tell you. He certainly won't tell me. He won't even discuss Uncle Donato with me anymore. He just starts in with his crazy crossword puzzle stuff."

"I think you're safe for now. Let's just give him a few days. We'll get him the clothes he wants from home. Maybe take him for a walk in town tomorrow. There's a costume parade and party this weekend. I thought maybe you'd like to join in on the festivities." Liam had no idea what made him say such a thing. He didn't do parades and costume parties, and certainly not in any way that involved a date.

Maybe the thought of seeing her in a naughty-nurse costume had made him bold.

"A costume party?" Her face lit up. "I love costume

parties!" She lay down beside him again, pulling the blanket over both of them. "I wonder what I should be. What are you going to be?"

"I don't know." He shrugged, staring at the ceiling. "I usually go as a vampire."

Chapter 13

Nothing in Mai's house or shop had been disturbed any further, but Liam had insisted they get in, get what they needed, and get out. Something didn't *feel* right to him, but he kept that to himself.

They had then driven to Rehoboth Beach, had lunch at a café, and stopped at a local pet store for Prince's dog food. Liam waited out in the car for Mai and her father, but they were inside so long that he began to worry. He was just crossing the parking lot when Mai exited the store, followed by Corrato and the dog. Mai was carrying two big paper bags.

Liam frowned, taking both bags from her. "Damn. How much food can this dog eat? He's not as big as a cat."

"Sorry." Mai opened the van door for her father. "They decided they needed dog toys and treats. Prince can be very particular." She looked at Liam over the seat and rolled her eyes.

Liam found himself smiling. He had nothing to smile about: global warming, the worldwide infestation of serial killers, zombies, and pedophiles, this crazy Weasel fuck with his vendetta. Liam didn't know why he was smiling. Mai just had that effect on him.

"We should probably get back to the apartment." Liam

gazed around the parking lot, that uneasy feeling coming over him again.

"I thought we were going to the costume shop." Mai climbed into the passenger seat beside Liam and buckled her seat belt. "I was kind of looking forward to it." She bit down on her lower lip, glancing around the parking lot. "But if you think we should go back..."

Liam pulled the minivan onto Route One. He had decided the whole idea of taking them to the parade and block party Saturday night was a bad one. There would be too many humans, too many vampires and other creatures of the night. He couldn't protect Mai and her father properly. But when he glanced at Mai now, he couldn't stand the disappointed look on her face.

He exhaled. *This* was why he tried to stay away from women. *This* was why HFs were particularly dangerous for a man like him. "Nah, it'll be okay. But I'll warn you. It's not really a costume shop. Just an old five-and-dime that gets all these costumes in for Halloween. They'll close for the winter after this weekend."

"I know the whole town shuts down. That's pretty amazing. It seems like no stores are seasonal anymore. They can't afford to be. Even though most of my business is in the summer, I know I can't."

He shrugged. "Just the way it's always been done here."

For the rest of the ride, they talked about other things: what was going on in world politics and the local elections. Corrato filled Liam in on this week's story line on *All My Children.*

The funny thing was, he didn't even mind.

Liam parked on the street just west of the boardwalk and they got out of the van.

"Says NO DOGS ON THE BOARDWALK, EASTER TO THANKS- GIVING," Corrato read from a posted street sign. He tucked the rat terrier under his arm. "We'll just wait here."

"*Babbo,* you can't stay here. It's not safe," Mai whispered.

There were a few people on the street, but not many. Most of them vampires, but of course she didn't know that.

"I can read, Mai." Corrato turned stiffly toward his daughter. "I might be crazy, but I can still read, gosh darn it."

"*Babbo,* no one said you were crazy." She glanced at Liam in frustration.

"It'll be okay to take him with us," Liam assured him. "Prince is barely big enough to be a real dog."

"You insulting the Prince of Dogs?" Corrato demanded. He was wearing brown corduroy pants a size too big, pulled up at least four inches too high, and a slouchy blue cardigan sweater, but when he threw back his shoulders, he actually had a certain air of intimidation. Liam wondered if he'd learned it from his brother. He wondered what other secrets the old man held.

"I meant no offense, sir." Liam studied the old man's cloudy blue eyes. "And I know everyone on the police force. It'll be fine. The sign is meant to keep tourists with dogs and no doggy bags off the boardwalk. Keep the place clean," he explained.

"Prince would never embarrass himself that way." Corrato pulled a little blue bag from his pocket. "But I carry one, just in case."

"Come on, *Babbo.* You can get a Halloween costume, too."

"I'm too old for a Halloween costume," Corrato grumbled, following them up the steps to the boardwalk. "Every time I look in the mirror and see this ugly old wrinkled man, I think I'm wearing a Halloween costume."

Mai cut her eyes at Liam and smiled. Like an idiot who didn't know about global warming or zombies, he smiled right back.

It was cool on the boardwalk, breezy but sunny. To the east, the waves of the Delaware Bay washed gently onto the shore. All the stores—the candy shop, a burger joint, a pizza place, and even the arcade that Liam's mother owned— were closed, but most had signs on their doors saying they would be open Friday.

Hilly's Five-and-Dime was flying a red, white, and blue flag advertising OPEN. A bell over the door jingled when they walked in. Usually, brightly colored blow-up rafts and beach chairs hung from the ceiling overhead, but in honor of the holiday, Fiona Hill had replaced them with paper bats, silky spiderwebs, and big rubber tarantulas that dangled on elastic bands. The smell of candy corn and apple cider dominated the store, instead of the familiar summer scent of suntan lotion.

"Welcome to Hilly's," greeted Seamus Hill, aka Hilly, busy stocking a shelf with Halloween candy. He turned around, offering a plastic pumpkin filled with treats. "Care for a sample?"

"Thank you." Mai reached in and pulled out a mini Tootsie Roll. "Want a piece of candy, *Babbo?* They're free."

"Not before dinner." The older man wandered down an aisle, the dog tucked under his arm.

"Liam?" Hilly offered the pumpkin. He was a vampire somewhere in his mid-sixties, a distinguished gentleman with salt-and-pepper hair. And a pirate's bandanna and eye patch.

Liam shook his head.

"Let's go down this aisle, *Babbo.*" Mai went after her father and steered him away from the maid miniskirts and toward the mummy and Frankenstein displays.

Liam stood awkwardly with Hilly, unsure if he should follow Mai or just stay put. This was exactly why he avoided social situations. He didn't know how to act. What to say. Where to put his hands.

Heard you were back in town, Hilly telepathed. *Sorry to hear about your trouble in Paris.* He adjusted the gold plastic saber he wore tucked into the brown leather belt that held up his chinos.

Liam nodded. *Not a big deal. It'll all get worked out.*

"Not what I heard." His wife, Fiona, didn't bother to telepath despite the fact that a family of humans had just walked in.

"Welcome to Hilly's. Care for a sample?" Hilly crossed the aisle to offer the pumpkin to two grade-school children shopping with their parents.

"Good to see you, too, Fiona," Liam repeated coolly. He kept an eye on Mai as she moved farther toward the back of the store.

Built early in the twentieth century, Hilly's Five-and-Dime was one of the last of the original buildings on the boardwalk. It was a true historic landmark, with high ceilings, wall-to-wall windows oceanside, and a musty smell of passing time the sickeningly sweet scent of candy corn couldn't quite cover.

"About time someone reined some of you boys in," she went on, arms crossed over her saggy bosom. "You think you're above our laws, but you're not. We all have to follow them, like it or not."

It was hard to take the sixty-year-old pillar of the community seriously in her country-girl costume: short, poofy, red skirt over pale, spider-veined legs, a red-and-white checkered shirt, a blond pigtailed wig, and a blacked-out tooth. Not to mention the straw hat.

Liam just nodded. He wasn't getting into this conversation with her, not here. Not now. Not ever.

"Prime example," Fiona said, lowering her voice a decibel, "those humans." She pointed at Mai and her father. "They shouldn't be here and you know it."

"Fiona, the whole town will be full of humans by Friday. They're here for the parade."

"*She's* not here for the *parade*." Her tone was filled with sexual connotations.

Mai was showing her father a dog sweater that looked like a tuxedo jacket. She held it up for Liam to see.

He nodded, but he didn't smile. He had known it was a bad idea to bring Mai here. Fiona had never liked him, at least not in the last couple of centuries.

"It's dangerous," Fiona hissed, straightening a stack of candy boxes. "There's a reason why we don't cohabitate with humans."

"We're not cohabitating. They needed a place to stay for a few nights."

"Why? She in some kind of trouble?" Fiona turned toward Mai, looking her up and down. "She looks like a young woman who could be trouble."

"It's a long story, Fiona. *None* of which is your business."

Mrs. Hill rested her hand on an ample hip. "Not my business?" She shook her finger at him. "You listen to me, Liam McCathal. That human *is* my business, and your mother would tell you so if she was here right now. That woman is every Kahill in this town's business. Having her here jeopardizes your identity; she jeopardizes all of us. Don't you think you're in enough trouble as it is without adding fuel to the Council's fire?"

"Liam," Mai called from two aisles over, "have a sec?"

"Excuse me." Liam smiled as he walked away from Fiona.

Mai watched him approach, waiting until he was out of anyone's earshot. She turned her back, blocking Fiona's view of them. "Who was that?" she whispered. She had several costumes draped over her arm. "I couldn't hear what she was saying, but she was really chewing you out over something."

"It was nothing." He leaned on a shelf. The store was overly warm; he was hot in his leather jacket. It was time to move on. Out of this store. Out of the position he'd gotten himself into with Mai. He had to find the Weasel and settle the matter between him and Mai.

"It was about me, wasn't it?" She searched his face. "I know. Small town. People talk."

"It's no one's business, Mai. So what'd you find?"

She grinned. "You have to help me pick one." She cut her eyes at him. "You're not going to believe what my father is insisting on wearing. Oh, and guess what I found for you." She held up a small cellophane package. "Plastic fangs!"

"This is fun and way beyond your comfort zone, I can tell," Mai said, looping her arm through Liam's. "Thanks."

They were standing on Main Street at sunset, watching the Halloween parade go by. They had a great place, right on the curb, a block off the beach. It was a big event in the area and seemed to get bigger with every passing year. There were local firefighters waving from the top of a fire engine, the nearby high school's marching band, all dressed in white sheets to look like ghosts, playing "Monster Mash," a motorcycle club with toy windup keys attached to the backs of their bikes, a pony club riding bareback, dressed like goblins, and a whole host of other entries.

"I mean it," Mai said when Liam made no response. She wasn't dressed as a naughty nurse, but the costume came close. She was an Indian maiden in a short, suede, beaded dress and tall moccasins that made her tanned legs look like they went on forever. She wore her long, dark hair in two plaits that made her appear so young that Liam felt like he was an old lech, just holding her hand in public.

"Something to take your mind off things," Liam muttered with a shrug.

"Yeah, well, we need to talk about that." She ran her hand over his chest, her hand warm through his T-shirt.

His costume consisted of black jeans, a black T-shirt, his black leather jacket, and his dark hair slicked back. He carried the plastic fangs she had bought him in his pocket.

"I've been waiting all week for you to tell me what you found out."

"I didn't find out anything."

She glanced up at him. A juggling pirate walked by, using plastic bones for batons. Corrato laughed and pointed, then held up Prince so the dog could get a better look at the clown/pirate's antics.

Corrato's costume was surprisingly good. He had bought a run-of-the-mill zombie outfit from Hilly's, but then had Mai do his makeup as per his instructions. The old Italian man looked so real that when Liam glanced at him quickly, Corrato gave him a start. He looked just like a zombie Liam had run into one night near the Coliseum in Rome last year. The spook had been a crazy son-of-a-bitch that had chased Liam five blocks before he gave him the slip.

"You're a lousy liar," Mai said, glancing back at the parade. "*Babbo,* you hand Prince over if he gets too heavy, okay?"

"Prince ain't heavy. He's my brother," Corrato the zombie said, chucking the little dog under the chin.

Prince was dressed in the dog sweater/tuxedo Mai had found at Hilly's.

"You asked my father about the Weasel at the dinner table the first night you came back," Mai said softly. The street was crowded with people, pushing, jostling, talking, and laughing, and they were close. She didn't want to risk anyone overhearing her.

"I didn't find out anything that directly related Donato to him," Liam argued. "Not exactly."

"Not exactly?" she asked.

"Let's talk about it later. The parade is almost over. Look, here comes the Queen of the Crypt and her court."

"We will talk about it later, very soon later," Mai said. She glanced out onto the street at the approaching convertibles. "What the hell is the Queen of the Crypt?"

"I don't know. It's just something silly we do. This year it's Peigi Ross." He waved at Peigi, who sat on the back of his Mercury Montclair. She was dressed in a dingy, shredded bride of Frankenstein dress, her sensible hair spiked so that it stood straight up, her face deathly white with fake blood oozing from the corner of her mouth. "And there's her court." He pointed. "Traditionally, the Queen of the Crypt is an older woman, and her court is always teenagers. See, there's Kaleigh. On the back of the Corvette." He waved at Kaleigh.

Mai craned her neck. "I see her." She waved. "Nice girl. Friendly. Smart, too."

Kaleigh, dressed in some sort of a dress of white rags, her face white with pancake makeup and a rubber hatchet through her skull, spotted Mai and Liam and waved wildly. She elbowed her friend Katy and Katy waved, too. She was wearing what appeared to be an old pink prom gown, covered in fake blood.

"I'm glad you liked her," Liam remarked, gazing around him. "I thought you might." It was almost sunset and the crowd was getting livelier. The spiked cider from the local tourist pub, O'Cahall's, was starting to kick in. Crowds made him nervous. Even crowds of innocent tourists. "Parade ends at the boardwalk. That's where they have the band. It's kind of a block party. You want to walk that way, or ... what?"

He wanted to take them home. What if the Weasel or one of his guys was in the crowd? It made no sense, of course. How could the Weasel find her here in Clare Point?

She looked up at him. "I don't know how long my dad will feel like staying out, but I'd like to go." She gave him a sly grin. "I haven't gotten out much lately, what with taking care of the elderly and a mob boss on my tail."

"Fine tail that it is." He leaned down and kissed the top of her head. "Come on, I know a shortcut. All these people are starting to make me claustrophobic. Corrato." He clasped the old man's arm. "We're going this way, buddy."

Liam led the way through the crowd of onlookers. Most were humans, but there were some locals. At least half of the people were in some form of a costume, whether it was an outfit, head-to-toe, or just a mask or face paint. "This way." At an alley that ran between a bookstore and a sandwich shop, he stepped back to let Mai and Corrato pass.

"Liam! Hello, there."

Liam heard his name called and, not recognizing the voice, he turned toward the street. He scanned the faces in the crowd, not able to match the voice with any of the people he saw.

"I'll be. You here for the parade?"

An older man dressed like Red Skelton in his famous Clem Kadiddlehopper sketches approached him. For a second, Liam still didn't know who he was. Then he recognized him.

Impossible.

Red pumped his arm, then leaned closer. "Looking good for the Eagles this weekend." He winked.

Liam growled, looked both ways, saw no one was paying attention to them, and grabbed the man by the arm and dragged him into the dark alley. "What the hell are you doing, following me?"

Chapter 14

"Liam?" Mai called.

Even in the dark, he could see her. "Keep going," he called. "I'll be right there." He pushed Anthony up against the brick wall of the bookstore. "I said, why are you following me? How the hell did you find me here?"

"I wasn't following you," the bookie protested. His voice trembled, but he didn't fall apart. Being a bookie, he'd probably had his share of getting roughed up over the years. Probably roughed up a few delinquent clients himself, in his younger days. "My sister Alice lives in Bethany Beach. I...I come here every Halloween weekend. We haven't missed a Clare Point parade in fifteen years."

He was lying. It was too big a coincidence. Wasn't it?

"You're going to have to do better than that," Liam ground out.

"I'm telling the truth, I swear on the Virgin Mary." His breath smelled of whiskey. "A...rrived on the 2:25 ferry. You can check the schedule. Alice DeFonso. That's my little sister's name. I'm staying with her. She's in the phone book. Look it up if you don't believe me. Widowed. Was married to Maury DeFonso from Bethany Beach. Clarkesville, actually. He...he had a heating and air conditioning business for thirty years before he stroked out last year."

"I'm not asking for a medical history of your family," Liam said, gritting his teeth, fighting the urge to beat the skinny old man to a pulp. The guy was just one more small-time thug.

"I swear. I wasn't following you. How could I? I had no idea you...I have no idea where you live. I just have this thing for faces. I...I recognized you. But...but I can forget you. Swear I can."

Liam loosened his grip on the old man's throat. He didn't need anyone seeing him beat up an old man in an alley. He looked over to where the crowd was spilling into the street. With all the excitement of the parade and the growing darkness, no one seemed to notice them. He glanced in the other direction. Mai and her father had reached the end of the alley and waited for him, her back to him. She was a smart girl.

"You swear this was an accident?" Liam said. As he spoke the words, he went over in his head anything he could have said to the bookie that night in the trattoria to give away where he lived. He hadn't. He would never do something like that. He wondered if the Rousseau brothers had anything to do with it, but that didn't make sense, either. The police had taken Anthony home; even if Dan and Levi had been crazy enough to follow them to Anthony's house and feed on him, they would have left him with short-term amnesia. He would have remembered nothing about them or anything they said.

It was a coincidence that he and Anthony had run into each other on the street. Pure coincidence, he decided. Life was stranger than fiction sometimes.

"Liam?" Mai called.

Liam slowly released Anthony. "You learn anything more about the guy I asked you about?"

"Got a lead," he said, raising his hand to his throat as he looked up warily. "My cousin's got a sister-in-law in the same parish as his parole officer. I'm working on it."

Liam knew he would never get the information out of Anthony if he scared him too badly. "I apologize for my behavior. A man can't be too careful. I'll make it well worth your while, should you locate the man in question. You have my number. I have yours," he added.

"So I can go?"

Liam nodded. "Sure. Have... have a good evening with your sister. Really. I apologize." He took one last look at the man in the Red Skelton costume and hurried down the dark alley.

"Who was that?" Mai asked, looking over her shoulder as Liam urged her across the street.

"It was no one. Come on."

"Didn't look like no one to me," Corrato the zombie said.

"How about some boardwalk fries?" Liam kept moving. "I know the best place in town to get them."

The zombie nodded. "Prince appreciates a decent boardwalk fry."

Mai rested her head on Liam's shoulder and, wrapped in each other's arms, they danced slowly to the music of the Isley Brothers. After the parade, they had sat on a bench on the boardwalk with her dad and shared a bucket of beach fries. The band had started playing and they'd sat for a while, watching everyone dance. It was a festive atmosphere, with people mingling and laughing, human and vampire together, and Corrato seemed to thoroughly enjoy himself. But then he said he was tired and it was time to go to bed.

Mai had asked Liam for just one dance before they left. He'd considered saying no. He didn't need anyone in Clare Point who hadn't yet seen him with her to see him holding her in his arms. Besides, he didn't dance.

But when he'd tried to say no, he hadn't been able to do

it. Her face had been too earnest. Too sweet. Before the words were out of his mouth, she was telling him it was okay. And then the song began. He'd always had a soft spot for the Isley Brothers.

"If you leave me now," he sang, mostly to himself, feeling ridiculously nostalgic, "you take away the biggest part of me...."

"Oh, baby," she sang softly. "Oh no, woman, please don't go."

"I like this one better than the Chicago song," he said.

"Me too."

Turning slowly, Mai in his arms, Liam noticed how the bare lightbulbs strung back and forth over the dance area cast a pale yellow light, a light so forgiving that he almost couldn't tell who was vampire and who was human. If only the world could be more like this.

Over Mai's shoulder, Liam spotted Kaleigh. She was slow-dancing with Rob. She lifted her gaze to meet Liam's and he realized her eyes were red. She'd been crying.

You okay? Liam telepathed, concentrating on keeping the message strictly for her, which wasn't easy to do with so many Kahills around. Liam's public telepathy skills were a little rusty and the whole sept was a bunch of Nosy Parkers. Living and working the way he did, he didn't usually have to worry about anyone else listening in.

I'm okay, she answered. Then she smiled. Sadly.

Want to talk? he asked, and then wondered what the hell was wrong with him. Sitting around like this, waiting on the High Council, was making him weak. He needed to get back on the road, track a serial killer or something and get out of touch with his softer side.

I don't know. Maybe. Might come by tomorrow after Rob goes back to school. Give you an update on your mom's house.

Come by tomorrow, Liam urged.

The song ended and Mai opened her eyes and looked into his. She was smiling more with her eyes than with her mouth. "Thank you," she whispered.

"For the dance? Sure." He kissed the top of her head and took her hand to lead her back toward the bench where her father waited.

"Not just the dance." She resisted and he was forced to stop. She was strong, for being so petite. "For everything," she said. "For letting us stay. For caring."

"I think he stole some diamonds." Liam just blurted it out.

Her forehead wrinkled in shock. "Uncle Donato? Diamonds?"

Liam nodded. People were walking around them, bumping into them on their way on and off the dance floor. The band began to play "Mustang Sally" and there were hoots and applause.

Liam glanced around. "We'll talk about it later."

"We'll talk about it *now,*" she said. But she let him lead her away from the crowd so they could hear each other above the music. Her father sat on the boardwalk bench, not too far away. "You think he stole diamonds from this guy? You've got to be kidding me." She set her jaw angrily. "How long have you known about this?"

He'd gone on the Internet at the Clare Point public library and done research on the missing diamonds Fia had told him about this week. He'd actually found some information about the diamond theft. The rare pink diamonds had been mined in Tanzania and disappeared during shipment after a private sale. Nowhere on the Internet did it indicate that the mafia or the Weasel had been suspected in the heist. Insurance had paid on the theft fifteen months after the diamonds disappeared. It was unknown if they had ever been cut down and sold on the black market, the only way they would not have been identified.

Liam didn't know why he'd kept the information from Mai until now; obviously, he had to tell her at some point. At her house the other day he'd looked around. There was no safe and whoever had been there had made a pretty good initial search. Donato wouldn't have been dumb enough to take the diamonds there anyway, would he? The diamonds had to be long gone, didn't they?

"How long have you known?" she repeated.

"Bits and pieces, a few days. I still don't have the full story, but it's not easy to track. A lot of the guys involved are dead now."

"They were murdered?"

He smirked. "Old age."

If she thought that was amusing, she didn't respond.

"The diamond heist was in the mid-eighties. Then the Weasel went to jail for twenty years."

She was still in shock. "The bastard had Uncle Donato killed over diamonds?"

"A lot of diamonds. Rare pink diamonds worth millions of dollars. I'm not positive that's what the Weasel is looking for, but if I find him, that'll be my first question."

She rested her hand on his arm. "That sounds like a bad idea, you looking for him. If...if the mob is involved in this, shouldn't I just take *Babbo* and run? Disappear?"

The sad fact was that that might be her best option, but it would be difficult with her father, the way he was. And how would they support themselves? He wasn't ready to tell her to run, not yet. "Give me a few more days," he said. "I'm going to be shipped out in the next week or two anyway, so I've got limited time. Let me use the time."

He could tell by the look on her face that she had a thousand questions: about her uncle, about his mob involvement, about Liam. Bless her, she asked none. Instead, she turned toward her father. He had gotten up off the bench and tucked Prince under his arm. Apparently, he was ready to go and intended to head out, with or without them.

"I guess we'd better go. He's getting antsy. I don't want him disappearing in the crowd. I don't know if he's got enough wits about him right now to find his way back to your apartment."

"Sure. We'll go." Liam hesitated. "But I want to ask you something. I'd like to ask your dad about the diamonds. See what, if anything, he knows. Would that be okay?"

She looked at her father, then back at Liam. "I can't imagine he—" She stopped herself, and raised her hand and let it fall. "Sure. Talk to him. But I've tried since this whole thing went down with Uncle Donato. I've never heard anything about these diamonds ever. The word *mafia* was never brought up in our household. We barely spoke of Uncle Donato over the years. We saw him at family gatherings, he sent birthday and Christmas presents, but that was the limit of my contact with him. And now, since Uncle Donato's murder, my father won't answer any questions about his brother. The minute I bring up the subject, he just starts in with the crossword puzzle nonsense. But go ahead. Have a try. You going to ask him now?"

Liam shook his head. "He's tired. It's time to go home. I'll try to catch him when he's in a good mood. Maybe feels like talking."

She gave a little laugh, but it was without humor. "Good luck with that. The man's so close-mouthed, he could have been a mobster himself."

That night, Liam stayed awake and waited for Mai to come to his room. After the sex, he'd almost asked her to stay. He had been tired but afraid to sleep, afraid of the nightmares. How having Mai in bed with him was going to change his dreams or what happened that night, he didn't know. He didn't ask and she had gone back to her own room. Eventually he had slept. And dreamed.

Last night he'd managed, in his dream, to reach the chamber where the brothers had been. He got as far as the little boy handcuffed to the cot. Then the blood had started. At first, he had just seen it at the boy's wrists, only a drop or two. Then it had begun to pour, first from the boy's ears and nose, then his eyes. Then the walls. The blood had slowly risen: to Liam's ankles, then his knees, then higher. First the pedophiles had drowned in the blood. It was funny how a vampire who consumed blood, who loved blood beyond all reason, could also be so repelled by it. In the dream, he reached for the boy, tried to save him, but the child was still handcuffed to the metal frame of the cot. Eventually the blood rose over their heads in a great ocean of thick, wet, warm death. Liam woke up coughing and choking, his eyes blurry with tears. As he sat up, gasping for breath, he could still feel the blood gushing down his throat.

Around four, he gave up on going back to sleep, rose, went for a run in the game preserve, and fed there. The blood of the deer he captured, then set free, didn't really satisfy him, but at least it nourished him, and he walked home, his head clearer. He showered and was early for 8 a.m. Mass. He was kneeling at the back pew when Father Kahill entered the church nave by way of the chancel.

Liam knew better than to approach him. They made eye contact, but then he went about his tasks, and soon two altar servers joined him and the congregation began to file in. Several people said good morning to Liam, but no one attempted to have a conversation with him, except for Mary Kay, Fia's mother, who stopped to suggest that *he* suggest to Fia that she attend Mass more often.

"I'm not sure anyone can tell Fia what to do, Mary

Kay." He looked up at her. "You ought to know that by now."

Mary Kay frowned. "Any word from your mother?"

"Not really."

"We all expected her back by now. You know, to have come to her senses." She looked around to see if anyone was listening, then, satisfied they weren't, she leaned closer. She smelled of blueberry muffins. Mary Kay Kahill could be a royal pain in the ass, but she made the best blueberry muffins he'd ever eaten, in twenty-seven life-times. "You don't think that Victor is holding her captive, do you?"

He flashed her a mischievous grin. "More like the other way around."

She drew herself up, puckering her mouth. "So you're not worried?"

"She'll come home, Mary Kay. She's pissed off because the Council wouldn't let her marry Victor, and I can see her point. My father is dead forever. Murdered. Why shouldn't my mother find a little happiness in Victor's arms?" He sat back against the pew. "She'll cool down and come back eventually."

After his father's death, Liam had suffered from guilt over the fact that he wasn't here to help his mother get through the ordeal. Not that he would have had much to offer, emotionally. And it angered him that he hadn't been able to help the sept catch the killers, but he'd been in the midst of several investigations in Europe and the High Council had insisted he remain entrenched.

"I just thought she'd come home by now," Mary Kay went on, "you being in all the trouble you're in. And now with you living with that human."

"I'm not *living* with a human," he corrected. "She's just staying a few days. With her father."

"*And* a dog," Mary Kay whispered conspiratorially.

"*And* a dog," he agreed, not sure what that had to do with anything.

"Well," Mary Kay went on, "I don't mind saying, everyone's talking about it and no one likes it much." She cupped her hand around her mouth. "Everyone's saying it doesn't make things look good for you. That your days on the you-know-what team might be coming to an end."

"Oh, they are, are they? I don't suppose you've heard when the Council will be discussing the matter with me? You are a member now, aren't you?"

"You have to have an interview first. And there's the investigation," she pointed out.

He looked up at her. "I don't suppose you know who will be conducting this interview?" *Or when the hell it's going to take place,* he wanted to add.

"No, but I'm sure you'll hear something soon." She looked away. "Oh, there's Roberta. You take care now, Liam. Stop by anytime. I know how you like my muffins."

Liam wanted to ask if he could skip the visit and just pick up some muffins, but he let Mary Kay go.

After Mass, he stopped for a Sunday paper for Corrato at the newsstand. While he was there, he picked up a crossword puzzle book. He found Corrato sitting out front of his shop on a chair Mai must have carried down from the kitchen. It was sunny and pleasant there and the sidewalk was wide enough that there was actually room for a café table and chairs, a possibility Liam had never considered. The rat terrier sat on the sidewalk beside him, standing guard. As Liam approached, he spotted Mai inside unwrapping pieces of china from a cardboard box. She waved.

"Brought you the paper, Corrato." Liam offered it. "And a crossword book."

The older man set the paper on his lap, removed his reading glasses from his shirt pocket, put them on, and read the cover of the book. *"New York Times Wednesday Crosswords."* He looked up at Liam. "Not hard."

"No, sir."

He raised a finger. "But not easy. See, they get harder as the week goes on. It can take a man half a day to do the whole Sunday crossword puzzle in the *New York Times*."

"Yes, sir." Liam sat down on the sidewalk beside the dog. Prince eyed him. He looked at Prince and the dog shifted his weight uneasily. Liam got the idea that the mutt was waiting for him to turn into a tiger again.

"I know you don't like to talk about your brother, Corrato, but I need to ask you a couple of questions."

"Seven-letter word, beginning with an L, meaning—"

"That's not going to work with me today," Liam interrupted.

Surprisingly, the old man went quiet.

"I'm not asking because I want to know your brother's business, or yours," he added. "And I have no intention of calling the cops or getting anyone into trouble. I'm only asking because I'm concerned about Mai's safety."

"He's looking for us, isn't he?"

Corrato spoke so softly that Liam had to strain to hear him.

The old man stared straight ahead. Maybe at the coffee shop across the street. Maybe at nothing. "That's why we're here and not home."

"Yes." Liam waited for Corrato to speak again, but when he didn't, Liam went on. "A man named Machhione. You know him?"

Corrato didn't respond.

"From what I've been able to figure out, your brother worked for Machhione for years." He watched Corrato closely. The man knew how to put on a poker face. "Some people called Machhione the Weasel. That ring a bell? He was from Union, same place where you grew up, but he worked out of Brooklyn."

"This has nothing to do with me or my daughter," Corrato said. He was angry; that was pretty evident. What was also evident was that he seemed to understand exactly what Liam was talking about and where he was headed. "I left Jersey in 1988."

"But your brother started working for the Weasel sometime in the seventies. Before Carlo DeCava disappeared."

"I don't know anything about that either. What's a four-letter word—"

"Do you understand that Mai's life is at risk?" Liam interrupted, looking the old man in the eye.

Corrato stood up, tucking the paper and the crossword puzzle book under his arm. "Do you understand that the less anyone knows, the safer they are? That means you too, buster. "

Liam was still sitting there alone on the sidewalk staring at nothing, trying to figure out what his next move was, when Kaleigh came down the sidewalk half an hour later. She wore jeans, flip-flops, and a hooded sweatshirt with the hood up, her hands shoved in the front pocket.

"You're up early," he called. "Been to Mass? I missed you at the eight o'clock."

She stuck out her tongue. She was still at that rebellious place in her life when she blamed God for all her woes and gave Him no credit for the good things. To Liam's knowledge, she hadn't attended Mass since she was reborn. "Maybe I was out late and that's why I didn't make Mass. Maybe I'm just getting in."

He raised an eyebrow and she dropped into the kitchen chair vacated by Corrato. "Okay, so I was home by eleven last night. But I *could* stay out all night if I wanted." She leaned back, looking every bit the sulky teenager. "I'm a wisewoman. I have a lot of power. People should respect me. Fear me."

He smiled to himself. He didn't know what was going

on with Kaleigh, but it was obviously important to her. "So what's up with my mom's house?"

"Pretty much cleaned. They sucked up the water in the carpet with this big vacuum and then they sprayed something to make it not stink. I think they've got big fans blowing in there now."

"Some of the hardwood was messed up," he intoned.

She exhaled as if it greatly annoyed her to go on. "Katy knows this guy whose dad has a lumber store. He lays down wood floors on weekends or something and they say they can replace the boards and make it, like, all match."

"Katy, huh? So she was one of the perpetrators."

Kaleigh frowned. "I told you I'd take care of the mess. I didn't tell you I'd squeal on my friends."

He smiled to himself. It was amazing how she could be so bright, so gifted, so mature at one moment, and then this in the next. "So what was going on last night? At the dance. You and Rob fighting?"

She crossed her arms over her chest. "I don't want to talk about it."

He watched a squirrel grab an acorn and run up a tree across the street. "And yet you're here."

"Kaleigh. Good to see you."

The teen sat up a little straighter when she saw Mai in the doorway. "Hey," she called. "What are you doing?"

"Let's see"—Mai glanced over her shoulder—"inventorying a set of post–World War I china made in Poland that looks like it has place settings for twenty-four." She frowned and looked at Liam. "Who has twenty-three people to dinner?"

He shrugged. "Must have been a good deal."

"Must have," Mai agreed.

Liam glanced over his shoulder at her. She looked so cute this morning, wearing her jeans and one of his black T-shirts. She wore a red bandanna around her head to keep the dust out of her hair. "Your dad okay?"

"Sure. He's upstairs watching TV now. Why wouldn't he be?" Her face immediately darkened and she looked up and down the street expectantly. "Everything okay? I thought it would be safe for him to sit out here."

"It's fine. He's fine out here. I should just find him a better chair."

Kaleigh got up. "Yeah, because a kitchen chair on the sidewalk in front of your shop—*lame*." She walked over to Mai, pushing back her hoodie. "So...want some help or something? With the dishes? I'm not too clumsy."

Mai smiled, stepping back to let her through the door. "That would be great!"

And Liam was alone again.

Chapter 15

"So what were you and Kaleigh talking about today?" Liam stood next to Mai at the kitchen sink, helping her with the dishes. Kaleigh had ended up staying all day, aiding Mai in her quest to organize his shop. The teen even stayed for dinner.

Tonight Mai had made baked ziti. Liam was going to have to start adding an extra mile to his run every morning or he would be out of shape by the time he got out of here.

The TV was on in the other room and Kaleigh and Corrato were watching the Cartoon Network. Liam had had the cable turned on Friday and borrowed his mom's TV. If the old man got pleasure from watching TV, it seemed a shame that he shouldn't have some decent choices.

"I don't know." Mai shrugged and handed him a plate.

Liam trusted Kaleigh not to say anything to Mai that would give her, or Liam, or the town away, but it had still made him nervous to see the two of them with their heads together, talking all day. Laughing. They couldn't possibly have been talking about him all that time, could they? "You don't know?" he pressed, drying the plate with a new hand towel that had mysteriously appeared in a kitchen drawer.

"I don't know. Girl stuff." She glanced down the hall, then back at Liam. "You and my dad. What did you talk about this morning? He seemed pretty miffed."

"Boy stuff."

She frowned and lowered her voice. "Diamond boy stuff? Mafioso boy stuff?"

"Something like that." He set the dry plate down and took another wet one from her.

"And did you get any response out of him?"

"Not the kind I was hoping for." Liam rubbed one side of the plate dry, then flipped it over. "But he knows something. Not sure I can get it out of him, but he knows more than he's saying."

"You think my uncle really stole diamonds?"

She still sounded as if she couldn't quite believe it, but in her world, it probably was pretty unbelievable. Liam, on the other hand, spent lifetimes among criminals. He knew the full extent of the possibilities of mankind's illegal activity, as well as their depravities.

"All the evidence points to that."

"But would he keep them all these years? Wouldn't he have sold them?"

"Maybe, but maybe not. Maybe he was afraid to sell them, afraid the Weasel would find out, and he was just waiting to see what happened. A lot of times guys never make it out of prison. The Weasel dies or is killed in prison, and Donato is home free." He turned the fact over in his mind. "Or maybe he didn't steal the diamonds for the money."

"What do you mean?"

"Maybe Donato stole them to get back at the Weasel for something. To hurt him."

"And my dad knows something about all this?"

"I don't know just yet. Your father is a hard nut to crack, but I think he'll come clean eventually."

She frowned. "You can't be mean to him, Liam. No matter what."

He looked at her. "Mean to him? Mai, I would never do that." He tried not to think of all the things he had done over the years that were far worse than bullying an old man. "What kind of guy do you think I am?"

She put a wet hand on his chest and he felt his heart soften. Her touch made him want to protect her, at any cost. What was amazing was that her touch didn't make him want her blood. Not too much, at least.

"What kind of a guy are you?" she asked softly. "I mean, let's be honest. I can guess by how you've treated us, but I don't know for sure."

He took her wet hand, brought it to his lips as if she were a fair maiden, and kissed it. "If it's any consolation, I'm not sure I *really* know what kind of man I am, either. But I do know that I wouldn't hurt your dad, or you."

"I know you wouldn't." She held his gaze a second longer and then pulled away. "So what do I do now? About this Weasel guy? What if Uncle Donato did steal his diamonds? What if they're in a safe-deposit box or something? I guess it's a possibility. My uncle was a pretty private guy." She gave a little laugh. "Which makes sense in light of the whole mafia thing." She shook her head. "It's still so hard to believe."

"You don't do anything right now, except stay here."

"And unload boxes."

He smiled, wiping water up off the counter with the dish towel. "Except unload boxes and get my store organized. But you and I need to go to your house and look around your uncle's room. See if there's any clues to this previous life he led. I'm trying to learn what I can about him, trying to find out if this beef the Weasel had with your uncle is genuine. We'll go from there."

She pulled the plug from the drain and watched the

water go down the sink. "I'd give them back, you know. The diamonds. If I had them."

He nodded. "Sure. The problem is, guys like this, sometimes that's not enough. Sometimes they want to eliminate their trail."

"So my father could still be in danger, even if we found the diamonds and returned them?"

He saw no reason to sugarcoat her situation. He wasn't a sugarcoating kind of guy. "Both of you could be in danger. It's very possible."

Tears suddenly filled her eyes, taking him completely off-guard. He hadn't expected that. Not here, now, over this. She hadn't even cried the night her uncle was murdered and was lying on her floor in a pool of blood. Mai was a tough chick.

"Hey," he whispered. Not really knowing what to say, he pulled her into his arms and held her tightly for a minute. She took a deep breath, then exhaled, and he felt her relax. She lifted up on her toes, gave him a quick kiss, and stepped back. She leaned against the sink.

Kaleigh laughed in the other room. They were watching *Scooby-Doo,* of all things. Liam recognized the canine detective's voice.

"She kind of wanted my advice," Mai said softly, nodding in Kaleigh's direction.

"What?"

"Kaleigh," Mai whispered. "You asked me what we talked about. I'm telling you. She kind of wanted my advice."

He glanced in the direction of the living room. Talking about Kaleigh, near Kaleigh was dangerous. Even thinking about her was dangerous. She was getting too good at reading minds.

He slid the stack of clean plates onto a shelf in the cupboard, making a little noise, trying to lull the teen into thinking they were still just cleaning up after dinner. "About what?" he asked.

"Sex," Mai whispered. She walked to the table and wiped it down with a dishcloth. Also new.

Liam hadn't known he even had kitchen linens down-stairs. What had ever possessed him to buy linens? "Sex?" he asked, trying to keep his voice down.

"Well, she *is* almost eighteen years old. She's been dating the same boy for two years."

More like fifteen hundred years, he thought. "What... what kind of advice was she looking for?"

Mai pushed in one of the chairs. "I probably shouldn't say. It was a private conversation."

He gave her a look that told her that wasn't an acceptable response.

She frowned, walking back to the sink to rinse the dishcloth. "I think he's pressuring her to have sex."

"What?" he blurted.

She glanced in the direction of the living room and shot him a look. "She'll hear you," she whispered harshly.

He exhaled, getting more aggravated by the second. What the hell was wrong with Kaleigh, talking about something like that with Mai? Vampire sex was no one's business, certainly not a human's. Kaleigh shouldn't have been talking to Mai at all. Mai was *his* human.

The minute that thought went through his head, he knew it wasn't right on *way* too many levels. Mai wasn't *his*. She didn't belong to anyone. There couldn't be a relationship here. Even if she wanted to be his, she couldn't be. She knew it, even if she didn't know why, and he sure as hell knew it.

This was all making him crazy. This crazy little town. The predicament he'd gotten himself into with Mai and Corrato. If only the Council would get the hell on with it, have his hearing, and let him go back to work. He needed to return to the world he knew, with rules he understood.

He chose his next words carefully. "So...what kind of advice did you give her?"

Frankly, Liam was a little surprised Kaleigh and Rob hadn't already had sex. They were life partners. They had been husband and wife before and would be husband and wife again. Of course, the sept strictly prohibited sex between vampires before they reached twenty-one years of age. Before then, they weren't always able to control their bloodlust during sex. Even with consensual vampires, things could get out of hand. A vampire drained of too much blood could become very ill and help had to be called in; it was an embarrassment he had suffered or caused on more than one occasion. The other problem with sex too soon after rebirth was that the lines between whom it was okay to have sex with and whom it wasn't, namely humans, were easily blurred; it was just easier to say no sex at all was permitted. Adult sept members agreed that the rules were good ones and should be enforced, but teens were teens and they didn't always follow the rules.

"Mai, what did you tell her?" he repeated.

"I told her she should talk to her mother."

He leaned against the counter, crossing his arms over his chest. "How'd that go over?"

"Not so well." She smiled mischievously.

"So...then?""

Mai took her time folding the dishcloth, then laid it over the kitchen faucet. "So then I gave her my opinion as a woman."

"Which was?"

"Which was and is none of your business," she said.

He grabbed her arm and pulled her roughly to him, playfully. For the most part. "None of my business?"

She laughed, struggling against his hold. "None of your damn business." She giggled, not seeming to mind that he was being a little rough. "That's why they call it *girl talk,* because *boys* aren't invited."

"I'm not invited?" He nuzzled her neck. She smelled so good, femininely musky and sweet at the same time. "Is that right?" he teased. "Not invited, am I?"

He felt her pulse against his lips and couldn't help wondering what she would say if he told her the truth about him. About how he wanted to bite her, to suck her sweet, hot blood...swallow it. How he wanted to throw her down on the kitchen floor right this minute and fuck her. Drink her blood and fuck her.

He had a feeling it wouldn't go over all that well. It usually didn't.

Liam kissed her mouth hard. With tongue. Then he let her go, leaving her breathless. "Dog been out lately?"

"What?" She looked almost dazed. He had that effect on women when he kissed them. Especially HFs. He wasn't exactly sure why, but apparently he was a pretty good kisser. Not all that impressive when you took into consideration how many centuries he'd had to practice. "The Prince of Dogs. Has he been out to pee?"

"No." She shook her head as if she could shake away the spell he had cast over her. "He hasn't."

"I'll take him out, then. Walk Kaleigh downstairs. She should be getting home. She's got school tomorrow."

Before Mai could protest, Liam walked into the living room. There was a commercial on TV for fruit snacks. "Okay, time to hit the road, kid." He gestured toward the door. "Prince, come on. Outside." He slapped his thigh.

Neither the dog nor the teen responded.

Liam wondered where the respect was. Didn't they know he was a trained killer? Well, Kaleigh knew. But he was pretty sure the dog suspected.

Kaleigh, he telepathed, *outside. Now. You, too,* he ordered the dog.

To his surprise, both jumped up.

Liam had never been able to speak telepathically to animals before. Was he gaining that gift? He stared at the little dog. It stared back, with bulging brown eyes, as if it knew what he was thinking.

Maybe the damned dog was telepathic and could read *Liam's* thoughts.... How weird would that be?

"I gotta go, Mr. Ricci," Kaleigh said. "But I'll be by later in the week. We can take that walk on the beach. Okay?"

Corrato didn't answer, just nodded. Kaleigh didn't seem to be offended. The two had obviously hit it off.

"Going outside?" Kaleigh asked the rat terrier in a high-pitched voice.

The dog danced a jig at her feet.

"Prince going outside?" she cooed.

Liam waited in the living room doorway to let them both pass, giving Kaleigh the eye as she went by.

"What?" she asked, throwing up her hands.

We'll talk about it outside, he telepathed.

Kaleigh stuck her head in the kitchen doorway. "Thanks for dinner." She pulled her sweatshirt over her head and flipped up the hood. "If it's okay, Mr. Ricci and I thought we might take a walk on the beach sometime this week. Collect shells or something."

Mai turned from the refrigerator where she was stacking containers of leftovers. "I think he'd like that." She glanced at Liam in the hallway. "If...if we can make it work."

"I think he'd be fine with Kaleigh," Liam responded, understanding that she was concerned for her father's safety. Of course, she didn't know that Kaleigh had the ability to protect Corrato and take on several mafiosi, should the need arise. "In fact, maybe we should go to your place and have that look around while your dad hangs here in Clare Point with Kaleigh."

Mai closed the refrigerator door. "That would be great. Thanks."

"Good night," Kaleigh called from inside the hood.

Liam waited until they were outside before he spoke. The air was cool and there was a breeze off the water. Leaves fluttered at his feet. He let the rat terrier down and Prince took off along the grassy spot he had marked as his own. "What the hell is wrong with you, talking to Mai about having sex with Rob?"

"She wasn't supposed to say anything to you," Kaleigh said from the shadows of the hood. He could hear the pout in her voice.

"That's not the point, Kaleigh. Mai is a human."

"You think I don't know that?"

Liam exhaled in frustration. "If you're having problems, if you need to talk to someone about a vampire problem, you talk to a vampire."

"Right. Like who? My mom?" she burst out. "Who likes to pretend I've never had sex in fifteen centuries? Katy, who'd have sex with everyone? Or how about you? Could I come to you and talk about my personal problems? You, who keep yourself so walled off that no one can reach you?"

The questions were obviously rhetorical. She kept going. "I'm the sept's wisewoman. You know what that means? That means I'm responsible for all of you. Every damned one of you." She sniffled and reached into her hood, to rub her nose, he suspected. "I have to listen to all your problems, help you solve them, and I'm not just talking little problems like who you are and aren't having sex with. I'm talking big problems. Like...like world peace and if we should kill some guy in Australia."

"Push back your hood," Liam said.

Kaleigh looked up. "What?" she snapped.

"Push back your hood. I can't see your face." He made a concerted effort to remove the antagonism from his voice. "I want to see your face when you speak."

"What if I don't want you to see me?" But she pushed it back and he saw her pretty face, her teary eyes, and her runny nose.

"That's better," he said softly. Then he looked around. "Where the hell did that dog go?"

"Prince!" Kaleigh called and walked along the side of the building. Liam followed.

"So ... what is going on with you and Rob?"

She threw him a look over her shoulder and went around the corner of the building. "There he is. Prince!"

"Kaleigh, don't make this any harder for me. I'm trying. I really am." He followed her across the grass in the dark. The next street over was residential. Faint light shone in the windows "Tell me what's going on with you and Rob."

"Like you would understand monogamy," she threw over her shoulder. "Prince, Prince, you can't run away. Your daddy would worry. We can't have that, can we?"

"Kaleigh, I don't have a life mate. That's not my fault."

"No, but it makes things easier sometimes, doesn't it?"

"Sometimes," he agreed. "Especially with what I do. But it makes it harder, too."

"How's that?"

They reached the sidewalk. Prince sashayed across the street just in front of them.

"You know. I don't *have* anyone."

"You have hundreds of people all over the world. You have the Kahills."

"It's not the same thing. I don't have one person who will ..." He groaned inwardly. This wasn't his style. He didn't like talking about this shit. But he genuinely cared about Kaleigh, and he sure as hell didn't want her running around sharing her problems with humans. The next thing he knew, she'd be at the guidance counselor's office in her human high school.

"You don't have one person who will *what?*" Kaleigh crossed the street.

"I'm going to kill that mutt when I get my hands on him," he muttered, flexing his fingers. He hadn't put his coat on and it was getting colder by the minute. "I have no one to come home to, Kaleigh. No one to hold me. No one who loves me, knowing what I am. What I do. If someone beheads me in an alley in Kandahar, no one would care."

She waited for him on the other side of the street. Prince had stopped to check out a dead beetle lying belly-up on the sidewalk. "A lot of people would care. I would care. I know it doesn't seem like it right now, but people here are thankful that you do what you do for us, for God's people—" She twisted her mouth. "That sounds corny, but you know what I mean. Some of us, we can't kill. No matter how right we believe it is, or how many humans we'll save, we can't do it, Liam."

"I know," he mumbled, feeling uncomfortable. He wasn't looking for compliments from her; he was just trying to explain how he felt. Maybe so it would help her. "But we're not talking about me, we're talking about you and Rob."

She started walking again. "You going to tell my mom?"

He laughed. "Have I ever told *your mom* anything? To your knowledge, have *Cassie* and I *ever* been tight?"

At that, she laughed. And hearing the sound of her voice, Prince sprinted forward.

"Just kill the dog. Throw a ball of fire at him, levitate

him and hurl him into a trash can, or something, will you?"

"Stop saying things like that. You're scaring him. That's why he's running. You're mean."

"You think I'm mean?" Liam fell into step beside her. He thought about what Mai had said about forbidding him to be mean to her father. That was two in one night. "Do I strike you as a mean person?"

"You strike me as a jelly donut." She prodded him with her finger. "Dipped in, like...cement. You're, like, all hard and manly on the outside and all soft and squishy on the inside." She laughed. He didn't.

"You and Rob, doing the nasty. That's what we're talking about."

She sighed, throwing up her arms. "Okay. He wants to do it. He says we've already been doing it for all these years, no big deal. Of course I can't *remember* that yet, so it's like I *haven't* done it yet. Big deal. I argue, I'm the wisewoman, I should be following sept rules. Blah, blah, blah. He says I'm the wisewoman, I'm more powerful than anyone in the sept—"

"Not yet," Liam corrected. "I could kick your ass in a fight, and I know Peigi can make a bigger bonfire than you can."

"Yeah, whatever." She stopped and watched as the dog sniffed a fire hydrant and cocked his leg. "So that's basically the problem."

"That Rob wants to have sex and you don't?"

"That he wants to have sex and if I don't, you bet he's going to do it with someone else. He's at Princeton, for God's sake. Free ass everywhere." She turned to look at him in the darkness.

"Aha," he said. "Which makes it more complicated."

"Which makes it more complicated." She exhaled. "Because I know, by sept rules, he's allowed to. I know we've all done it. It just happens, some lifetimes more than others." She pushed her hair behind her ears. "I just don't want it to happen right now. I don't want him to have sex with another girl. I want him to wait for me to be ready. And I don't want to feel like he's pushing me into doing it when I don't want to," she added quickly.

"So you're not ready?" Liam asked.

"No, I'm not. Yeah. Maybe. I mean, I think about it. And it's not like I haven't done it before. No big deal, right?" She threw up her hands, looking at him. "I don't know! That's the problem. *I don't know.* I'm supposed to be so smart and here's this little, tiny, itty-bitty problem, and I don't know what to do." She walked toward the dog. "You move again, Prince," she threatened, "and you're a weenie on a stick."

The rat terrier froze. Kaleigh walked over, picked him up, tucked him under her arm, and walked back toward Liam.

"You know what I say?"

"What do you say, Liam?"

They walked side by side, back down the sidewalk toward the shop. He stuffed his hands into his jeans pockets for warmth. "I say wait until you're ready. Don't listen to Rob. Don't give in to his pressure. Don't listen to the sept, either."

"I don't think you're supposed to say that. You're supposed to be an adult. You're supposed to tell this unformed creature to follow the rules."

He stopped and turned to her. "Follow the rules of your heart," he told her. "Have sex with Rob when you're ready, whether it's tomorrow or when you turn twenty-one or sixty-one. If he wants to go have sex with someone else, you can't let that be your problem. That's his problem."

She hugged the dog. "You think so?"

"I know so. Hand him over."

She held the dog up in front of her as if he was an infant and spoke directly to him. "That's a good boy. I'll see you another day. Now, be a good boy and no more running off." She handed him over. "If you need me to come over one day this week and hang with Mr. Ricci, I can do that. No problem. Then you and Mai can do whatever it is that's so top secret." She giggled.

"*That's* not what we need to do." He snatched the dog from her. "We need to go back to her house and look for something."

"You going to tell me what's going on with them?"

"No."

"I could just read your mind, you know."

He smiled. "Guess you could try."

She grinned back. "How about Tuesday? I've got Honor Society after school tomorrow."

"Works for me." He turned to go, then turned back. "Hey, Kaleigh."

She had started to go the opposite way. "Yeah?"

"Another favor?"

"Maybe."

"Poke around, see what you can find out about my hearing. I'm supposed to have an interview, then be put on the docket to appear before the Council. I haven't heard a word about even the interview yet."

"I'll see what I can find out." She headed back down the sidewalk. " 'Night."

"Good night."

Liam walked back to the apartment, dog under his arm, kind of smiling to himself. It was nice that Kaleigh had talked to him about her problem with Rob, even if she did need a little coercion to do it. It was nice to think that she trusted him enough. That she valued his opinion.

As he approached the outside door, Prince began to growl.

"Hey, knock it off," he told the squirming pooch as he started up the stairs.

Then the dog began to bark, softly at first, then louder and more ferociously. Liam took the steps faster. Something was wrong upstairs. Just as he put his hand on the doorknob, he heard something heavy fall, then breaking glass.

"Take another step closer," Mai threatened from the other side of the door, "and I'll knock the hell out of you."

Chapter 16

Liam halted, one hand holding the dog under his arm, the other on the doorknob. Was Mai talking to *him*?

No, it couldn't be. In a split second, he realized what was going on. He'd been so wrapped up in his conversation with Kaleigh that he hadn't been paying attention to his surroundings. *Intruders. Vampires.*

He jerked open the door at the top of the stairs and shoved the dog in, pushing him across the floor and, hopefully, out of harm's way. Instead of racing toward his master in the living room, tail tucked between his legs, however, the pooch hung a left, directly into the kitchen, barking his little head off.

"Elwood! Back off," Liam growled. His fangs vibrated and he stretched his lips over them, trying to keep them from protracting. He didn't want to scare Mai any further.

"I got this," Mai called, her voice amazingly steady, considering the circumstances.

Elwood had her backed up against the kitchen counter, his fangs bared. But she was holding a chair over her head, threatening to hit him with it. "I tried to tell him Halloween was over," she quipped.

"But technically, it isn't," Elwood responded. "It's the 31st."

"It's Sunday," she corrected. "Halloween was observed this year on Saturday, October 30th."

At that moment, Prince growled and dove for the vampire's ankle. Elwood gave a yip as the dog clamped down on flesh.

"Ouch! *Condamnez-le! Appel outré du chien!* I meant no harm!" Elwood cried, trying to shake the dog loose.

Liam reached out, grasped Elwood by the collar of his black suit jacket, and yanked him backward, off his feet, laying him out flat on the kitchen floor. "What the hell are you doing here?" Before Liam could get turned around and sink a knee into the jerk's chest, Prince hopped up on the prone vampire and thrust his little snout in Elwood's face. The dog growled, baring vicious little needle teeth.

"Please," Elwood whimpered, looking at the dog. "*Je voulais pas de mal.* I meant no harm. I only came to call on the little lady."

"Dressed in that stupid costume?" she demanded, slamming the chair to the floor and thrusting it under the table. She was royally pissed.

Liam kind of liked seeing her this way. Defending herself. It made him less worried about her future when he was long gone.

"I only came to say hello," Elwood insisted.

"So when I told you to take a hike, you pushed your way in?" Mai demanded as she stomped by. "*Babbo?* You okay?" she called as she went down the hall, leaving Liam and Prince in charge of the intruder.

The Road Runner was now beep-beeping on the TV.

Liam pressed one knee to the floor and looked at the dog, still poised to snap off Elwood's nose. "I think I got this one," he said respectfully to the rat terrier. "Go check on the old man."

Prince turned his face, looked into Liam's eyes, then hopped off Elwood's chest and trotted down the hallway toward the living room.

"What the hell are you doing here?" Liam grunted under his breath.

"Trick-or-treating?" Elwood pleaded hopefully.

"*Again,* a day late." Liam grabbed him by his shirt and tie and, in one movement, rose to his feet, taking Elwood with him. "I thought I was clear the other day that you weren't welcome here."

"I...I just wanted to be sure the little lady felt the same way."

"I could seriously hurt you. You know that, don't you?"

"Aren't you in enough trouble?" He put up his hands to protect himself. "How would this look to the Council, you harming me over a human?"

"Fuck the Council." Liam began to half-carry him, half-drag him out of the kitchen. "I think I'd like to hurt you."

"I'd like it if you didn't," Elwood managed as he clawed at Liam's hand, trying to catch his breath. "I meant no harm. Truly. We were just goofing around."

"We?"

Elwood's eyes got bigger than they already were. He broke into a sweat.

"Where is he?" Liam demanded.

"I—"

Liam gave him a shake for good measure.

"Down the hall! I...I don't know! Maybe he had to take a leak!"

Liam thrust Elwood through the open door so hard that the would-be blues singer hit the wall before he started the long tumble down the steps.

"Jake!" Liam bellowed as he headed down the hall. The first door was Liam's bedroom. It was closed. Ahead, he saw the bathroom and the second bedroom doors open, lights out. He felt Jake's presence as he threw open his bedroom door.

"Surprise?" Jake said in a tiny voice. He crouched on Liam's bed, in the dark.

"Get out!"

"Like Elwood said, we—"

"Get out!" Liam shouted, pointing toward the door. He was so angry he was shaking. These two were relatively harmless, considering what was out there in the world, but it angered him that they had crossed his turf. Scared *his* girlfriend. "Get out now, or I'm throwing you out the window." As his last words came out, he was unable to control himself and his fangs came down.

Jake, dressed in full Blues Brothers' garb, took the opportunity to leap off the bed and sprint for the open doorway. A couple of seconds later, Liam heard the door to the apartment slam shut and Jake clamber down the staircase. No doubt, Elwood was still lying at the bottom of the steps in a heap, if Liam was lucky, with a broken leg.

Standing in the dark in the middle of his bedroom, Liam took a deep breath and exhaled. He couldn't let Mai see him like this. He flexed his fingers, curled them until his fists were balls, and did it again. Adrenaline raced through his body. His heart pounded. In this state, his natural instincts were much sharper, but that made him more dangerous to a human like Mai.

As if thoughts of her conjured her up, Mai appeared in the doorway, silhouetted against the light coming from the kitchen and living room. "Liam?"

"Lock the apartment door," he said, turning his head to speak to her, his voice deep as he struggled to gain control of himself.

"I did."

She took a step into the dark room and even at the distance of a few feet, he could feel her heart beating. He could imagine the blood pumping from her heart, through her circulatory system. Just a tiny nick on her neck and—

"Mai! Go check on your father!"

"I already—"

"Get out!" he barked.

Startled, she backed out slowly, staring at him. In the dark, he knew he was concealed well enough. She couldn't see his fangs.

"Close the door," he said, quieter. "Please."

She did as he instructed and he felt, as much as heard, her retreat.

Liam waited a full ten minutes in the dark in his room. He touched his fingertips to the crucifix around his neck. He prayed to God to give him the strength to spare this woman the curse of being marked by a vampire. By him.

His fangs retracted. His heart slowed to a normal pace. Only when he was sure he was himself again—his safer self—did he leave the room. He found Corrato and the dog, perched on the couch beside him, watching TV. The cartoons had ended. They were watching an episode of *Mister Ed.* For a moment, Liam stood in the arched doorway and watched. It was the episode where Wilbur removed the phone extension from the barn, angering the horse because he could no longer make phone calls.

The Prince of Dogs looked no worse for wear, having momentarily held down a vampire. If Corrato knew his daughter had had an altercation in the kitchen, he gave no indication.

Liam glanced over his shoulder, wondering where Mai had gone. The apartment wasn't that big. It couldn't have been far. He could see she wasn't in the kitchen. The bathroom door was still open, the light out. Her bedroom door, however, was closed, light streaming from beneath it.

Liam walked down the hallway, leaned against the wall, and knocked.

She didn't answer, but he could feel her on the other side. "Mai? Can I come in?"

She still didn't answer. He could hear her moving around in there. He took a chance of being hit with a chair and opened the door. She had her gym bag on the bed and was stuffing clothes into it.

He walked in and closed the door behind him. "What are you doing?"

"What's it look like I'm doing?"

"It looks like you're packing."

She didn't respond.

Liam stood there for a second. His first impulse was to just walk away, open the door, and walk out. It was the smart thing to do. For everyone: for Mai, for him, for the whole sept.

He got as far as putting his hand on the doorknob before he turned back to her. "I didn't mean to snap at you like that. I'm sorry."

She was facing the wall, her back to him. She dropped a T-shirt into the bag. "You scared me," she said softly.

He had one last chance to make his escape.

He let go of the doorknob and walked up behind her. He very gently put his arms around her. Any anger left inside him was gone, drained out of him. "I didn't mean to scare you. I...I was upset. Those guys, they—"

"What is with them, anyway, walking around in those stupid costumes?" She turned in his arms, looking up at him with those big, dark, innocent eyes of hers. "The Blues Brothers didn't have plastic fangs."

He almost laughed aloud. With relief, as much as amusement. She still didn't realize the fangs were real.

Thank God. Because how was he going to explain that one? If she became too suspicious of the Hildegard brothers, of Kaleigh, of him, or of anyone in Clare Point, he'd have no choice but to take her blood. The Kahills had a way of erasing a human's short-term memory when they partook. It was a safety mechanism for both humans and vampires.

"I guess they just like Halloween," Liam said lamely.

She frowned. "Nut jobs is what they are."

He looked down at her, closing his arms around her. "Will you come tonight? To my room?" He kissed her very gently. "To me, and let me make love to you?"

She groaned, letting her eyes drift shut. "This is getting weird, Liam. Maybe I should just go home."

"No, no, you can't go home. You're still in danger."

She opened her eyes. "Really? Do you really think there could be any truth to this diamond thing?" She exhaled. "With every day that passes, I wonder more if I just...I don't know, imagined the whole thing. What if it really was just a burglary that Uncle Donato got caught up in?"

He stroked her back. "That doesn't explain the phone calls."

She pressed her cheek to his chest. "Not just prank calls, were they?"

"Not just prank calls. And having your house tossed wasn't a prank, either."

She was quiet for a second and Liam took the opportunity to enjoy the feel of her in his arms. However this played out, he knew she'd be gone soon. He knew their time together was going to be brief and he wanted desperately to hold on to this feeling as long as possible.

"I'm going to get to the bottom of this. I swear I am," he told her.

"Soon," she insisted. "Otherwise...otherwise I'm going to, I don't know. Go to the police?"

"If you didn't go before, if you didn't answer their questions completely honestly before, they're going to be suspicious now, Mai."

"I know." She smoothed his T-shirt under her hand.

"Just give me a few more days, a week." He stroked her long hair, liking the feel of its silkiness in his fingers. "A week. Two, tops. Come on, it's not so bad staying here with me, is it?"

She smiled and looked up at him. "Not so bad." She patted his chest and pulled away. "You want some dessert? I made pumpkin pie."

"Pie would be good." He still held on to her hand, even as she moved toward the door. "Will you come tonight?"

She cut her dark eyes at him, a playful smile on her lips. "Guess you'll just have to wait and see, won't you?"

"So, exactly what are we looking for?" Mai asked, standing in the middle of the mess that had been Donato's bedroom. They'd spent some time in her shop, but they both thought it less likely her uncle would have hidden the diamonds there. He was rarely in there, and where could he have put them that he wouldn't have had to worry about her selling the item, with the diamonds in it?

Just looking at her uncle's room made her want to cry. The entire house was trashed like this. It would take days to clean up.

They had left her dad with Kaleigh, watching TV. Unfortunately, it was raining, so a walk on the beach was out of the question. But Kaleigh had taken a checkerboard, and the two had big plans to watch *Oprah*.

Liam had decided that Donato's bedroom was the place to start looking for clues as to the mystery of the pink diamonds. They'd pretty much ruled out her shop for various reasons and would concentrate on the house. Mai didn't have high hopes of finding anything, but it was nice to be in her own house again, even for a couple of hours. Staying with Liam wasn't bad, but she missed her home; she missed the life she'd had before Uncle Donato was murdered in her store.

Mai gathered sheets that had been thrown on the floor when the intruder or intruders had searched under her uncle's mattress. The room was small with pale cream walls; Mai had picked the color out, thinking her uncle would find it soothing. She'd painted the room herself, making the trim a crisp white. The furniture was all treasures she had accumulated over the years, sturdy but comfortable pieces. There was a double bed with a maple headboard, a dresser and nightstand in pine, and a painted bookshelf. Turned upside down on the floor was an oak rocking chair with a seat that had been re-caned. Her uncle had seemed pleased when she'd shown him the bedroom the day he arrived. It was small but neat, he said. Everything an old man needed.

It didn't look so neat now. The closet door was open, shoes and clothing tossed on the floor in front of it. The whole floor was covered in her uncle's meager belongings: mostly clothing, but some books, magazines, and what appeared to have been a picture album before the pages were yanked out and strewn across the carpet. When Mai inhaled, she could faintly smell her uncle. It wasn't a bad smell, but a familiar one—a mixture of old-fashioned shaving soap and old age, she supposed. And lemon drops. He had loved lemon drops, and the evidence of that was on the floor under the bed. Someone had ripped open a bag and thrown the pieces all over the floor.

"We're not looking for the diamonds, are we?" Mai asked, adding the quilt to the growing pile on the bed.

Liam picked up books, flipped through them, and set

them on the bookshelf near the door. "You can certainly let me know if you find any, but no, we're not really looking for diamonds. I was thinking more like bank statements, some sort of paperwork. Do you have his will?"

"I hadn't even thought about a will. He never said anything to me about one. I can ask *Babbo,* but who knows what kind of answer I'll get there? His wife and parents are dead. He had no children." She tossed the bedding onto the bed. "My aunt Francisca, his sister, died a few years ago and she and her husband had no children, either, so I guess I'm his closest relative. After my dad. If there is a will, I need to find it."

Liam slid another book onto the shelf. "He bring these with him?"

She glanced at the books he was cleaning up. "Yup. He didn't bring much, but he was very particular about his books." She smiled sadly. His books had been one subject he had been able to converse on. They often talked about what they had read. "As you can see, he liked the classics."

"Some good ones here: *Treasure Island, Oliver Twist, Gulliver's Travels.*"

She righted a lamp on the nightstand. "Any treasures in *Treasure Island*? You know, like a hole cut in the pages and diamonds stuffed in them?"

"That's actually what I'm checking for, but I think the guys who got here ahead of us did the same thing."

She righted the rocking chair.

"Hey, it looks like he also liked Amish romances." He held up a handful of paperback books. "Beverly Lewis, Emma Miller, Wanda Brunstetter?"

She grinned. "I know, weird. We used to go to the bookstore regularly to see if there were any in he hadn't read yet. I think Emma Miller lives around here somewhere. He was hoping she'd have a book signing in Rehoboth Beach and he could meet her. He had me check her Web site." She began to gather shoes, pairing them up with their partners and neatly lining the floor of the closet, just the way her uncle had done. "Hey, you think it would be okay if I took my laptop back with us? I must have a ton of e-mail." She held a shoe in each hand. They were the same worn leather shoes, just different colors. "I mean, he can't track me by the Internet, right?" She lowered the shoes. "But you don't have wireless Internet, do you?"

He gave a look that needed no further explanation.

"I bet your library does, or one of the shops in town."

"I can probably have Internet added to the cable package." He was still working on the books.

She turned to him after she set the shoes in the closet. "You don't have to do that. We'll be gone in another week or so." She looked down at the row of shoes she'd just made on the closet floor. "What am I thinking? I shouldn't be putting all this stuff in the closet. I should be bagging it up to donate to charity." She was surprised by the emotion in her voice. She hadn't been that close to Uncle Donato; over the years, much of their contact had been about birthday gifts and stilted greetings at Thanksgiving dinner. Then, of course, he'd been in prison all those years. She didn't know why his death was affecting her this way. But it wasn't just Uncle Donato and this nonsense about diamonds, or even the death threats; it was about Liam. It was about the fact that she had finally met a man she could love and yet she knew, in her heart of hearts, it was not meant to be.

Liam glanced in her direction. "Hey. You okay?"

She felt stupid. There might be mafia thugs after her and her father and she was getting teary over an old man's shoes? An old man who could very possibly have gotten her into this predicament, fully knowing he was putting her and his brother at risk.

She crossed her arms over her chest, refusing to cry in front of Liam. She faced the closet, trying to give herself a second. "I'm fine."

She heard him push another book onto the shelf and then he walked over to her. "Yeah?" He wrapped his arms around her from the back and kissed the nape of her neck, directly under her ponytail.

"Yeah." His kiss felt delicious. But then, every kiss they shared was delicious. Never in her life had she known such a generous, virile lover. She sighed, closed her eyes, and leaned against Liam, letting him nibble her earlobe.

Even with the overhead light, the room was dim and in shadows. Rain pattered on windows that faced south.

"Think maybe it's time to take a break?" Liam whispered huskily in her ear.

She smiled, closing her eyes again. "A break? We haven't been here an hour yet," she teased.

"But it's hard work, shelving books."

He nipped at her ear, then touched it with the tip of his tongue, sending a shiver of pleasure right to the tips of her toes.

"Hard work?" She turned in his arms so she could face him and tilted her chin up to invite another kiss. "Poor thing."

His kiss was long and painfully sweet. He always tasted so good, never like food or toothpaste, but like...Liam. The scent of his skin, his hair, the taste of him on her mouth—she would never forget it. It had been plain from the start that he didn't want a relationship. And somehow, that was okay with her. But knowing that made her want to savor every moment they had together.

Liam slid his hand under the band of her Bethany Beach

sweatshirt, under her cami, then under her bra. She groaned as he covered her breast with his warm hand and squeezed gently.

Suddenly, despite the fact that she had turned back the thermostat the day she left, she felt hot. Beads of moisture gathered above her lip. She grabbed the hem of her sweatshirt, caught the hem of the cami, and tugged them both over her head. She tossed them on the floor onto a pile of Uncle Donato's pajamas. Liam assisted her with her bra. She arched her back, giving him easier access to her breasts, now tingling with anticipation.

He caressed each of her small breasts as if they were treasures, then stroked her nipples with his tongue until they were hard points. She looped her arms around his neck, no longer feeling completely stable on her feet. "You think we'd be more comfortable on the bed?" she whispered.

He raised an eyebrow. "Your uncle's bed?"

"It was mine first." She turned toward it, but then Liam surprised her by lifting her in his arms. She had never had a man carry her to bed. Liam McCathal was full of surprises.

He laid her down gently on the tangles of sheets and then stood up. His gaze locked with hers; he pulled his black T-shirt off. Then his fingers found the button of his jeans.

It was like her own personal male strip show. A surprising turn-on.

Mai lay back on the bed and watched him. Without taking his gaze from hers, he kicked out of his shoes and slowly pushed down his jeans. Standing in front of her in black boxer briefs, he pulled off his socks.

Still watching him, she took a moment to kick off her sneakers.

He looped his thumb into the waistband of his boxer briefs. She could already see the evidence of his desire for her, but she liked watching him spring forth from the fabric. She licked her dry lips and he grinned.

She was embarrassed. A little. But she laughed. "Come on," she called, opening her arms to him. "We already know you're hot, my mystery man."

Before crawling onto the bed, he unbuttoned her jeans and pulled them off, adding them to the pile of strewn clothing on the floor. As he leaned over her, his fingers found the strings of her bikini underwear. He looked at her questioningly. She lifted her hips to let him peel them away. Then, feeling silly to be wearing nothing but white shorty socks, she pulled them off as she scooted back on the bed to make room for him.

He didn't lie on top of her, though. Instead, he stood over her, his hands on her thighs. He stroked them lightly and then lowered his head. First he kissed her knees, then one inner thigh, then the other. By the time he reached the object of both their desires, she was practically writhing beneath him.

The guy was good. The best.

Mai came twice before she opened her arms, begging him to join her on the bed, begging him to push inside her. She wrapped her arms around his broad shoulders, crying out with amazing pleasure as he took her. He felt so good. He made her feel so safe. So . . . maybe not loved, but *cared for. Treasured.*

They rocked the old maple bed hard. Mai managed to come twice more before Liam's cell phone rang somewhere on the floor. They both laughed, ignoring it. But the spell of the moment was broken and he came fast and hard, both of them panting, gasping for breath.

The phone stopped ringing and Liam eased himself onto the bed beside her. She was thinking to herself that she'd have to wash the sheets for sure now, when the phone began to ring again.

He looked at her. He was still panting, his bare chest rising and falling.

She smiled and lifted up on her elbows to kiss him. "Answer it. It might be Kaleigh."

Chapter 17

Standing naked in the middle of the bedroom, Liam fished his cell phone out of his jeans pocket. He checked the screen before answering it. The name that came up surprised him. He had been half afraid he'd never hear from him again.

"Anthony." He pointed to the doorway to let Mai know he was going to step into the hall to take the call.

"Mr. McCathal."

Liam stepped into the hall and walked toward Mai's bedroom, putting some distance between him and her. "Anthony, you don't need to call me Mr. McCathal. I apologize again for my behavior the other night. You just took me by surprise."

"Wanted to let you know I've made contact with the rat in question."

Liam frowned. He assumed the bookie was referring to the Weasel; he hadn't asked the old man to talk with him, only to try to find out where he was living, maybe what he was up to. "I see," he said slowly.

"Living with a nephew in Brooklyn. Nice coffee shop around the corner from the place. I bought him a cannoli."

"You weren't supposed to talk to him," Liam said, not liking this turn of events. He wasn't in the habit of getting old men into trouble, not even an old bookie who had probably created plenty of his own trouble once upon a time.

"No need to worry. I've been dealing with his kind longer than you been alive, sonny." He chuckled. "He's a pretty old guy."

"How...how did you end up having cannolis with him?" Liam walked into Mai's bedroom. It looked as if it had been tossed as thoroughly as Donato's. The only difference was that there were girly things on the floor: panties and bras, makeup, some jewelry, and a black lacquered jewelry box, its contents strewn.

"Easy. Asked him if he was interested in a piece of my action...if I was to go into semiretirement. Which reminds me, Eagles beat the Saints. I owe you a buck twenty."

He was referring to the bet Liam had made on the Eagles as a joke to tell Fia. "Keep it. Part of your fee." Almost stepping on the jewelry box, he picked it up and set it on Mai's dresser. "Now tell me what Machhione had to say."

"Not much. We talked about the business and then about stuff."

"Stuff?" Liam questioned. He pulled back the edge of the lace curtain and looked down on the backyard. Mai's minivan was parked in the driveway but he saw no sign of anyone else, suspicious or otherwise.

"You know, about old times."

"You said you never knew him," Liam said into the phone. He was beginning to wish he hadn't enlisted Anthony's help. The guy seemed to think this was some kind of game. Maybe he didn't like getting old and losing the identity he'd made for himself, being the tough-guy bookie. Liam wasn't sure; he just knew he didn't like it. Anthony made him nervous.

"I didn't know him. But we have acquaintances that go

way back. You know, he once owned blocks of this borough. Everywhere he went, Machhione got respect. We were in the same business, he and I."

Not exactly, Liam thought. *While you were beating up trash collectors to get what they owed you on a losing bet, the Weasel was stealing rare diamonds and ordering hits on his enemies.* But Liam didn't go there. What was the point? "So...what *did* you find out? Is he...working?"

"Didn't get a lot of personal information. I was trying to make him comfortable. Keep him from getting suspicious. It worked. I'm just a lonely old guy like him, met at the coffee shop. We're having dinner Thursday night. A little trattoria down the street from his nephew's place. Clam linguine to die for, he says."

"I think that's a bad idea. Just give me the address where he's staying and I'll take it from there. I'll wire the money I owe you. And a bonus," he added. "Maybe you should take that trip to Bethany Beach to see that sister you were telling me about." *If something happens to this old geezer,* Liam thought, *it would be my fault.*

"I got this," Anthony said. "I'll make the meet. I got his address in my phone. Can't remember a thing these days. I'll have to text it to you."

"No, Anthony, just—"

"Coming!" Anthony called to someone. "Call you Friday," he then said into the phone.

"No, call me after the"—the line went dead—"meeting," Liam finished.

"Everything okay?" Mai stood in her bedroom doorway, naked, and awfully damn sexy.

"Um. Yeah. Sure."

She walked to her dresser. The top drawer was lying on the floor, turned upside down, panties under it. She opened the second drawer and took out a lacy pink bra. "You sure?"

"It's all good. Nothing from Kaleigh. She and Prince must be holding down the fort."

Mai smiled as she squatted, flipped over the drawer on the floor, and chose a pair of pink panties that matched the bra. "I'm going to jump in the shower." She walked past him, headed for her bathroom. "Want to join me?" she asked over her shoulder.

He didn't need a second invitation.

"What are you doing today?" Liam asked Mai from across the table. They were eating breakfast. Actually, her father, who sat between them, was eating breakfast and doing a crossword puzzle. Mai and Liam were drinking coffee.

"I don't know. So many choices." She cupped both hands around her coffee mug, enjoying the warmth of the pottery. It was a gorgeous, hand-thrown mug Liam said he had "picked up in the south of France." She had carried so many household items up from the shop that she was beginning to feel guilty. Like she was taking over his apartment, or playing house or something. But it seemed like such a shame to her, leaving such beautiful things in boxes when Liam, well, when they all could enjoy them.

She glanced out the kitchen window. After four days, it had finally stopped raining and the sun shone, but the house was still chilly. Only a few days ago, it seemed as if the air conditioner had been running nonstop. Last night, Liam had had to turn the heater on, her dad had complained so cantankerously about being cold.

"I could sort books," Mai said. "I could put those two Tiffany lamps together, *or* I could start sorting silverware, which should only take ten years or so." She frowned and leaned forward, elbows on the table. "You've got some gorgeous silver down there, including a mint Gorham Versailles set. Whatever possessed you to dump *silver* silver-ware into boxes, mixing the patterns?"

Liam shrugged. "Busy?"

"What? For the last hundred years?"

He gave her that boyish grin that he knew made her melt. That was all he had to do whenever she was the least bit frustrated with him and he knew it. One smile, and her irritation was gone, as if it had never existed.

"Seven-letter word meaning 'eager and serious,' " her father announced. He munched on his cereal. "First and fifth letter, an E."

"*Earnest.*" Liam glanced at Mai over the rim of his coffee mug. "You know you don't have to do any of that. I made the mess. I'll clean it up."

"In, what, *another* hundred years?" She leaned back in her chair, taking her coffee with her.

"I just don't want you to feel as if you, you know, you have to. You're starting to make me feel bad. Like I need to put you on the payroll or something."

"It keeps my mind occupied," she said, looking across the table at him. "Off other things," she added meaningfully. "And this way, I don't feel like such a moocher."

"You're not a moocher. I invited you here." Liam got up to pour himself more coffee. He took his black; she liked hers sweet with heavy cream. Not surprising.

"The cable company is coming today," he continued. "You should have Internet by this evening. At least you can read your e-mail."

"And you can Google the five-letter word for a journey in search of something," her dad injected.

Mai looked at Liam and had to suppress a giggle. She didn't even know her father knew what it meant to Google. He had refused to even *attempt* to use a computer.

Her father poured more Rice Krispies into the milk in his bowl. "Last letter, T."

"*Quest.*" Liam picked up the coffee press to offer her a refill.

She shook her head, not wanting to tip the balance of the perfect cup of coffee she had right now. "You're good."

"You shouldn't have told me so quick," her dad grumbled. "I knew that one."

Again, she smiled at Liam. "How about you? You up for silverware sorting?"

"Um..." He lingered at the stove. "I've got someone I need to see this morning. But after that, sure. You okay with waiting here alone for the cable installer? The company said he'd be here midmorning. He'll have to come inside to hook up the modem in the living room, but I know the guy. Name's Shawn. He lives down the street. Perfectly trustworthy."

"Sure, I'm fine with that."

"Anyone going to bother to ask me what I'm going to do today?" her father asked, drinking the last of the milk from his bowl. He didn't look at either of them.

Mai wondered whom Liam needed to see. He didn't seem to have any friends. He never went anywhere but church and the grocery store, and no one ever came to visit, except Kaleigh. She was curious, but she didn't ask him. He wasn't the kind of guy you quizzed. Yet another reason why she was still pretty sure he worked for the State Department.

"*Babbo,* what are you going to do today?"

"Same thing I do every day," he grumbled. "Nothing. Pretty dull existence, I'll tell you that."

"Not so dull." She patted his hand, feeling badly for him. She knew he missed his home, his bed, his routine. He was as frustrated as she was, but while she could barely sleep at night for worry, he didn't seem to be all that concerned that they were basically in hiding. He didn't seem to be all that upset about his brother being dead, either. He didn't bring up Donato's name and when she did, he brushed over the subject or responded with a crossword puzzle question. But maybe he didn't understand that his brother was really dead. That he had been murdered. It was hard to tell.

"I like to walk," the old man said. "I miss my walks. I was supposed to walk on the beach with that girl. The one with the red hair." He scooted his chair back, making sure Prince was out from under his feet. He rose to put his bowl in the sink. "We were going to go for a walk on the beach. You think she'd like to go now?"

"Kaleigh's in school, *Babbo*. But you and I could go for a walk, I suppose."

"I don't want to go with you," he said matter-of-factly as he ran water in his bowl in the sink. "I'm tired of hanging out with you two. Both of you. A man needs his own friends. Not his daughter and her lover."

Liam raised his eyebrows at her.

Mai had to cover her mouth with her hand to keep from giggling out loud. How did her father know she and Liam were lovers? She was very careful about public displays of affection and he was always asleep when she left the bedroom and when she returned before dawn. At least she thought he was. Maybe he didn't mean *lover* literally. Once again, it was hard to tell with him.

"I need some friends," her father went on as he shuffled out of the kitchen, the dog trotting behind him. "The redhead and I, we're friends."

"I'm going downstairs to the shop in a few minutes," Mai called after him. "Get your sweater and you can sit outside in the sunshine and do your crosswords."

"Six-letter word for *dull*," he muttered over his shoulder as he went down the hall. "Third letter, R."

Liam started to answer, but before he got the word out

of his mouth, her dad shouted it in a sing-song voice. *"Bor-ing!"*

She laughed. What else could she do?

"So I'll see you after a while?" Liam poured his coffee into a stainless-steel travel mug she'd found behind the counter in the shop with what appeared to be years of mold on the inside. A little soap and hot water, though, and it was as good as new.

"Sure. No need for you to stick close to home. There's no *weasel* after you," she quipped.

Liam kissed the top of her head on his way out of the kitchen. "I'll take care of it. I swear I will." He sounded so serious. It was so sweet.

"Could you stop for bread on your way home? And potato chips, the ones in the blue bag? Dad likes his chips."

"Anything else?" he asked.

She turned in her chair so she could see him as he went out the door, thinking he sounded a little irritated. "I don't mind going to the market myself."

"I'll take care of it." Liam walked out of the apartment, closing the door behind him.

He took his leather coat off the hook in the stairwell and tossed it over his shoulder. He took the steps two at a time.

He'd woken up feeling as if something wasn't right and he was jittery. Something crackling in the air made him jumpy. That worried him. Last night Anthony was supposed to have met Machhione for dinner. He'd feel better once he heard from him. He'd tried to call Anthony several times since the other day. He'd left phone messages, but the old man was ignoring his calls.

At the bottom of the steps, Liam slipped into his jacket and, with his coffee in one hand, dialed Fia with the other.

She'd called him earlier this morning, but he didn't want to talk to her while in the apartment; he didn't want Mai or Corrato overhearing their conversation.

"Hey," Fia answered. "Can't talk. Headed into a meeting with a bunch of bigwigs from Washington. Call you back?"

"You called me at six-thirty this morning," he complained.

"I found info on your Riccis. I was calling to tell you what I found."

"You were at the office in downtown Philly at *six-thirty* this morning?"

"No rest for the wicked." She chuckled. "Or the FBI. Gotta go. Call you later."

She disconnected and Liam tucked the phone back into his pocket.

Fia had said she had info on the *Riccis*. As in plural. He fully expected there to be intel on Donato, but did that mean the FBI had information on Corrato, as well?

Liam was rarely surprised by human behavior, but that one shocked him.

Chapter 18

Liam walked down the street, heading east, and sipped his coffee. The air was cool, though not cold, and the sun shone brightly. He pushed his sunglasses onto his head, closed his eyes for a second, and enjoyed the feel of the sunshine on his face. Humans thought vampires abhorred the sun, that it made them melt or ignite or something equally ridiculous, mostly because of what they had seen on TV. The opposite was true for Liam. The sun made him feel alive; it made him feel God's presence, even as cursed as he was, and each time the sun rose, it reminded him that he had another day to prove himself. To strive for redemption.

He opened his eyes and slipped his sunglasses back on. He had more pressing business right now than the redemption of his soul.

What could Corrato possibly have had to do with his brother's business? He had moved to Delaware when Mai was a little girl. Maybe Liam had misunderstood Fia. Maybe she meant she had information on Donato.

And maybe vampires couldn't fly. . . .

His cell rang. That was two calls in one morning. Pretty unusual. This time it was his mother.

"Liam."

"Ma."

"Mary Hall tells me I had a leak in the pipes and my house flooded."

"What the hell are you doing talking to Mary Hall on the phone? I thought you hated her."

"All water under the bridge now," his mother said.

Mary Hall and Liam's father had been having an affair at the time he was murdered. In all fairness, his father and Mary Hall had been having an affair on and off for centuries, and his mother had had her share of affairs, as well. It was the way it worked when one was doomed to perpetual life. Vampires were no more monogamous than humans seemed to be. That didn't mean his mother had approved.

"Don't avoid my questions," she went on. "How bad is my house? You should be staying there. I told you to stay there."

"Your house is fine, Ma."

"She said thousands of dollars of damage. My house could be a total loss."

He'd been there the day before. Kaleigh had been true to her word. Not only had the water damage been repaired, but the entire hardwood floor in the living room had been refinished; it looked better than it had in fifty years. "Ma, the house wasn't a total loss. Everything is fine there. Better than fine."

"You haven't even asked me how I am, Liam."

He exhaled, wishing he'd brought a bigger mug of coffee. "How are you, Ma?"

"I'm fine, but Victor, he's not so good."

"I'm sorry to hear that."

"He's short of breath. He can't even play nine holes anymore. It's his heart, I'm afraid."

"Maybe it's time you came home." Liam tried to keep the annoyance out of his voice. No one told Mary

McCathal what to do, not even Liam McCathal. "You don't want to be stuck there if Victor dies. It will be a mess getting him home in time."

Whenever a Kahill died, he or she was brought to the St. Patrick's cemetery in Clare Point so that on the third day, the vampire could be reborn again. The ceremony, if necessary, could take place elsewhere; Liam had once died in the Sahara Desert. But it was an inconvenience, what with sept members having to be present at the time of rising. Then the newly born teenager, full of questions, had to be escorted safely back to Clare Point. It was just easier when the process could take place at home.

"It won't be a mess!" his mother argued. "I'll just toss him in a car and drive back." She was now clearly as aggravated with him as he was with her. "You don't think I can drive that far alone, do you? You don't think I'm capable of handling a little problem like a dead husband?"

Liam exhaled. He'd heard that everyone suspected his mother had married Victor and had wondered if it was true. Even if they did marry before humans, the marriage didn't count. Not here in Clare Point. That was why she had left in the first place. "I was thinking it wouldn't be easy for you to get him in the car. *Physically*. Once he dies. Rigor mortis, Ma."

"So, I'll have to move him fast, before he stiffens up on me!"

Liam had to smile. His mother, if nothing else, was a practical woman. "Fine, whatever. Come home. Don't come home. Do what you want. You always do."

"Maria says you haven't had your interview." And just like that, she had moved from one combative conversation to another.

"She would be correct in that observation." He walked past The Hill and waved to the proprietor, Tavia, who was sweeping her sidewalk.

"Liam, don't be such a stranger," she said as he walked by. "Stop by and have a beer one night."

He nodded, then held out the cell to show her he was talking. *My mother,* he telepathed.

"Tell her to come the hell home," Tavia shouted. "You hear that, Mary McCathal? It's time you and that crazy Victor came home!"

Liam smiled. "Hear that, Ma?"

"Tavia says it's time we go the hell home," his mother said, talking to Victor, he presumed, and not him.

Liam heard the rumble of a male voice and then his mother spoke into the phone again. "Victor says to tell Tavia to kiss his hairy white ass."

Liam chose not to pass that tidbit on. "What do you want to know about my hearing, Ma? You know as much as I do. I haven't been interviewed and no one has told me what's going on."

"You need to relax more, Liam. You're too uptight."

He clenched his coffee cup tighter.

"So what about the girl? The one living with you? You know better, Liam McCathal. An HF!"

"Mary Hill tell you about that, too?"

"No, that was Mary Kay. Now, what's going on? Frankly, Liam, I'm worried. First you pull that stunt in Paris and now you have an HF living in your apartment? In the winter?"

"And a dog," he quipped. "Surely she told you about the dog."

"Actually, I did hear there was a dog, but I'm being serious, son. You're treading on thin ice with the Council. Why would you poke them with a sharp stick? I mean, honestly, Liam..."

After that, Liam didn't say anything more; he just let her talk. Five minutes later, he was off the phone. He walked by the Lighthouse Motel and waved at the octogenarian proprietress, Mrs. Cahall, who was standing out front wearing a white tennis skirt and sweater, smoking a cigarette. She was all skinny, white legs and bright pink lipstick. She waved wildly at him. She didn't play tennis, but she played a mean game of gin rummy and had won two hundred dollars off him last time he'd been home.

"Closed for the winter! Come by tomorrow night for cards!" she hollered after him. She was hard of hearing, so she assumed everyone else was. "I'll beat your pants off!"

He smiled and waved and kept going. There were a lot of crazy vampires in this town and she was definitely one of them. Maybe *crazy* was too harsh a word. Maybe *eccentric* better described her. Because there were some definite crazies around here.

A block off the bay, he turned north, leaving the quaint shops and eating establishments, mostly closed now, for a residential area. Most of the Victorian cottages had been built before the turn of the twentieth century and were painted bright, historically accurate colors: pink, turquoise, and yellow. All the homes, even those rented out in the summer, were owned by locals. And now that the summer season was over, the vampires were back in town. They were everywhere: raking their lawns, repairing mailboxes, sweeping their sidewalks. Liam waved and smiled.

Liam tried Anthony's phone again as he walked. But Anthony didn't answer. All he got was a recording. He didn't leave a message. Liam crossed Rose Street and turned onto Geranium. He waved to several residents but didn't stop to chat with anyone. It just wasn't his thing, making nice with sept members. Even now, when how they viewed him could make or break him.

Liam found Gair Kahill at his yellow house, seated on his front porch, in a bright pink Adirondack chair, smoking a pipe and reading the *New York Times*.

Gair was the chieftain of the sept. He had led them here

to the colonies all those years ago when they'd been forced to flee Ireland, running for their lives from the vampire hunters. Some sept members gave him credit for saving their lives, perhaps their souls. Liam was one of them. It was Gair who had brought them to the conclusion that the only way to regain God's favor was to protect his humans. Liam adored him. Feared him. Nearly worshipped him.

"I wondered how long it would take you to come," Gair said, turning the page of his paper. In his sixties, he wore his gray beard close-clipped, but he needed a haircut. He was wearing a windbreaker that advertised a popular local brewery; Gair was a fan of pop-culture clothing. He had an entire collection of vintage T-shirts.

Liam walked up the steps. "Good to see you, Gair." He offered his hand. Gair didn't get up, but he shook his hand.

"Sit down." He pointed to a matching turquoise-colored chair.

"That's okay. I'm not staying." Liam leaned against the porch rail, finishing off his coffee.

"You come to talk about your hearing or those humans you've got at your place?"

Liam smiled to himself, glancing down at the worn floorboards of the porch. "I came to talk to you about the hearing. Do I have a choice in the matter of the humans?"

"You do not." Gair slowly folded his paper, taking care not to wrinkle it. "I don't have to remind you that keeping humans isn't permitted during the winter months."

The way he said it, it sounded like Liam was keeping *pets*. "It's temporary. They're in a jam. I'm trying to help them out." He considered how much he should say. "Someone's after them."

"There are police for that sort of thing."

Liam lifted his gaze to meet the old man's. His skin was leathered and wrinkly, but his eyes were the clearest blue.

He looked a lot like Spencer Tracy in *The Old Man and the Sea*. "You know that's not always an option."

"She in trouble, or him?"

"Both, I'm afraid." He set his coffee cup at his feet.

Gair thought for a minute. "The dog in trouble, too?"

Liam grinned. What was with these people and the damn dog? Vampires kept cats and dogs as pets, too. "The dog can hold his own."

Gair nodded. "They didn't rob that minimart in Rehoboth, did they?"

Liam shook his head. "Nothing like that."

"Good, because as far as I'm concerned, people like that should go to jail." He set down his paper, eyeing Liam. "So what kind of trouble they in?"

"Someone killed the old guy's brother. Tried to make it look like a robbery but it may have been a hit. Sort of."

"So who's after them?"

Liam looked away. "I don't know. I'm not sure."

Gair wasn't buying it. He waited.

"I think they got caught up in some mafia thing from years back. This old guy called the Weasel got out of jail and is looking for something he misplaced."

"So *your* old guy stole *that* old guy's money?"

"Not really, but *that* old guy thinks *my* old guy has his money." It was the truth. Sort of.

"And the Asian HF? Where's she work into the mix?"

"My old guy's daughter."

Gair sucked on his pipe, then exhaled, and Liam watched the curl of smoke drift heavenward. The smell was pungent and sweet; it smelled of apples. "But they're not staying long with you?"

"Not staying long."

"Because, you know, it's going to be added to the Council agenda. An infraction of the rules like this is serious. It has to be added to the agenda."

"Right," Liam agreed. "But that gives me, what, a month by the time it's actually brought up at Council? They'll be long gone in a month." He glanced at the azalea bush that still had a green tint to its leaves. "And my hearing should come before that. Right?" He looked at Gair.

The older man slid his pipe to the corner of his mouth. It bobbed as he spoke. "Now, that I can't tell you. Good guess, though."

Liam closed his eyes and rubbed them in frustration. "So you don't know anything? About the investigation? The interview?"

"No one ever tells me anything. You should talk to Peigi."

"I did talk to Peigi. She said I should be patient."

"So be patient. Doesn't look like you're left with any choice." He hooked his thumb in the direction of the house. "You got a minute? My garbage disposal is acting up. Could you take a look at it? You know me." He was already out of the chair. "Never good with mechanical stuff."

When the chieftain of your sept asked you to look at his garbage disposal, you looked at his garbage disposal. No matter how good a trained killer you were. "Sure." Liam pushed off from the porch rail. "I can take a look."

When the guy sent to hook up the Internet arrived, it was almost eleven. Mai spotted him out front chatting with her father. Actually, he was talking to Corrato; Corrato was busy watching a squirrel carrying what looked like a piece of a hot dog bun across a branch in the tree nearby.

Mai stuck her head out of the shop doorway. "You're here to hook up the Internet, right?"

"Yes, ma'am." He was a burly guy with a buzz-top haircut, wearing a shirt with the name of the local cable business over the breast pocket. He carried a toolbox in one hand, a new modem in the other. "To tell the truth, I was surprised when I saw the work order." He followed her inside when she motioned to him.

"I'm just running upstairs, *Babbo*," Mai called from the doorway. "You and Prince sit tight. I'll be right back."

"Almost lunch," Corrato announced. "Could use a pastrami on rye. Antonia's, one street over from where I grew up in Jersey, always made a good pastrami on rye."

"We don't have pastrami, *Babbo*," she said as she followed the workman into the shop. "How about turkey? I can bring you turkey."

"I hate turkey."

Mai offered the workman a quick smile as she closed the front door. "Sorry. Right up those steps. You were saying you were surprised about the work order?"

"Yeah, right." He glanced around. "Wow, this place looks better than it has in years."

She smiled, looking at the displays she had arranged: a dining room, a bedroom; she'd even made a work area for Liam with an area rug and an old Victorian desk. "Thanks."

"Liam's not home much. Doesn't usually have the cable turned on when he *does* come home." He glanced at her over his shoulder as he went up the steps. "You staying long?"

"Just a few more days. Top of the stairs, turn right. Living room."

"This won't take me long."

Mai waited until he went into the living room and then she entered the kitchen. She was digging in the lunchmeat drawer when the cell phone in her pocket rang. The screen read CALLER UNKNOWN. She debated for a second, then let the phone keep ringing. She set it on the counter, grabbed the turkey and cheese and mayo, and set them beside the phone.

It stopped ringing. She pulled out a loaf of bread. The

phone rang again while she was making two sandwiches. That was one of the weird things about living with a senior citizen; you started wanting lunch before noon.

The third time it rang, the cable guy stepped into the hall. "Everything okay?" he asked, looking at her.

She found the question odd for a guy who installed Internet modems. "Yup," she said. "Fine." When he went back into the living room, she opened her phone and switched off the ringer.

As she put away the lunchmeat and mayo, the phone vibrated on the counter. It was still reading CALLER UNKNOWN.

What if it was Liam? What if he was calling from someone else's phone?

But she knew it wasn't Liam. She knew who it was. Somehow, he'd gotten her cell number.

The smart thing would have been to let it ring. Better yet, shut it off, but by call five, she was standing there watching the phone vibrate on the counter. She grabbed it and flipped it open.

She waited. She knew someone was there. "Liam?"

"No," said a male voice. It was the same man who had called her at home, then at Suzy's. It was the Weasel.

"What the hell do you want?" she demanded softly. She didn't want the guy in the other room to hear her.

"You know what I want."

"No, no, I don't," she said. She wasn't so much scared as she was angry. And frustrated.

"The diamonds," he hissed.

"I don't know anything about your damn diamonds! How did you get this number?"

Getting the awful feeling that someone might be watching her, she drew back the curtain she had hung just the day before. She couldn't see anyone on the street. Her father was out of view; he was sitting too close to the door for her to see.

"Your father's next, you know. Maybe I'll have better luck getting the information out of him. Maybe not. Good thing is, I know right where to find you, thanks to a little bird."

A sound behind Mai made her whip around.

Chapter 19

She gave a startled cry as she turned to find not the Weasel standing in the kitchen, as she had feared, but the cable guy. She slapped her chest with her free hand. "Jesus! You scared me."

"Sorry." He eyed the phone. "Everything okay in here?"

She closed the phone, hanging up on her uncle's killer, as she tried not to cry. She hadn't really believed it, not even when she had gone to her house with Liam to look for the diamonds. But Uncle Donato really had stolen diamonds and this guy wasn't going to go away. And if he could find her unlisted phone number, how long would it be before he found her and her dad?

"Ma'am?" He was still looking at her. "Should I call Liam?" he asked.

"No." She exhaled, trying to slow her pounding heart. "What's your name?"

"Shawn. Shawn Hill."

"Lots of Hills in this town," she said. Her thoughts were scattered. She felt like she couldn't quite catch her breath. It was as if, suddenly, the severity of her situation was just hitting home, after weeks of living it. "A lot of Kahills, too. Weird." She walked toward him. "I don't want you to call Liam, Shawn. And I don't know what you overheard, but you don't need to tell him any of that, either. You...I just need you to install whatever needs to be installed so I can have Internet service and then you need to go."

He started back down the hall. "I didn't hear anything. Swear I didn't. I only came to the kitchen because I need to follow the original cable wire." He hooked a thumb behind him. "It goes to another room, probably to the end of the house, and I didn't want to—you know—walk around the house without your permission."

She took another breath and started down the hall. Everything he said sounded perfectly reasonable. Perfectly innocent. So what was it about the guy that made her suspicious? Was he really watching her with too much interest right now, or was it just her imagination? Had the Weasel just spooked her? "Okay. Where do you need to go?"

"Liam's bedroom."

She glanced back at him, but she didn't ask him how he knew which room was Liam's. He said they were friends. Maybe he'd been in the apartment before. She walked past the living room and flipped on the overhead light in the bedroom. It was as austere as it had been when she moved in two weeks ago. The only thing that adorned the walls was a very old, very creepy—in her opinion—crucifix.

Shawn glanced at the single bed that was neatly made, then at the wall shared with the living room. "Aha."

Mai waited at the door, her hand on the doorknob. What was she going to do? She had to get out of Clare Point. She had to run. What other choice did she have? She knew Liam had said he would get to the bottom of this, and she had sort of agreed to let him try. But that was before she found out that her uncle really *had* stolen diamonds. Or at least the crazy old guy on the phone thought so.

"See, it goes this way." Shawn pointed to a thick black cable stapled between the floor and the wall. He followed it from one side of the room to the other. "Shoot."

"It goes into the next room, too?" Mai asked, hoping it didn't.

"Sorry." He grimaced and walked out of the bedroom and waited in the hall for her.

She led him to the end of the hall, pushed open the door to the bedroom she and her dad shared, and let him pass. "How much longer is this going to take?" She had thought about calling Liam, but the thing she needed to do right now was to take a minute and think. If her uncle really had stolen the diamonds, and he hadn't sold them, then they had to be somewhere. Maybe if she found them, if she gave them back, then the Weasel would just leave her and her dad alone. She knew Liam had said it wouldn't be all that simple, but he was exaggerating, wasn't he?

"You sleep in here?" Shawn asked, walking to the wall this bedroom shared with the other. He had noticed a bra and panties she'd left drying over a chair. She snatched them up and dropped them on the seat so at least they weren't hanging for the guy to see. It had never occurred to her that the cable guy would need to get into the bedroom.

Like that mattered right now.

"Just get the Internet up and running," she said.

Shawn followed the cable to the far wall and knelt, examining where it appeared to come into the house. "Here we go. Here's the problem."

She closed her eyes, running her hand over her face. "Look, is this going to take a long time? If it is, I don't want to hold you up. We can just..." She felt so overwhelmed, she wanted to sit on the floor and have a good cry. "I don't know, reschedule?"

"Nah." He got down on his knees. "A simple splice job and that will be it."

Mai gazed down the hallway. She'd been making the sandwiches before the Weasel called. She should take a sandwich to her dad.

What if he called again? Did she answer? Not answer? Did she try to reason with him?

"I'll be in the kitchen if you need me," she said.

Mai retraced her steps and finished the sandwiches. She took the time to put them on a plate and add some chips.

When Shawn shouted "almost done" from the living room, she got carrots from the refrigerator, peeled two, and cut them up to add to the plates. Her father liked carrots on his lunch plate. Not in the least bit hungry, though, she left her plate on the counter.

"All done," Shawn announced as she headed for the door to go downstairs.

"Great." She let him go in front of her. "So . . . you'll just send a bill?" Liam hadn't said anything about paying him.

"Yup."

She followed him down the steps and through the shop. "Thanks. Have a good day."

"You, too. Tell Liam I said hey." He held open the front door for her.

"Thanks." Mai walked out onto the sidewalk and it took her a second to realize what was wrong. "*Babbo?*" Holding the plate in both hands, she looked up the street, then down. A block away, she saw the postman pushing his cart, but no sign of her dad.

"*Babbo?*" Her heart thudded in her chest. "Prince?" She spun around to Shawn. "My dad. He's gone." She didn't say it, but all she could think of was that while she was on the phone with the Weasel, someone was downstairs, kidnapping her father. Images of her uncle lying in blood on the floor of her shop flashed through her head and a moan escaped her lips.

"It's okay. He's got to be here somewhere." Shawn put down his toolbox and took the plate from her hand.

"Maybe he just went for a walk." He set the plate on the little table Liam had put out for her father.

Her father's crossword puzzle book and pen were still lying there. "He...he didn't go for a walk." She shook her head. Her brain was working too slowly. She didn't know what to do.

"How about if I take the van and drive around the block? I bet he didn't get far."

"I...I have to call Liam." She couldn't take her eyes off the crossword puzzle book. How long could he have been gone? She wasn't upstairs more than half an hour. "I...I need my phone."

"Okay, you go upstairs and get your phone and call Liam." He grabbed her arm, forcing her to focus on what he was saying. "I'll go around the block."

"I should look for him," she said.

"No. No, you need to stay here. Do you understand?" Shawn had the clearest blue eyes. She hadn't noticed that before. "You have to stay here," he insisted, "in case he comes back. You understand?"

She nodded. "Right." She turned to run into the shop, then turned back. "His dog. Keep an eye out for his dog. It's a rat terrier. His name is Prince. My father would never voluntarily leave his dog somewhere, or let him run free."

"Prince. Got it." Shawn picked up his toolbox. "And your dad's name?"

"Corrato Ricci."

Shawn headed for his van.

Mai ran into the shop. She considered locking the door behind her. What if the Weasel had taken her dad? What if there was someone lurking around the building, waiting for the cable guy to go so they could snatch her as well? But what if her dad came back? What if he really had just gone for a walk? She wouldn't want him to return to a locked door.

She hurried up the steps, through the door, leaving it standing open, and grabbed her phone off the counter. When she opened it to call Liam, she saw that she had missed a call. The caller ID feature listed the number as CALLER UNKNOWN.

"Just one more quick thing," Gair said, coming out of his laundry room with an air filter in his hand. "Could you replace the filter in my air handler? It's in the attic." He passed Liam in the hallway and grabbed a string hanging down from the ceiling.

"Gair, I really need to—"

The older man tugged on the string, and the pull-down stairs to the attic groaned, cutting Liam off. A ladder stairs sprang down. "It'll just take a minute." He pushed the filter into Liam's hand.

Liam considered arguing with him but decided it would be faster just to climb the creaky steps and replace the air filter. Then he was out of here. He'd already been gone longer than he intended. He'd "fixed" the garbage disposal by removing a cap from a beer bottle from it, tightened the hinges on the back door so the door hung square again, carried porch furniture to the shed, and set three mousetraps.

"I've got things to do," Liam said, tucking the filter under his arm and climbing the steps. He stuck his head through the opening in the attic floor. "Left or right?"

"Left. Oh!" Gair snapped his fingers. "Lightbulb. It blew out. Let me get one for you."

"I'm a vampire, Gair. I don't need a light."

"Take my word for it. Save your eyesight. You'll be glad you did when you get to be my age."

Ignoring him, Liam stepped onto the attic floor and carefully walked on the narrow walkway laid down in plywood strips. "You ought to nail this down. Someone's going to fall through your ceiling doing this one of these days." He squeezed past a pile of neatly stacked boxes and a beautiful leather trunk that had to be more than a hundred years old.

Spotting the air handler, he searched for an opening. He was just sliding the old filter out when his cell rang.

Damn, he was a popular guy today.

He added the dirty filter to a pile of them on the floor and checked the direction the airflow was supposed to go on the clean filter and slipped it in place. His phone stopped ringing.

"Got a bulb," Gair shouted up.

"Don't need it!"

"What?" Gair hollered.

Don't need it, Liam telepathed, trying not to be impatient. He'd been old once. He'd be old again, before he knew it.

The ladder creaked and Gair's head popped up through the opening in the attic floor. "Got it. Goes right over there." He pointed to the opposite side of the house from where Liam stood perched on a two-by-two-foot piece of plywood.

"Do you really think—"

"Humor me," Gair interrupted. "I like everything in working order in my house."

As Liam leaned over to snag the five dirty filters, his phone rang again. He considered not answering it but then shifted the filters to one hand to answer it. Afraid he wouldn't get to it fast enough, he answered without checking who it was.

"Liam, he's gone." It was Mai; she sounded terrified.

"The dog?"

"My dad. And the dog. And... and he called again. On my cell." She sounded as if she was barely keeping it together. "The Weasel. He... he said Uncle Donato stole his diamonds and he wanted them back. He said he knew where to find us. Liam, what if he took my father?"

Liam strode toward the stairs. Did the Weasel really know where Mai and her dad were? How? Surely Anthony wouldn't have told him. Damn, but he wished the old geezer would answer his phone! "Corrato just wandered away," he insisted, trying to reassure Mai.

"But he's never done it before. He's never even gotten out of that chair. I shouldn't have left him."

I have to go, Gair, Liam telepathed.

Gair stood on the top rung of the ladder. "But my lightbulb. I wanted you to—"

Liam dropped the filters and sprang through the air, twisting so that as he fell through the opening in the floor, he would stay clear of Gair and the staircase. He hit the hallway floor with a loud thump but landed upright. *Gotta run,* he told Gair.

"Liam? Liam, are you still there?"

"I'm here." Liam strode out of the house, across the porch, and down the painted white steps. He slipped on his sunglasses. "Now tell me exactly what happened."

Chapter 20

Liam listened to Mai as he hurried down the sidewalk, keeping a lookout for Corrato. He was sure the old man was somewhere nearby. There was no way the Weasel could have found them in Clare Point, he reasoned, ignoring the niggling detail that Anthony was now AWOL. Sort of.

He got off the phone as quickly as he could, insisting Mai stay put while he found Corrato. He was going to need some help. With an entire town full of nosy vampires, someone had to have seen the old guy. He only hesitated a second before he used his speed dial. He knew just whom to call. The phone rang once, twice, three times.

"Come on, come on, Tavia," he muttered, looking both ways before he crossed the street, headed south toward Main Street, which ran perpendicular to the bay.

It rang a fourth time, a fifth. But Liam knew she was at The Hill; she was always there. When she wasn't behind the bar giving orders, she was in the brewery, mixing her magic. She slept upstairs in an attic apartment that she built after Hurricane Hazel washed her house off the beach and into the bay in '54.

"Come on, Tavia."

"The Hill, what do you want?" Tavia demanded on the other end of the line.

"Tavia, it's Liam. I need a favor." He was surprised how worried he was. He was actually upset that Corrato was missing.

"There's a lot of things *I* need, Liam."

"I'm serious. The old guy staying with me—"

"The one with the ugly little dog with the bulgy eyes?" she interrupted.

He exhaled. "The one with the dog. He...apparently, he wandered away from my place about half an hour ago."

"Where were you? You have to keep an eye on humans, you know. They tend to wander."

"You're a barrel of laughs, you know that? I was at Gair's."

"Trying to find out what's up with your hearing, huh?"

"Tavia, this is important. This old guy's daughter doesn't know where he is and she's scared to death. He's a little forgetful, if you know what I mean."

"Crazy?"

"No, no, he's definitely not that. I'm not even convinced he's all that forgetful, but the point is, we need to find him. Now."

"You don't think he and the dog have gone for a walk and they'll wander home when they get hungry?"

"Tavia, there are some concerns for his safety. That's why he and his daughter are staying with me."

"Aha! I didn't believe you were holding the HF captive and making her your sex slave, not for a minute."

"What?" he demanded as he hurried down the sidewalk. He saw Mrs. Malarkey walking her Siamese cat on a leash and Sorcha and John Hilton sitting on their front porch, watching a game show on a portable TV, but still no sign of Corrato. "Who the hell told you I was holding someone captive as my human sex slave?"

"Don't worry your handsome little head about it. I'll see what I can do. Where'd you say you are now?"

He refrained from reminding her that she hadn't let him tell her where he was. "On Petunia. Almost to Main Street. Shawn Hill was at my place doing an installation, so he's checking my neighborhood."

"Okay, when you hit Main, walk toward the beach. I'll check this side of town, see who's seen what. I could use a little exercise."

He sighed, relieved. "I appreciate it, Tavia."

The water was cold when Corrato hit it, so cold it took his breath away. He felt guilty for leaving Prince on the shore, but there were some things a man had to do in life. Things he had to do without his dog.

Tasting the saltiness of the ocean on his tongue, he took a deep breath and dove under. A numbness came over him, a numbness that was comforting, in a way.

As he held his breath, he wondered if this was what it felt like to die. He thought of Donato. Of the blood pooled on the floor. He once read somewhere that when you bleed to death, you just sort of go to sleep. He wondered if Donato had just fallen asleep.

It was a nice thought, but he doubted it. The knife had to have hurt.

Sometimes people got what they deserved. Which wasn't all that comforting, because some might argue he deserved the same.

Even though Liam was breaking the rules by having Mai and Corrato at his place, and he was in hot water over what had happened in Paris, the members of the sept were still willing to come together to help him find a human and his dog. None of them knew Corrato; it was Liam they were doing this for, and the thought was pretty humbling.

Within minutes of placing the call to Tavia, the entire town seemed to come alive. Suddenly, Kahills were coming out of the woodwork. They left their comfortable seats in front of their TVs, pulled half-baked cookies out of the oven, and even walked away from serving lunch at the diner. All for him. As Liam walked on Main Street toward the bay, a sea of voices greeted him in his head. Familiar voices, voices he'd been hearing since the fifth century.

Gotta be here somewhere.

Not to worry, Liam. Dog that small can't walk far.

Donal saw him walk past the police station half an hour to forty-five minutes ago.

Petey's out in his patrol car having a look.

No sign of any other humans. He's fine. We'll find him.

Not to worry, Liam.

We'll find him. We'll find him. We'll find him....

Their words echoed in Liam's head as word was passed telepathically all over town. Most Kahills couldn't telepath with anyone out of their sight, though some had a decent range of a few blocks. A very few could telepath long-distance, but working this way, as a single unit, rather than as individuals, it wasn't long before the entire town knew what was going on.

Liam dialed Mai.

"You find him?"

"Not yet, but someone saw him not long ago. He's fine, Mai. I'm sure of it." He hesitated. "You get any more phone calls?"

"No," she murmured. "He didn't call back, but Liam, we have to do something. I can't just sit here and wait for him to find us. I think it might be time for us to go. When we find him," she added.

"Go where, Mai?"

"I don't know. Out West? My dad's talked about seeing the Grand Canyon."

"You don't think he can send someone after you *out West?*"

"You got any better ideas?" she snapped.

He was silent for a second. He knew she was just scared. She wasn't angry with him, just her unfair situation. "Let's take care of one problem at a time, okay? Let's find your dad, and then we'll talk about this. Okay?"

"Okay." Her voice was shaky.

"I gotta go," he said. There were so many voices bouncing around in his head that it was hard for him to concentrate on the conversation with her. He waved to one of his mother's friends who was standing in front of her closed T-shirt shop. She nodded and smiled.

Tell Liam he was seen on the boardwalk ten minutes ago.

He was seen on the boardwalk.

Yo, Liam. The old guy with the dog was seen on the boardwalk ten minutes ago.

Liam looked up to see his mother's nemesis-turned-buddy, Mary Hall, pulling up in her Honda Civic. She put down her window. "Want a ride? Jim and Sugar saw him headed north on the boardwalk. Apparently the little dog was willing to go head to head with Sugar."

Sugar was Jim's Irish greyhound. He walked her for hours a day, often on the boardwalk or on the beach.

"Thanks, Mary, but I'm almost there." Liam waved as he jogged across the street in front of her. He took the wooden steps two at a time and stepped onto the north end of the boardwalk. He hadn't gone fifty feet when he spotted Jon Kahill, one of the young guys on the local police force. He was in uniform. In previous lives, Jon had served on Kill Teams with Liam. He was a good man, steady, dependable, but sometimes he got too emotional. Jon had asked not to serve on the team this lifetime, just to have a break.

Jon pointed toward the beach. "That who you're looking for?"

Liam couldn't help but chuckle when he looked in the direction Jon pointed. A skinny old man stood thigh-deep in the bay, his back to them, his arms open wide as if calling to the powers of the water, his wedding band glimmering in the sunlight. He was stark naked. It was Corrato; even from this distance, Liam recognized the back of his mostly bald head. To confirm the identification, sitting patiently on a pile of clothes on the beach was the Prince of Dogs.

"Need help with your human?" Jon asked.

"Nah. I got this. Thanks." Liam's gratitude was genuine.

"I grabbed this blanket out of my car for him. You want it?" He offered a red blanket. "He's probably going to be pretty cold when the adrenaline wears off."

"Thanks." Liam took the blanket and made a quick call to Mai telling her which street to pick them up on. He took his time crossing the beach. Corrato was just standing there in the water, letting the gentle waves lap at him. When Liam got within thirty feet of Corrato, the Prince of Dogs turned and regarded Liam for a minute. Then he turned back to his master and gave a sharp bark of warning.

Corrato glanced over his shoulder at the dog. "Who is it?" he asked, squinting. He wasn't wearing his glasses.

Liam wondered if he was asking him or the dog. "It's Liam, Corrato." He halted beside the dog, holding the blanket on his shoulder. "Water's a little chilly, isn't it?"

"Invigorating. Twelve-letter word. Third letter v. You don't see it often in crossword puzzles." He slowly waded toward the shore.

As Liam watched him, he studied the old man's withered body, remembering his own body at that age. It always seemed to Liam that his flesh betrayed him in some way. When he hit his seventies, his body began to deteriorate: hard of hearing, poor eyesight, weakness of muscle. But his mind was always sharp. He wondered if Corrato felt that betrayal now.

"You shouldn't have wandered away without telling Mai. She was worried about you." He held out the blanket. "Wrap yourself in this. Dry off and then we'll get your clothes on."

Corrato snatched the blanket from him. "I didn't *wander* away. I *walked* away. The girl and I, we were supposed to go for a walk on the beach, but it rained."

"With Kaleigh, right." He handed him his glasses.

The old man clutched the blanket around his shoulders, shivering, and fixed his glasses on his wet face. "Kaleigh," he said. "That's her. Cute little redhead."

"You can't walk away, Corrato, without telling Mai."

"If I told her, she wouldn't have let me go," he grumbled.

"Fair point."

"You know what it's like, having your daughter tell you where you can and can't go, what you can and can't eat? I used to change her diapers!" His pale blue eyes flashed with indignation.

"She's just concerned for your safety."

"Afraid I'm going to get it like Donato, isn't she? Afraid the Weasel will come for me."

Liam watched him carefully. "I thought you said you didn't know anything about the Weasel."

"No, I don't know anything about his diamonds, but you think I'd tell anyone if I did?"

Liam stared at the old man standing before him, naked under the blanket, his stick-thin white legs trembling. *Sweet Jesus,* he thought. *He does know something about the diamonds.* "Corrato, you have to tell me what you know. If you know where the diamonds are, you have to tell me. Otherwise, I'm afraid you *will* end up like Donato."

Corrato ran his hand under his runny nose. "Maybe that's the way to go, eh?" He held the blanket with one hand and drew the other across his neck.

"But you're putting Mai at risk, too," Liam snapped. "You want her to die?"

"I suppose you called her," Corrato muttered, completely ignoring what Liam had just said. "Come on, Prince." He started across the sand toward the boardwalk and the dog followed.

"Corrato, your clothes."

"*Babbo!*"

Liam turned to see Mai standing on the boardwalk waving wildly. "Oh, *Babbo,* thank God you're okay." She leaped down from the boardwalk onto the sand and ran toward her father.

Liam looked back at the pile of clothes and after a second, reluctantly picked them up and started across the sand, behind the dog.

That evening, after dinner, Liam decided to escape downstairs and go over some paperwork. Mai had inventoried so many items that he needed to compile the lists before they got out of hand. He went down to do that, and to be alone.

He had tried to talk to Corrato in the afternoon, after the old guy took a nap, fatigued from his swim in the bay. Liam had tried to get him to talk about the Weasel, about his brother, about the diamonds, but Corrato wouldn't give up anything. Crazy like a fox he was, reverting to his crossword puzzle questions whenever he didn't want to talk about something.

Liam hadn't had any more luck getting ahold of Anthony. Now his phone was going straight to voice mail. Liam was beginning to worry. Seriously worry. He still couldn't shake the feeling that something was wrong. Something had gone *wrong*. If he didn't hear from him in another day, he wondered if he should go look for him. But that would mean leaving Mai and Corrato alone and he wasn't crazy about that idea.

He'd tried Fia three times today and she hadn't called him back, either. Damned long meeting.

He sat at an ornate Victorian desk and tried to concentrate on the inventory lists, but he couldn't keep his mind from wandering. Going to bad places. If Corrato had the diamonds, the Weasel would kill him for them. He'd kill Mai, too. Those were the simple facts. The question was, how was he going to turn this thing around?

Liam thought he wanted to be alone, but when he heard Mai's footsteps on the stairs, he welcomed them.

"Hey," she called as she walked toward him. She had changed into sweatpants and a T-shirt. Her sleeping attire.

"Hey." The Tiffany lamp on the desk shone a soft pink light over her, making her almost glow. She parked her bottom on the edge of the desk as she rubbed her neck.

"Your dad go to bed?"

"Sound asleep. Said he enjoyed his swim. Was thinking of making it part of his daily constitution."

Liam smiled and took her hand, turning it so he could study her palm. "He was restless, that's all. He just went for a swim."

"What am I going to do, Liam?" she said suddenly. "Maybe the Weasel was just bluffing. Maybe he doesn't know where I am. Yet. But he's going to find me."

Liam wanted to deny it, but considering the facts that Anthony had never gotten back to him after the meet with the Weasel and he wasn't answering his phone, he hesitated. What if Anthony hadn't played it as safe as he insisted he would? What if the Weasel had figured out that Anthony had been talking to Liam? And even though it was by complete coincidence, the fact of the matter was that Anthony knew where Liam lived. At least he knew what town he lived in. A guy like Machhione wasn't above torture to get information.

Liam hung his head.

"What is it?" Mai asked, sliding over until she was seated on the desk in front of him. She took his hand and raised it to her cheek.

He shook his head. "I told you I'd get to the bottom of this. I don't want you to have to run. This guy, he shouldn't be able to do this to you."

"This is not your fight," she whispered, letting go of his hand and leaning down to kiss him. "I should never have involved you."

He closed his eyes, his heart suddenly pounding. He didn't want to feel this way, like he was letting her down. Like he had let those kids down, trapped in that cellar all those months in Paris while he paced that tiny apartment and waited as proof of the pedophiles' heinous crimes piled upon proof.

A lump rose in his throat.

"Not your fight," she whispered.

Liam rose, wrapping his arms around her. He covered her mouth with his, kissing her hard, forcing his tongue into her mouth. She clung to him, wrapping her arms around his neck and her legs around his hips.

Her scent was intoxicating, the embodiment of a fragile, human female. Fragile of body, but strong of heart. He covered her face with kisses: her cheekbones, the tip of her nose, her eyelids. He kissed his way along her jawline, then downward until he pressed his lips to her throat.

She moaned softly.

He refused to think about the blood that pulsed through

her veins. Instead, he drew his hand up under her T-shirt. She was braless. He cupped her breast in his hand, liking that it fit perfectly. Nuzzling between her breasts, he lifted her shirt.

"The light."

"What?"

"The light. Someone will see us." She stretched out and turned the key on the lamp, surrounding them in velvety darkness.

He didn't have the heart to tell her that anyone who lived in Clare Point who walked by the shop and bothered to peer in the window would have seen them anyway. Not that anyone would pay any attention. It was one of those crazy unwritten rules pertaining to their super hearing and sight. They had just learned to look away or not listen, giving each other some semblance of privacy. Of course, this wasn't typical vampire/vampire sex, but human/vampire, so someone might stop to gawk.

He pushed her up onto the desk, her legs dangling over the front. Pushing up her shirt, he took a nipple between his lips, then his teeth, and sucked. Gently, then more eagerly. She pulled the shirt over her head and tossed it on the floor, then cradled his head, running her fingers through his hair.

He could smell her, damp and ready. He tugged at the waistband of her sweatpants and she lifted her hips so he could slip them off her.

Then, laughing, she sat up. "Why am I always the one naked and you're always dressed?"

Perched on the edge of the desk, she unbuttoned his jeans and pushed them down over his hips as she kissed him gently, then nipped at his lower lip. As she pushed down his boxer briefs, she ran her hands over his buttocks.

"I've always liked men with nice butt cheeks," she whispered in his ear.

He nipped her back, this time a little harder than she bit him. She laughed, caught his lower lip between her teeth, then sucked it, digging her nails into his lower back.

Liam wrapped his arms around her waist, pulling her hard against him. She slipped her arms around his neck again, kissing him, liking the feel of his hot, hard body pressed against hers. She loved everything about this man's body, about him.

She loved him. Not that she was going to do anything about it. She had known from day one this was something that was never meant to be, that had no future. But she was thankful to have him right this minute. Maybe that was a fatalistic attitude, but it felt good to have someone looking out for her, if just for a few minutes.

Breathing hard, Mai parted her legs, moving closer to Liam.

He grabbed her by the waist, lifted her off the desk with his powerful arms, and knelt on the area rug she'd unrolled the other day.

"The desk was working for me," she said playfully.

"Eh. Someone might see us."

She looked up into his dark eyes. "It's dark, silly. No one can see us."

He silenced her with a hard kiss and Mai parted her legs again. She didn't need foreplay tonight. She just needed to feel like a part of him; somehow that gave her strength. She lifted her hips to meet his, accepting his first thrust.

Pausing for a moment, he nuzzled her neck, whispering something in a language she didn't recognize. His voice in her ear sent delicious ripples of pleasure through her whole body.

But it wasn't enough.

She raised her hips again, meeting him, taking him fully.

She groaned and her mouth found his. They moved faster, finding a rhythm that sent her pulse soaring. She came almost immediately and he slowed his pace, giving her a second to catch her breath. Never had she known such a giving lover; she'd never forget Liam for that.

After a moment, she pressed her hands into his bare buttocks and they began to move again as one. She rode wave after wave of pleasure until again, she cried out as her body convulsed in ecstasy. The man had amazing stamina; it wasn't until her third orgasm that he finally let himself go. His last thrusts were so hard that he pushed her across the rough wool carpet, only adding to the sensations that still rippled through her body.

She hugged him tightly as he came inside her, every muscle in his body tightening before his final release. Smiling and falling back on the rug, she kissed his damp forehead.

"I love you," she whispered. He was silent, but that was okay. She just needed to say it, because something told her she might not have many opportunities left.

Chapter 21

Kaleigh strolled into Liam's shop midmorning. He was busy writing on boxes of silverware that Mai had separated into patterns and boxed in sets of twelve. He didn't feel like messing with eBay but, in the past, he'd had Regan Kahill list items, mail them, and collect the money, taking a fee. Regan was Fia's younger brother, twin to Fin. There had been a while there when Liam hadn't been able to trust him with money; he'd developed a drug problem that had made him unreliable. But Regan had been to rehab the previous spring and was doing well, according to everyone Liam asked. He'd given Regan a call that morning and Regan offered to come over in the afternoon and see what Liam was ready to sell.

"Hey. Heard you had some fun yesterday," Kaleigh said. She was carrying a brown paper bag that smelled like fresh bagels. "Mr. Ricci okay?"

"He's fine."

"Everyone in town was talking about it last night. My mom said everyone was looking for him. She said he was skinny-dipping."

"I wouldn't bring that up to him, if I were you."

She grinned. "So why all the fuss over an old guy and his dog going for a stroll...and a dip?"

"Mai was afraid something might have happened to him."

"You going to tell me why they're here?" she asked.

He glanced back at the box of silverware on the counter. "Nope."

"I'll find out," she warned in a sing-song voice.

He didn't look up as he closed the cardboard box and wrote in black Sharpie on it: *W. Rogers, Elberon* so he could easily identify the pattern later. "Not from me you won't," he sang back. As he wrote, he blocked her thoughts from his head. He felt her tapping, but she didn't break through.

She exhaled with what sounded like a mixture of frustration and boredom. "I brought bagels." She held up the bag. "Mai said you guys had cream cheese."

"You already talked to her this morning?" he asked, surprised.

"I called her cell phone. *Hello.* I had to know if she liked 'everything' bagels or not. That a problem?"

"No. I just don't want you to...you know, get too attached to her." He reached for another box to store another set of Elberon pattern silverware. It was unique because the nineteenth-century silversmith had extended the decorative edges from one end of the handle to the base of the working part of the utensil. "Because she has to go back to her life and we...we have to go back to ours."

She watched him for a moment, swinging the paper bag. "You like having a girlfriend, don't you?"

"She's *not* my girlfriend." He glanced up at Kaleigh. "Did she say she was my girlfriend?"

Kaleigh smiled an *I'll-never-tell* smile. "When you go back to work, *if* you go back to work, you'll miss her."

"Things never work out between vampires and humans. You know that. It's better if I just go before things get too complicated."

"But you'll miss her?" She watched him. "Come on, Liam, you know you will. I mean, you do what you do because it's your job, but you're not as heartless and unfeeling as you want everyone to think."

"I missed Roxanne," he said quietly. "For years." *Missed her and felt guilty about what happened,* he thought. *If I hadn't gotten tangled up with her, gotten so involved, maybe she would have died of old age, instead of dying the way she had.*

"You weren't responsible for what happened to her," Kaleigh said, as if she could read his mind. Which, of course, she could, if he would have let her.

"Maybe," he agreed, counting out forks.

"For sure. And she knew you were a vampire. But you haven't told Mai. You've protected her from that."

"I just want to get her back in her house, safe again. Then I hope I'll be on my way again. Back to Paris, or Beijing, or Dublin—wherever the sept wants to send me."

"You want to go back? You can still do it?"

He frowned, dropping the twelfth fork into the box. "Of course I can do it. I wouldn't be asking to go back if I couldn't handle it, Kaleigh."

"And you don't think you'd...you know, *lose it* again?"

His hands fell still. He thought about the moment he walked into the room where the Gaudet brothers had taken that little boy. A rage had overcome him; he had done things he shouldn't have done, but it had been a controlled rage. He had known what he was doing at every moment.

"I'm not a risk, Kaleigh. I didn't wait for the High Council's okay, because they were going to get away again. What I shouldn't have done was what I did once I got there. I fully admit that, but they deserved it." He lifted his gaze to meet hers. "You know they did and maybe, just maybe, what I did will make someone think twice before they tie a child to a bed and do what they were doing to that little boy."

She reached out and ruffled his hair, like she was fifty and he was ten. But it didn't make him feel bad. It made him feel good, as if she *got* him.

She stepped back and swung the paper bag. "So, you think it's okay if Mr. Ricci and I take Prince for a walk later? Maybe just over to the park? I asked Mai when I talked to her on the phone but she said I should ask you."

He glanced up. "I'm afraid it's not safe."

"How about if we just go around the block?" she begged. "We'd practically be within sight of you." She paused. "If you don't give him a little leeway, he's going to take off again. You know he is."

Liam frowned.

"Come on, a walk around your block," Kaleigh repeated.

He thought about it. Kaleigh was a pretty powerful vampire, powerful enough to have faced a werewolf the year before. And she was perceptive; she knew when to be on the lookout for danger. Surely a couple of mobsters couldn't best her. She could hold them off long enough to get help.

His thoughts weren't purely unselfish. If Kaleigh took Corrato for a walk, it would give Liam some time alone with Mai.

It had disturbed him last night when she told him she loved him. He didn't think she really expected him to say it back, but it bothered him that he couldn't. Which was exactly why he needed to get the hell out of Clare Point as soon as possible.

"Nice day," Kaleigh said, stuffing her hands into the front pocket of her hoodie. Even though it was November,

it was still pretty decent out, mostly because it wasn't raining. Kaleigh hated the rain. It got dreary here in the winter,
so dreary that it made her long for places like Southern
California. Better yet, the south of France, Greece, Rome.
Places she feared she would never, ever live again.

"Blank for your thoughts," Mr. Ricci said.

"What?" She looked at him.

"*Blank* for your thoughts. Five-letter word, second letter E, fourth letter N."

"Hmmmm," Kaleigh said. They were still within sight
of Liam's antiques shop. It wasn't much freedom for the
old guy, but she figured it was better than nothing. "Five-
letter word, second letter E, fourth letter N." She looked
back at the rat terrier that ran just a foot behind his master on a leash. "What do you think, Prince?"

"He's not good at crossword puzzles," Mr. Ricci said,
seeming apologetic.

Kaleigh smiled. "*Penny.* But I don't understand. What
do you mean, 'penny for your thoughts'?"

"It's an old saying."

He crept along slowly, not seeming to mind too much
that they weren't even walking around the block, just up
and down the street in front of the shop. It was all Liam
would agree to. Kaleigh didn't know what was going on
with these two humans, but she was beginning to suspect
it was something pretty interesting.

"It's the way we old guys ask you what you're thinking," Mr. Ricci went on. "But in broader terms, I guess it
means, '*Whassup?*'"

She chuckled at the way he said it.

"You've been nice to me, Kaleigh. I appreciate it. I
know a teenager like you has better things to do than to
walk an old man."

She wrinkled her nose. "You say that like I'm walking
you on a leash. End of the sidewalk. We have to go back

the other way." She turned around. "How about I carry Prince for a while? Give his little legs a break."

"He's a tough dog." Mr. Ricci, teetering on the curb, glanced back. "But if you want to carry him, he'll let you." He slowly turned around.

Kaleigh scooped up the dog, taking the leash from Mr. Ricci. "I was thinking how nice it is outside, even though it's November." She lifted her face to the sun. "But it's going to get cold here soon. And rainy. I get tired of the rain. I was thinking it would be nice to go somewhere, like California, or even Italy. You know, to live for a while."

Mr. Ricci walked slowly, kind of shuffling. He was wearing a cardigan sweater, a scarf around his neck that smelled like Liam, and a weird hat, kind of like Dick Tracy's. The hat was definitely not Liam's.

"So why don't you go to college in California? Wouldn't be my choice." He made a funny face. "Earthquakes. But you might like it. Or you could be one of those exchange students. I saw the world when I was a young man. It's good to see the world. It makes you appreciate what you've got."

She held the dog over one arm, her opposite hand under his chest so that he sort of sat up in her arms, his little head thrust forward so he could see everything. It was quiet for a Saturday morning: not a lot of cars going by, not many people in their yards. Everyone in Clare Point was preparing for winter, getting cozy in their living rooms, or cleaning out closets, like her mother was doing this morning.

"I thought about going to college somewhere like California." She glanced at Corrato. Mai said he was seventy-four but he looked older to her. "But I also thought about staying here and going to the community college, at least for two years."

"Go to California," he said, waving his hand.

The way he talked, the way he acted, made her think of the old guy in the movie *Up*. She loved that movie, and the old guy in it.

"You've got your whole life to stick around," he told her.

"Yeah, but I've got responsibilities here. I kind of think I should stay. It's complicated," she finished, knowing she couldn't very well tell him she was a wisewoman for a bunch of vampires who needed her guidance.

"I don't need to know your business, but I can tell you as a person who's done *many* things because he had responsibilities, you should think it through. Something tells me, any responsibilities a young girl like you has got"—he looked at her—"could wait a few years."

Kaleigh waved and smiled at Liam and Mai as they walked past the shop. Mai waved back. Liam looked as grumpy as Mr. Ricci acted.

"I don't know," Kaleigh told Mr. Ricci. "It's a lot to think about."

"It is." He looked at her. "So what's a girl like you do when you're not in school? You have hobbies?"

Kaleigh thought about how much time she spent practicing her mental telepathy, moving objects, reading minds, levitating, but that wasn't the kind of thing she could share. "I like to read," she said brightly.

"Classics?"

She made a face.

"Me neither," Mr. Ricci said. "My day, it was Westerns. Adventure books. Zane Grey was one of my favorite authors."

"I've never heard of Zane Grey. I'm reading this book my friend gave me about this girl who falls in love with a vampire. But she kind of likes her werewolf friend, too. I'm only on the first book. There's a series. There's movies based on the books, too, but I haven't seen them."

"I think I saw that on TV. I don't get it." He shook his head. "That she would go for a vampire. A human girl and a vampire guy, sounds to me like a bad ending waiting to happen."

Kaleigh smiled to herself but decided she should probably keep her mouth shut on this subject. "We're almost at the end of the street. You think Prince wants to walk again?"

"Why do you keep checking your phone?" Mai asked from where she sat on the floor, sorting books. "You waiting for a call?"

Liam stuck his phone back in his pocket. "Can you see your dad and Kaleigh?"

"They just walked by." She flipped open the book on her lap, looking for a copyright date. "Dad seems to be enjoying himself. I think the exercise is good for him. It was nice of Kaleigh to offer to walk with him."

"Yeah." He carried a box to a stack he was making near the door. Regan would photograph the items and list them on eBay.

"She's a nice girl."

"Yeah."

Her hands fell. "Liam, what's going on?"

"What do you mean?" He set down another box, not looking at her.

"You've been acting weird. Has something happened?"

"I forgot to ask you," he said. "Did you return the detective's phone call?"

"I called him back yesterday. He just wanted me to know that my uncle's case would remain open. That they'd continue to follow leads as they presented themselves." She frowned. "Meaning they know nothing about the Weasel. Or the diamonds. They're still assuming it was a robbery. But you're changing the subject. Why are you so antsy?"

Liam's phone rang, saving him from having to answer Mai. Seeing that it was Fia, he stepped outside, closing the door behind him. "Hey."

"Two messages, Liam? You've really got it bad for this HF, don't you?"

He watched Kaleigh and Corrato turn at the end of the block and start back toward him. The dog ran ahead for a second, then dropped behind them, as if on patrol, guarding them. "You said you'd call back after your meeting. What did you find out about the Riccis?"

"Donato Ricci worked for Machhione, closely, but I'm guessing you knew that since he was the object of your first inquiry."

"What else have you got?" Liam asked.

"Actually, not a hell of a lot. Donato Ricci was picked up for questioning a few times in the eighties when the Feds were trying to nail Machhione for some murders. After the Weasel went to jail, it was Ricci's turn to sit in the hot seat over some murders, but nothing stuck. He actually ended up going to prison for tax evasion, which is often the only way we get these guys. But it wasn't a big case. I think he only did a couple of years." She was quiet for a second. "But you probably knew that, too."

"How about the diamonds Machhione stole? Was Donato ever questioned concerning the diamonds?"

"No record of them I can find."

Liam massaged one temple. He could feel a headache coming on. "Any contact with the Feds after he got out of prison?"

"Apparently he laid pretty low after that. No record of him after the jail term. But power was shifting in Brooklyn by then. Hard to say what happened. He may have chosen to live a quieter life, or the decision could have been made for him by someone higher on the food chain."

Liam exhaled. He didn't know what he had been hoping

to hear, but he was disappointed that Fia hadn't learned more. He was beginning to feel like he was banging his head against a wall. "You said you had info on the *Riccis* when you called. What did you find on Corrato?"

"Nothing."

That was good news.

"But he was questioned half a dozen times between 1985 and 1989, when his bro went to the pen," Fia said.

Liam thought for a second. "You sure you've got those dates right? He and his daughter were living in Delaware by 1988. The guy had nothing to do with his brother's business. He was an electrician, for Christ's sake."

"Doing electrical work for Christ or not, I'm telling you, he was interviewed. Let's see, in New York and here in the Philly office. I suspect he had *something* to do with his brother's shenanigans; we just never came up with enough evidence."

Liam was genuinely shocked. Corrato involved in criminal behavior? It was possible that federal authorities might question an innocent person, but it was a lot more likely they had good reason.

She paused. "So, now you want to tell me what's going on? I saw that Donato is recently deceased and the case is an open homicide. You aren't trying to protect that old guy in your house from the cops, are you?"

"Corrato didn't kill his brother, if that's what you're asking," Liam snapped. He turned around and looked through the window at Mai. She was still seated on the floor, sorting a pile of books. "Sorry, Fee. I'm not angry with you. Just frustrated with the situation." He took a deep breath. "Corrato didn't kill his brother."

"Okay, so what's going on? Don't tell me Corrato's got the missing diamonds." She was quiet again for a second before she went on. "I can come to Clare Point. Help you out with this."

Liam turned back to face the street. The threesome was walking slower now; Corrato seemed to be tiring. "Are you at work now?" he asked Fia.

"It's Saturday morning. Of course I'm at work."

"I've got another name for you. Anthony Thomas Pallota. P-A-L-L-O-T-A. Can you see what you can find and call me right back? I need this as soon as possible, Fee. Please."

"I suppose," she conceded.

"Talk to you soon." He hung up as Kaleigh and Corrato walked up to the shop.

"See," Kaleigh announced. "Safe and sound. You got a DVD player?"

Liam frowned. "No."

Kaleigh turned to Corrato, passing Prince's leash to him. "I'll run home and get my DVD player and the movie and be right back." She backed away. "Mr. Ricci and I are going to watch this lame vampire movie. Want to watch it with us?"

Liam didn't even dignify her question with an answer. He turned to Corrato. "You headed upstairs?" He held open the shop door for him.

The old man stood in indecision. "Sciatica's acting up, but Prince needs his wee." He glanced around. "Not much grass here. He likes the backyard better."

Liam took one look at Corrato's weary face and put out his hand to take the leash. "You go upstairs. I'll take Prince around back and then be up."

Liam and Prince walked along the side of the brick building, then around to the back, where there was still grass. He was just getting ready to carry the rat terrier up the back staircase when his cell rang. He was surprised that Fia was calling him back so quickly.

He shifted the phone from one hand to the other so he could scoop up the dog. "That didn't take long."

"That's because the latest on Anthony T. Pallota, of Brooklyn, New York, is hot off the press."

Liam halted on the bottom step, tucking the dog under his arm. "What do you mean?"

"Last night his body washed up on the shore of the East River."

Chapter 22

Late in the day, when Regan appeared at the door of the shop, Liam considered sending him away. He wasn't up to messing with the eBay stuff, but Mai was upstairs in the kitchen making dinner and Kaleigh and Corrato were having some sort of movie marathon, so he had no real excuse not to take care of business. And maybe it would take his mind off Anthony Pallota floating in the East River. Fia hadn't had much more info to give, other than that Anthony hadn't gone into the river voluntarily; his hands and feet were tied. His throat had been cut.

"Thanks for coming." Liam glanced out the door, looking up and down the street. It was beginning to get dark and the temperature had dropped significantly. "You walk here from your house?"

"Yeah. Brought my camera." He slipped a digital camera from his denim jacket. "Figured I'd just take the pictures, run the listings, and ship from here, if you don't mind. You don't mind, do you?"

"Works for me." Liam could see nothing unusual on his street, but he was sure now that the Weasel, or rather his envoys, were going to come after Corrato in Clare Point. It was only a matter of when. "See anything unusual out there?"

"Annie Hill was walking her dog, wearing that pink bra of hers, the one with the tassels, over her anorak. But nothing unusual. Why?"

Liam closed the door, fighting a smile. Annie was eighty years old. Kahills rarely lived to be that old before they died and were born again, but it was up to God as to when that happened. "You didn't see any humans?"

"The only humans I know of in Clare Point right now, buddy, are the ones you've got upstairs." He pointed over his head. "Jeez, that smells delicious. Egg rolls?"

"Vietnamese spring rolls. They're made in rice paper."

"She cook for you like this every night?"

Liam began to pull down the old-fashioned roller shades he'd spent most of the afternoon installing on the door and windows. He was short one, but he was sure he had another box of them somewhere. The shades would give them a little protection. It wouldn't be as easy for the Weasel's thugs to see into the shop.

"So, just out of curiosity, why are we looking for humans?" Regan asked.

"We're not *looking* for humans," Liam explained grimly. "But they might be looking for us."

"Meaning *them?*" He pointed in the direction of the second floor again.

Regan Kahill was a good-looking guy who appeared to be years younger than his thirty-something age. Before the drug problem had resurfaced, he and Fin had pretended to be college students while investigating cases for the sept. It had been a good cover and Liam liked working with them; he hoped Regan would be deemed well enough to join an investigation team again soon. Liam hoped he'd be cleared so he *could* work with Regan and Fin again.

Regan set his camera down on a cardboard box and began to help Liam close the shades. "You need some help with these humans? Because I can help. I'm clean, you know. You can even ask Fia. Or your mom. I helped her out with the arcade this past summer. We had that one dead human in the NASCAR seat, but I kept my shit together through the whole thing. Helped Fin solve the case. You heard all about that, right?" He pulled down the last shade. "Turned out this Italian vampire girl, here on vacation with her family, had flipped out and was killing humans. Kaleigh found this crazy rule about being able to make her one of us and absolve her of her crimes, so we didn't have to execute her. Sort of. So she's here." He knitted his eyebrows. "Well, not *here,* here, because she's in some kind of vampire boarding school right now trying to get acclimated to being a Kahill, but—but you heard all this, right?"

"I heard." Liam went to the pile of boxes he'd stacked near the door. "I put descriptions of each item and the starting price in with it. You can take the pictures on that table set up over there." He pointed toward the counter. "There's a blue tablecloth and a white one. Use whichever works better as a background for the item. Have any questions, just holler."

"Okie-dokie."

Liam was seated at the desk, going over the book inventory Mai had created, when a short time later, Kaleigh came down the stairs. "Hey, Regan," she called.

"Hey, girl."

Kaleigh wandered over to Liam.

"Going somewhere?" he asked, looking up from the list in front of him.

"Home." She sighed, obviously not pleased. "My mom's flippin' a bitch about my clothes being all over the floor of *my* bedroom, and she thought I was supposed to clean the upstairs bathroom, only it's really Connor's turn, but he lied and said it wasn't." She rolled her eyes. "The usual family drama. I tried to tell her I couldn't come home, that I was on sept business, but she said I had to come home or she was going to ground me for, like, the next decade or something. She doesn't respect me or my position as the wisewoman. And I really wanted to try Mai's spring rolls. She made them with shrimp."

"You told your mother you were on sept business?" He lifted a brow. "Since when has watching movies about teenage vampires and werewolves and eating my chips and salsa become sept business?"

"See?" She held out her hand to him. "No respect from you, either. How do you guys know if I'm on sept business or not? What if it's *private* sept business?"

"She's got a point," Regan put in.

Liam glanced in his direction, then returned his attention to Kaleigh. He hadn't realized Regan was listening to their conversation. He lowered his voice. "Look, things have heated up here—"

She plopped her hand on her hip. "Concerning...?"

"Concerning business that's none of yours. Anyway, I need you to keep an eye out for strangers in town. Humans."

She let her hand fall from her hip. "Bad humans, I'm assuming?"

"Bad humans." His thoughts were going a mile a minute. He could feel the whole situation with Mai and her father building toward a climax, possibly a bad one, but he didn't know how to stop it. He'd considered sending them away and just waiting for Machhione and his crew to come for Corrato and Mai, but Liam didn't know how far-reaching his contacts were. If he somehow found out Mai and Corrato had fled, he might reach them before Liam did. He had the same problem with just going after

the Weasel and killing him himself. He wasn't sure that
would end the problem. What if there were other men
working for Machhione who were willing to take up the
torch if their leader fell?

"I don't suppose Corrato said anything to you about
who's looking for him?" He watched the teen carefully,
hoping maybe the old guy had confided in her and she just
hadn't said anything yet. "Or why?"

"Actually he did." Her phone vibrated and she read the
text. Then she smiled. "It's Lia."

"We were just talking about her," Regan said. "How's
she doing?"

"Good." She turned to talk to Regan across the store
from them. "She hates boarding school, but she thinks if
she does what she's supposed to, she can come here over
spring break." She wrinkled her nose, turning back to
Liam. "Whoever heard of boarding school for vampires?
Where do we come up with this crap?"

Liam rose from his chair. "Come on, I'll walk you out."
He waited until they were on the sidewalk, the door closed
between them and Regan. He shivered in the cold. "Okay,
so what did Corrato say to you?"

"It didn't really make sense." She started texting on her
phone.

"Kaleigh, hon, this is important." He closed his hand
around her fingers, stopping her from texting. "I need to
know what Corrato said to you about the guys looking for
him. His and Mai's lives could depend on it."

With a sigh, she stuck her phone back in her hoodie.
"He said he was pissed off that his brother put him in the
middle of something. He didn't say what the something
was, but I assumed that what he was talking about had to
do with why he was here. Brrr. It's cold out here." She
flipped up the hood on her sweatshirt. "Mr. Ricci said he

wanted to go home. That he didn't know where the package was and he'd just tell them that when they came for it. I asked him what package, but he didn't answer. He just said he liked the salsa he bought better than what you buy."

"That it?" Liam asked.

"Pretty much." She walked away and called over her shoulder. "Oh, but he did say Prince wanted to go home, too."

Liam fought as he was pulled down into the depths of the nightmare, but he wasn't strong enough. He never was, and soon he found himself in the cellar of the Gaudet brothers' *palais*. As he took those last steps into their private chamber, he felt the dampness of the stone walls and smelled the terror of others who had been there.

The two men were far easier to overtake than Liam had anticipated. It was over so fast, it almost seemed anticlimactic. Maybe the Gaudet brothers were too shocked to see a vampire in their cellar to defend themselves. Or maybe they had been waiting for someone like him to stop them because they could not stop themselves. He would never know.

The child handcuffed to the cot saw Liam first but didn't make a sound. Only stared at him with round, empty eyes.

The older of the two brothers, and the larger, Anatolle, reached for a pistol on a table. Liam flew at him, intercepting the attempt, and knocked Anatolle backward with a well-placed boot to his jaw. Anatolle hit the stone floor so hard that his head bounced and he lay there dazed.

Seeing his brother knocked to the floor, Donat did what any pedophile would do; he turned and ran. Liam leaped into the air, landing on his back, and because his neck was bare, he sank his fangs into the bastard's flesh. It was purely an instinctive reaction. The blood that gushed out was so foul that it made Liam gag.

They hit the floor and Liam rolled him over, slamming his fists into Donat's face until the Frenchman stopped struggling. It was as Liam climbed off the unconscious Donat that he saw the nylon rope hanging from a hook in the ceiling. Gazing up, he realized that there were several of the shiny objects, all resembling meat hooks in a butcher shop.

The sight of the rope and hooks brought Liam's rage rushing back, overflowing until he could barely think. What he did next, even in the dream, was hazy. He cut short lengths of rope with his ceremonial dagger and tied the men's hands together. Then he found the keys to the handcuffs, released the child, and carried him to the outer room. There, he deposited him on a chair, murmuring that he would be right back for him. Then he returned to the chamber where the Gaudet brothers were both just beginning to reach consciousness again. Anatolle's jaw appeared to be broken and Donat was bleeding from the wound in his neck.

"Que faites-vous?" Anatolle muttered, his speech affected by the broken facial bones "What do you want of us?"

"S'il vous plaît, nous avons de l'argent." Donat's eyes were glassy with fear. "We have money," he repeated. As he spoke, he was trying to scoot backward on the floor.

Liam kept an eye on them as he cut lengths of the nylon rope, but he had no fear they would escape. They knew they would not escape. He saw it in their faces.

Donat screamed as Liam hoisted him into the air. Screamed like a little boy. Like all the little boys whose screams had gone unanswered in that fetid cellar.

Anatolle, the braver of the two, or perhaps the dumber, made no more than a grunt of pain as Liam hauled him into the air by the bindings around his hands and hung him from the meat hook.

The pain would increase by the second, though, until Anatolle would be screaming.

Still trembling with anger, Liam slipped his knife from his belt and gazed up at the men hanging before him. "Who will go first?" he asked, in French.

It was Donat's screams that woke Liam, transporting him back to the present, back to Clare Point.

"Liam. Liam," Mai whispered, hovering over him, pressing her palm to his cheek. "Wake up, Liam. You're dreaming."

His eyes flew open. He was breathing hard, his pulse racing. "Dreaming," he panted.

"Only a dream," she insisted. "I'm here. You're safe here." She snuggled beneath the quilt on his narrow bed, and lying on her side, molded her slim, naked body to his. She wrapped her arm around him. "Such terrible nightmares," she whispered, kissing his bare shoulder. "Have you always had them?"

He let his eyes drift shut, thankful for the warmth of her body. He was sweaty, but shivering with cold. "On and off," he answered.

"I'm sorry."

"Why would you be sorry? They've nothing to do with you."

"I'm sorry that you have to feel this awful, night after night. I'm sorry to see you suffer."

He leaned his head back, covering her hand with his. He sensed it was very late. Nearly morning. "Will you stay?" he asked.

She kissed him again. "I'll stay."

*   *   *

Liam woke to find the morning dull and gray. After lying there for a while, he decided he needed a hot shower. It might not wash away the guilt he was feeling over Anthony's death, but at least it would prepare him for whatever the day brought.

He slipped out of bed, leaving Mai to sleep, and walked down the hall to the bathroom, his clothes under his arm. He'd probably been standing in the shower for five minutes, hot water streaming over him, when the bathroom door opened, then closed.

Through the steamy glass of the door, he saw Mai.

"'Morning," she said, sounding as if she was not quite awake. "Mind if I brush my teeth?"

"No. No, of course, not." Feeling awkward, he squirted some soap into his hand and began to lather his whole body. He wasn't used to sharing his morning ablutions and it felt weird to have her in the bathroom while he showered.

But as he washed, listening to the sound of her running water, dropping the cap from the toothpaste, brushing, he realized that it was kind of nice to have a woman brushing her teeth in his bathroom. It was nice to have had her in his bed last night when he'd woken from the nightmare.

He thought about what she'd said the other night, about loving him. He felt like it was hanging over his head. He'd had other women who'd confessed their love for him and he'd never responded to them, either. But it had never bothered him. He'd told himself they deserved honesty. And they certainly deserved to love and be loved by a better man than him. So why did he feel like such a jerk this time?

The sound of the shower door startled him and he

turned around. Mai was standing there, naked. "I need a shower, too. Mind sharing?"

He grinned, stepping back. "Not a lot of room, but, sure, come on in."

She closed her eyes and backed up toward the shower spray, letting the water cascade over her head, washing her long, dark hair.

Come to find out, Liam liked a woman in his shower, too. Not that he'd never bathed with a woman before, but this somehow felt different. More...domestic.

"Turn around. I'll shampoo your hair," he told her. "All I've got is the herbal stuff from the drugstore. I can get something else, if you want." He squirted some into his hand. He was babbling. He didn't know why he was babbling.

She turned in the tight quarters, presenting her bare bottom...and wet head of hair. "Mmmm," she said with a sigh as he lathered up her hair. "This is as good as sex." She backed up, massaging his groin with her bottom. "Okay, not quite."

He smiled, digging his fingernails into her soapy scalp. "Sorry about that," he said, apologizing for his growing erection.

"Don't be." She turned to face him, lifting up on her toes to kiss him.

Liam drew his soapy hands over her slick shoulders, enjoying the feel of the hot water streaming over him. "Did you check on your dad?" he murmured, nuzzling her neck.

"Bedroom door's closed. Still asleep."

"You don't think he'll"—he pressed his lips to her throat—"get up and—"

"Locked the bathroom door," she said, her breath already coming quickly.

"So this was preplanned?" he teased, reaching up to wash the last of the shampoo from her hair.

She lifted her wet lashes to look into his eyes. "That a problem?"

"No." He kissed her softly on the lips. "Not a problem." The next kiss was more forceful.

Mai ran her hands over his buttocks, stroking, kneading. He pushed her back against the wall of the shower stall and she lifted one leg, wrapping it around him, pulling him closer.

Liam cupped one breast, kissed it, stroked her nipple with the tip of his tongue, lapping the warm water, then lowered his hand over her hip, across her belly, and then lower to the triangle of dark hair.

Mai moaned. She was wet for him, ready...

He kissed her collarbone and drew a trail of wet kisses up to her neck again as he drew his fingers between her legs, stroking her.

Mai slid her arms around his shoulders, holding tightly to him. "I can't balance like this long," she said with a laugh. "Get over here."

She wrapped her fingers around his cock, guiding him into her, and Liam was powerless to argue. Not that he really wanted to. He pinned her against the shower wall, sinking into her, both of them wet and slippery.

She was warm and welcoming and he groaned with pleasure at the first stroke, closing his eyes, reveling in the feel of Mai in his arms and the water pouring over them. In a way, it was as if the water formed a curtain around them, isolating them from the harshness of the world, if only for a few minutes.

It didn't take them long to finish. Mai dug her fingernails into his back until it almost hurt, making that sweet sound that he knew meant she was coming. Which was a good thing because he wasn't sure how much longer he could hold back.

Mai cried out and Liam gave in, bursting with pleasure. He had to make a conscious effort to hold on to her to keep them both from falling in the wet shower. She laughed as he withdrew from her, then she clung to him, resting her cheek on his chest. "I'm going to miss you, Liam," she said.

He started to say something, though what, he wasn't sure. Before he could, she reached up and pressed a finger to his mouth. "Don't say anything. Please. It's one of the things I like most about you. I don't expect you to respond, just like I didn't expect you to respond to what I said the other night."

She leaned back, looking into his eyes. They both knew what she was talking about. "I don't need you to say those things. I don't want you to." She lifted up on her toes, kissed him, and then pushed on the door and stepped out. "I'm going to steal all your clean towels."

She closed the shower door and grabbed a towel off the rack to wrap up her hair. Then she wrapped herself up with the towel he'd left on the toilet seat to dry off with.

Liam squirted body soap into his hand and began to soap up again. "There's more in the hall."

He watched through the steamy glass as she went out the bathroom door into the hall, one towel wrapped around her slender body, the other in a turban around her head.

He reached down with sudsy hands to wash his groin.

"*Babbo?*" Mai called from the hall. Her voice got louder as she passed the open bathroom door, walking toward the kitchen. "*Babbo?*"

There was something in her voice that told him he

needed to get the hell out of the shower. He rinsed off and stepped out, dripping wet. "Mai?"

She came back to the bathroom door. Seeing he was naked and wet and without a towel, she pulled off the one on her head. "He's gone," she said, tossing him the towel. "I can't believe this. My dad and the dog are gone again."

Chapter 23

"I can't believe he would do this again," Mai muttered, her wet hair dripping down her back.

Liam ran the towel over his muscular body, then his hair, then dropped it on the floor and walked out of the bathroom. "Get dressed."

"I told him he couldn't go to the beach without one of us." She went to her room and put on a bra and panties. Sometimes she felt like her father was a child, *her* child, instead of the other way around. In her underwear, carrying jeans, a sweatshirt, and socks, she went down the hall to Liam's bedroom. "I thought he understood clearly why he couldn't go out alone."

Mai found Liam at his chest of drawers, already wearing boxer briefs and a black T-shirt. Mai had left his clothes there just the night before. She'd fallen into the routine of washing Liam's clothes when she washed hers and her father's. She washed and folded Liam's things but never put them away for him—some sort of concession. As long as she didn't do his laundry *completely,* there were no real ties between them to break when this nightmare was over and they both went back to their own lives.

Stupid.

She closed her eyes for a second and groaned. "You

know, I'm tired of his games. I'm tired of all of this. Maybe it's time I go to the police, tell them about the Weasel and about my uncle's involvement with the stolen diamonds."

"I don't know that the police can protect you from them, Mai. There are only a certain amount of resources."

"I know. I don't really want to go to the police. We'd be in so much trouble by this point, we'd be lucky if we didn't all go to jail. I just want my life back, Liam." She stepped into her jeans. "The way it was. That's all I want. I want—"

"I think we need to hurry."

The annoyance she felt slipped away and was replaced with sudden fear. The look on Liam's face told her he was genuinely worried about her dad. His eyes told her he didn't think Corrato had gone for a walk. Not this time.

"He's just gone down to the beach again, right?" she said, quickly pulling the sweatshirt over her still slightly damp body.

Because she believed Liam. She trusted him. He was a strange guy, she'd give him that. And she knew he held deep, dark secrets that she was better off not knowing, but she sincerely believed he had her best interests at heart. And her dad's, too. "Maybe he's skinny-dipping, like the other day?" She tried to laugh, but the sound didn't come out right. Here she had been thinking terrible thoughts about her dad and he might really be in trouble.

"We have to find him." He pulled on jeans that he'd left thrown over the chair the night before. "The Weasel killed someone else, an informant who provided me with information. I think."

"You *think?*" She sat down in the doorway to pull on her socks. "You think he gave you information? Or you think the Weasel killed him?"

He threw her a look that told her he meant what she thought he meant.

"Grab the keys to your van." He took a key from his pocket, a key she'd never seen before, and unlocked his closet door. She'd never gone into his closet, so she'd never noticed the doorknob *had* a lock. From the closet floor, he slid out an old hard-sided suitcase that had been pushed to the back. He went down on one knee and popped the latches.

Mai watched from the doorway wondering what the hell he was doing with the suitcase. When he opened it, she covered her mouth with her hand. *This* was why she didn't have a boyfriend, a husband, a significant other.

Tears welled in her eyes as she scrambled to get to her feet.

She didn't have a man in her life because she was lousy at picking men. It was always the crazies she was attracted to. The *dangerous* crazies.

He only opened the suitcase for a second, but it was long enough for her to see several guns, including some sort of high-tech automatic rifle nestled in foam. He pulled out a pistol and a clip of ammo, slammed the suitcase shut, and locked the closet again. When he turned to her, he was holding the pistol.

"You have a *gun*, Liam?" She looked at him. "What is it you do for a living?"

"We need to go. Now."

"Who are you?"

"The man you've been sleeping with for the last couple of weeks." He looked down, checked the gun, and slipped it into the rear waistband of his jeans. Like he knew what he was doing. Like this wasn't the first time he had armed himself. The spare clip went into his pocket.

"I'm the man trying to help you. I can't tell you much more than that." He grabbed a long-sleeved T-shirt from the pile on the dresser. "Are you going with me, or you staying here?"

"I'm going with you, but not with that gun." She stared at him accusingly. "You'll scare my father half to death."

"I don't intend to use it if I don't have to." He grabbed his shoes. "But don't be so naive as to think your father hasn't seen one before."

Mai dropped her gaze to the floor. All of a sudden, she felt like she was going to crumble into a million pieces. All this time she'd been telling herself that her father was innocent, that he knew nothing of Donato's dealings with the mafia, nothing of the diamonds.

But she'd been lying to herself since she found Uncle Donato's body.

They cruised the streets of Clare Point for an hour, checking the boardwalk, the beach, the closed five-and-dime they had visited before Halloween. They checked everywhere they thought Corrato could have gone.

With no sign of him, Liam pulled up in front of The Hill. "Wait here," he told Mai. "Lock the doors when I get out. You see anything suspicious, you hit the horn. You *do not* get out of the car. Do you understand?"

She'd barely said a word since they'd left the apartment. She was upset about the guns in his closet; it was stupid of him not to have waited until she left the room to retrieve his Glock. He didn't know why he'd done it. Was it a subconscious ploy to chase her off? To hurt her before she hurt him?

It didn't matter why at this point. And there was no sense trying to explain the guns to her. No lie, no matter how plausible, was going to satisfy her right now. Now he had to find Corrato. Later they'd talk about his munitions cache. Or not. He hadn't decided.

He walked up the crumbling brick sidewalk to the old pub. The door was locked. It was Sunday morning. What

else would he expect? He banged on it. When Tavia didn't
come, he tried her cell. Then he stepped back and hollered
at the window over the street that he knew was her living
room window. Finally, with *still* no answer, he resorted to
mental telepathy, which he probably should have tried
first. But he'd been away from Clare Point so long and
spent so much time with Mai and Corrato that he sometimes forgot he had alternative means of communication.

Tavia! Tavia, it's Liam. I need your help.

Liam?

My old guy is missing again.

Where the hell are you?

Downstairs. At your door. Let me in.

*Wait a damn second. I've still got conditioner in my
hair.*

As he waited, rocking on his heels, he glanced in the direction of the minivan. Mai sat stiffly in the passenger seat,
looking straight ahead. She looked so scared. So vulnerable. So damned beautiful. It was funny, but until he'd met
Mai, he'd never had any strong feelings one way or the
other about Asian women, vampire or human. Right now,
he thought Asian humans were the most beautiful in the
world.

He heard the window open on the second story and
stepped back. Tavia had her gorgeous red hair wrapped up
in a towel turban, just like Mai had had this morning. She
was toweling off, not caring how much of her body she
bared. He and Tavia had been lovers, though not in this
lifetime.

He glanced back at the van. Mai was watching them.

"You say your guy's gone again?" Tavia called down.

"Yeah, but I've got a bad feeling this time. He's not
skinny-dipping. I need your help. I need everyone's help. I
think he's been kidnapped."

She hesitated for a second. "You know, this is where I

could say I warned you. That more than one of us warned you that keeping them here was a bad idea."

"You *could* say that."

She exhaled, taking her time before she spoke again. "Okay, fine. You take your HF back to your place. I'll rally the troops."

"Maybe I should keep Mai with me. Keep her safe. Her life could be in danger, too."

"Take her back to your place, Liam. I'll send Kaleigh over to sit with her. I'm sure everyone in Clare Point will look for the old guy, but they don't want to get involved with your little HF girlfriend. I'll call you in a few minutes. Now I'm freezing my ass off, so if you don't mind..." She slammed the window shut.

Liam went back to Mai's van and waited while she unlocked the door. He got in.

"Who was that?" she asked.

"A friend."

She bit down on her lower lip. "She's pretty. She was also naked."

"An old friend, okay?" He turned the key in the ignition. "Tavia's going to let everyone in town know your dad's gone on walkabout again. If he's here, they'll find him."

She drew her knees up, hugging them to her body. Her hair was still damp and hung over her face so that he couldn't see her eyes. "He's not on walkabout," she said softly. "Not this time."

Liam knew in his gut that she was right, but he didn't say so. The truth became pretty clear when they pulled up in front of his shop. The Prince of Dogs sat waiting for them at the door, his leash dangling from his collar. He was alone.

Liam returned to his antiques shop two hours after he'd left Mai and the dog in the care of Kaleigh. He carried a plastic grocery bag. When he walked into the kitchen, Mai was stirring a pasta sauce while the teen sat at the dinette table. He'd known Mai long enough to know that cooking was one of her favorite emotional outlets; she cooked when she was happy, when she was sad, when she was scared out of her wits.

Everyone turned to look at him, including the dog, when he stopped in the kitchen doorway. It was the look in the dog's eyes that made him feel sick to his stomach. *I tried, buddy,* he telepathed.

It might have been Liam's imagination, but the dog's face seemed to soften. *I know you did,* he seemed to say.

"You didn't find him." Mai stirred her sauce with a wooden spoon.

"He left of his own volition this morning, I'm guessing, with the intention of walking home. On his way to Mass this morning, about seven, Father Kahill saw Corrato. He assumed he was walking his dog and that I knew." He set down the plastic grocery bag and Prince ran over and stuck his nose in it.

"We found the bag on the road that leads south out of town," he told Mai. "It's your dad's. Dog food and a crossword puzzle book. The one I bought him at the newsstand the other day." Liam's limbs suddenly felt heavy. He was exhausted, so exhausted he felt like he could sleep.

Mai stared at the bag on the floor. "So now what?" Emotion caught in her voice and he walked over and put his arm around her. "We just wait?" she whispered.

"I think we wait," Kaleigh piped in. "If they were going to kill him, they'd have done it there and then. Killing him would be a last resort. You know very well that the night they killed his brother, that wasn't the first contact they had with Donato."

Liam looked at Kaleigh, seated at the table, then back at Mai.

"I told her," Mai admitted. "The whole story. I...I needed to talk to someone. We can trust her. I know we can."

He exhaled, walking over to the table and dropping into a chair.

"You think Mr. Ricci knows where the diamonds are?" Kaleigh asked Liam.

He shrugged. "Hard to say with Corrato."

"But he's smart. If he doesn't know, he'll buy himself some time. If he does know, he might tell, but he'll do it in a way that at least gives him a chance of walking out alive."

Liam looked up at Mai. "I think we have to go back to your house. Go over everything again, this time paying attention to your father's belongings. Just in case..." He let his sentence trail into silence.

"I'll go, too." Kaleigh popped up out of her chair.

Liam's first impulse was to tell her no. She needed to stay here and wait for Corrato, should the old guy turn up. But everyone in the room, including the Prince of Dogs, knew Corrato Ricci wasn't going to just *turn up*. Not alive.

Mai turned the stove off. Kaleigh rose from her seat. "Come on, Prince. Let's go find some diamonds."

The dog beat them all to the door.

Chapter 24

"There's nothing here." Mai dropped onto the couch that had no cushions; though no longer strewn all over her living room, they were still in a pile on the floor. She leaned back and closed her eyes. "I'm tired, I'm hungry, and they're going to kill my dad and there's nothing I'm going to be able to do about it." She sounded beyond feeling any emotion. She'd been working for hours, going through her shop with Kaleigh while Liam worked in the house, but now she was out of energy, and hope, it seemed. She opened her eyes. "How long before they come after me, Liam?" she asked matter-of-factly.

He was picking up books off the floor and passing them to Kaleigh. They'd already gone over the entire upstairs, the laundry room, and the half bath downstairs; the only room left after they finished the living room was the kitchen. He was checking each book for papers or hidden objects before he gave it to Kaleigh to replace on the bookshelves. They'd been at it for almost six hours. In the end, Liam had been glad he'd brought Kaleigh with them. She'd served as a pair of extra eyes and hands in the search. She'd also provided a buffer between him and Mai.

Mai was pretty upset. Upset with him, with her father, with herself, and Liam didn't know how to handle her. He didn't know what to say to make her feel better, which made him feel inadequate. He didn't like feeling inadequate. But maybe there was nothing *to* say.

"How long?" she repeated.

"There's no way to say." He held a coffee table book that featured glossy photographs of antique clocks. He had the same book somewhere. "But I have a feeling the Weasel will be contacting us before it comes to that."

"Before or after they kill my dad?"

He saw no reason to sugarcoat the situation. It was bad. But it wasn't hopeless. "Before. The Weasel's top priority is to get his diamonds back."

He wasn't sure Mai was really listening.

"It's getting dark." She glanced at the windows. Shadows were lengthening in the room and they'd had to turn on the lights a little while ago so Kaleigh and Mai could see what they were doing. "He's got to be scared. What if he's hurt?"

"Your father's a smart man. A survivor. He made it out of Saigon, didn't he?" Liam passed the clock book to Kaleigh. There was nothing in the books, nothing in the house to help him help Mai. "He'll be okay. At least for now."

Mai pressed her lips together. "You think so?"

He walked over and sat down beside her. The couch was hard without the cushions. He got up and retrieved the sliced-up cushions from where they'd stacked them. "Get up," he said. She rose and let him replace the cushions.

She sat down again. "You really think he'll be okay?"

He took her hand in his. "I do. I don't know how to explain it to you, but I just have this feeling in my gut that, at least for now, your father isn't in imminent danger." He paused for a second. "Now, we need to think through this again. Go about it logically. We have to accept the fact that Donato had the diamonds, otherwise the Weasel wouldn't be going to all this trouble, not at his age. So, if the diamonds aren't here, where could they be? You said neither your dad nor Donato drove a car anymore."

She shook her head, clasping his fingers. "Dad lost his license a year ago. A couple of fender-benders, then he accidentally ran a red light and almost caused an accident. He actually surrendered his license before the state revoked it. Uncle Donato didn't have a license or a car when he came to live with us."

"No public transportation here, so that means you had to drive them where they wanted to go," he said, thinking out loud. "Think back since Donato arrived. Did he ever get you to take him somewhere like a storage facility, maybe?"

"No."

"To meet someone you didn't know?"

"No."

"And, to your knowledge, he didn't own any property anywhere?" Liam hadn't been able to find any public record of her uncle owning property, but he just wanted to be sure.

"No," Mai answered. "Not as far as I know."

Which didn't really make sense, Liam thought. He'd found records where the IRS had seized multiple properties, as well as bank accounts, when Donato went to jail. But he'd had time to make money and buy property after he got out. A man like Donato, who was even reasonably successful in his day, would have made plenty of money. Of course, maybe he just got good at hiding it after tangling with the government and going to jail.

"What do you think, Prince?" Kaleigh asked. She walked over to where the dog slept in a little wicker bed near the foot of the stairs. She sat on the floor and began to stroke his smooth back. "Did Uncle Donato hide the diamonds here in the house, or somewhere else? Did your daddy Corrato tell you?" she crooned. "Does the smart little doggie know where the jewels are hidden?"

Liam stared at the dog, then shifted his gaze to the dog bed. He remembered the night he'd brought Corrato and Mai back to the house to collect their belongings. Corrato had tried to bring the dog basket, but Mai had made him leave it. The incident had seemed meaningless at the time. Now he wondered. Why had Corrato wanted the dog bed and no other possessions beyond a change of clothing and some crossword puzzle books? Was he just worried about the comfort of his canine companion, or was it something else?

"You're a good boy. You know that?" Kaleigh scratched behind the dog's ears. "Sometimes I wish I had a dog," she said over her shoulder to Liam and Mai. "But Mom says no dog. She doesn't want to clean up after it in the yard. You ever have a dog, Liam?"

"Pick up the dog," Liam said, letting go of Mai's hand and springing off the couch.

"What?" Kaleigh frowned, looking at him like he was crazy.

"I said, pick up the dog."

Kaleigh pulled the rat terrier into her lap protectively and scrambled to her feet. "What's wrong?"

"Nothing's wrong." He grabbed the dog bed and began to examine it carefully. It consisted of a fuzzy faux-sheep-skin cushion in a little rattan or wicker or some kind of crappy basket. He flipped the bed over; there was nothing on the bottom. He pulled out the bedding and dropped it on the floor. He found nothing on the inside of the basket and no place to hide anything. The weave was loose enough that he could see his hand through it. He picked up the sheepskin cushion. It smelled like dog. And dog food. He began to squeeze it, starting at one side and moving toward the other. He'd almost given up the idea when he felt something hard.

"I'll be damned," he whispered.

"What is it?" Mai asked.

"Kaleigh, scissors, a knife, anything I can use to cut this open."

Kaleigh ran to the kitchen, carrying the dog under her arm.

Mai got up to join Liam. "What did you find?"

"Feels like a key," he said, trying not to get his hopes up. "A small key."

Kaleigh was back in a few seconds. She handed him a steak knife. Mai and the teen watched as he cut open the dog bed and extracted a small brass-colored key on a plastic key chain. It looked shiny and new.

"You recognize this?" he asked, holding the key up for Mai to see.

She shook her head. "I have no idea what it is or where it came from. I certainly don't know how it got in there." She studied it in his hand. "Is it for a drawer or a box or something? It looks too small for a door on a storage facility."

"It's a key to a bank lockbox." He read aloud the name of the bank.

"That's where we do our banking," Mai said, staring at the key.

Liam fingered the key. "You have a lockbox?"

She shook her head. "I don't have anything of value to lock up. I keep car titles and stuff like that in one of those fire boxes in my office."

"Do you know if your dad or your uncle rented a box recently?"

"I don't know how they could have. As I said, they don't drive. I take them to the bank once a month for them to deposit their Social Security checks."

Liam looked at Mai. "You use the drive-through window?"

She chuckled. "A drive-through for two seventy-something guys? Of course not. My dad and Uncle Donato always insisted on going inside. They got all dressed up once a month just to walk in and cash their checks."

"And you didn't go in with them?" he guessed.

"No, I wanted my dad to feel like he still had some independence. I always waited in the car."

Liam smiled.

"You think Uncle Donato put the diamonds in a lockbox at the bank?"

"Possibly, but since the key was in Prince's bed, I'd bet you the lockbox belongs to Corrato, not Donato. Or at least the box is registered in Corrato's name. Donato has nothing in his name that I've been able to find, so he probably doesn't have any bank accounts or lockboxes...at least not under his own name. "

"We have to get into that box!" Mai looked up at him. "But I don't know how we're going to do that. My name's obviously not on it. The bank won't let me go into it, even if I have a key." Her shoulders slumped. "So the key is useless."

Liam glanced at Kaleigh. "Did I hear Aedan was in town?"

The teen's tired face lit up in a smile. "Yup. Got in two nights ago. A tussle in London with some—" She cut herself off and offered a quick grin in Mai's direction. "He's home," she said quickly.

Liam slid the key into his pocket. "I think it's time to call it a night, ladies. We can't get into the bank until tomorrow morning anyway." He offered his hand to Mai. "Come on," he said quietly. "Let's go back to my place and get some sleep."

"I don't understand how you're going to get into my father's lockbox. Does this guy, this Aedan, work at the bank or something?" She looked at Kaleigh. "What kind of trouble was he in, in London?"

Liam put his arm around her waist and kissed the top of her head. "You're going to have to trust me on this one. We'll get in that lockbox."

She turned to him, looking into his eyes. "I don't like these secrets of yours." She searched his gaze. "But I guess it's a little late for me to say that now." She pressed her lips together. "You think the diamonds are in that lockbox?" She sounded afraid to be too hopeful.

"I think something is important enough in that box that your father was willing to deceive you."

"I'll kill him," she murmured, shaking her head as she walked out of Liam's arms. "If you live through this, *Babbo,* I swear to God I'm going to kill you."

"You got some salsa?" Corrato ignored the big ox with the gun near the door and spoke to the skinny guy seated at the opposite end of the rickety kitchen table.

He didn't know exactly where he was. They'd put a cloth bag over his head when they pulled him into the van. But he was pretty sure they were in New Jersey. He'd been able to tell when they went through the toll booths on the Jersey turnpike. No E-ZPass, so they'd had to stop to pay tolls. They were holding him in a crappy apartment, possibly in an abandoned building. He couldn't hear any neighbors, but he could hear the sound of cars driving by, through the blackened windows. He was two stories up.

Corrato stuffed a forkful of chicken enchilada into his mouth. It was takeout, served in one of those tinfoil pans with a cardboard lid, but it was decent. The corn chips in the paper bag were stale.

The two thugs who had kidnapped him hadn't hurt him. Just scared him. The scariest part was when they'd grabbed him off the road and he'd dropped Prince's leash. Corrato had begged them to let him bring his dog, but then Prince had taken off, something he never did. Corrato had cried as the dog ran away, but later, lying on the floor of the van that stunk of old fast food, he'd decided that Prince knew what he was doing. His faithful companion would go back to the apartment and warn Mai and that odd boyfriend of hers. Liam would know what to do. He'd come for Corrato. And if he didn't? *C'est la vie.* Corrato figured he'd lived a good life. Everyone had to die someday. He just hoped it wouldn't be too painful.

He looked up at the skinny guy again. He'd heard the big one call him Alejo. The Weasel hadn't even hired Italians. These guys were Mexican. They'd spoken Spanish all day and Corrato hadn't been able to understand a word. He'd always meant to learn some Spanish. It would have come in handy beyond knowing the four-letter word for *hand.* "You hear me, Alejo?" Corrato said. "I asked if you got salsa. These enchiladas are a little dry." He pointed at the takeout container with his plastic fork.

The other two weren't eating, which ordinarily would make him feel uncomfortable; his mother had taught him better. But they were the ones who kidnapped him, right? They could starve for all he cared. They weren't getting his chicken enchiladas or his rice and beans. Or the stale corn chips. This was the first thing he'd eaten today.

"Shut up, old man. We got no salsa." Alejo sucked on a cigarette.

Corrato waved his hand in the air. "You shouldn't be smoking in front of me," he complained. "You'll give me lung cancer. The Weasel won't be happy. And don't call me old man. My name is Corrato Ricci. Mr. Ricci, to you."

"What would make the boss happy, *old man,* is if you tell me where his property is. Then we all go home."

"Right." Corrato scooped up a forkful of refried beans.

"Like I would believe a man who would leave a defense-
less dog alone on the street." He raised the fork to his
mouth. "I don't know where those damned diamonds
are." He stuffed the soft, warm beans into his mouth.
"Not that I'd tell you if I did."

The next morning, Liam drove south on Route One
with Aedan beside him in Mai's minivan. Liam and Mai
had argued this morning because she wanted to go with
them to the bank. There was no way for Liam to explain
to her why she couldn't come, which had made her so
angry, she hadn't even said good-bye when he left. Kaleigh
had cut school to stay with her, the only way Liam could
be sure Mai would stay put, and stay safe. Kaleigh, of
course, had been all for the plan; she was missing a calculus quiz.

"I appreciate you doing this for me, Aedan." Liam
glanced at him.

Aedan was a big guy, even for a Kahill. He was six-five,
and not thin, like most sept members. While physically fit,
he easily ran two-fifty. He could fill up a doorway like a refrigerator, which sometimes came in handy in the field.

"Anything for you, Liam. I still owe you for saving my
ass in Prague two years ago." He grinned. He was good-
looking, with long, dark auburn hair and blue eyes, an
unusual combination for a Kahill vampire. He looked just
like his mother, Brigid, whom he'd lost a few centuries ago
to vampire slayers while on an assignment in Scotland.

"You don't owe me anything." Liam turned his attention back to the road. "If we're keeping tabs, which we're
not, I probably owe you."

Aedan's job was to investigate the men and women
whose names had been brought to the Kahill sept's attention. He was particularly good at rooting out serial killers,
tracking them, watching them *at work*. His unusual

shape-shifting ability often allowed him to go where other sept members could not, making him extremely useful to them. His good nature was a bonus.

"We could argue about this all day." Aedan picked up the photo of Corrato Ricci from his lap. "Like I said, this is going to be tricky, between me having to use a photo and you wanting me to add on a few years."

"Sorry. She couldn't find a more recent picture. It's only three years old." He glanced at the picture Aedan was studying. It was of Mai and Corrato, arm in arm, posing at a wedding reception. He was wearing a suit; she was in a cute pink dress, smiling and gorgeous. "But you can do it, right?"

Reaching Five Points, he got in the turn lane, heading down Savannah Road. The bank was in a new shopping center not far off Route One.

"I can do it. I just have to get the image in here." He tapped his temple. "I have to take the photograph, then superimpose the older image, as I see it in my head, on top. And you don't want him in this suit, right?" He pointed at the photo.

"Nope. Think old-man clothes. Old man who's lost weight and never likes to buy anything new: baggy shirt and pants, a cardigan sweater. All gray or brown."

"No glasses?"

"He doesn't wear them all the time, so they're not necessary." He pulled into the parking lot. "We're here." He cut the engine, glancing at Aedan again. "You ready?"

Liam had seen him do it hundreds of times, but it still surprised him, amazed him, every time Aedan morphed. Instead of Aedan Kane, it was Corrato Ricci who climbed out of the van.

Chapter 25

Liam waited nervously. He drummed the steering wheel with his fingers. He turned the radio on, cruised the stations, turned it off again. Occasionally, he glanced in the direction of the bank's double glass doors. Things had to be going all right, so far. Aedan hadn't come tearing out, morphed as a dog or an orangutan, waving for Liam to pull up the getaway van.

Aedan had this sick sense of humor. Whenever he got in a bad spot, like the time in L.A. at a party, when he'd morphed into a drug dealer, only to run into the real one, he'd morph into something or someone who totally didn't belong there, and take off. That time it had been an orangutan—perhaps not so far-fetched, considering some of the people Liam had met in L.A. over the years. Aedan said he did it to throw people off-guard just long enough to escape, but Liam thought he liked messing with people's heads. He'd once been caught in a harem in the Middle East romancing some sheik's third wife, morphed into a rhino, and gotten away before the guards had had the sense to stop him.

Liam went back to drumming the steering wheel. Then he flipped down the visor to see what Mai had tucked up there. He found a hotel brochure, a bank deposit receipt, and an old shopping list. The list was in Mai's delicate, loopy handwriting. She had needed chickpeas, basil, oranges, and cereal.

He'd miss her.

When this was over. When he went back to work. When she returned to her quiet life and her antiques shop.

If he ever got to go back to work. If she survived.

Suddenly impatient to have this done, over, no matter what the outcome, he slapped the visor up and took his cell phone from the console. He dialed Peigi. She didn't pick up. When the answering system beeped, he considered hanging up. Instead, he spoke.

"It's Liam, Peigi. Look, I don't know what's going on, but the Council's dragged their heels long enough on this. I have a right to a speedy hearing. I have a right to tell my side of the story. So..." He hesitated. "Can you talk to someone? Can you get the ball rolling, because—" He was surprised by the lump of emotion that rose in his throat and almost kept him from continuing. He'd gotten too involved with these humans. He cared too much. "I need to get back to work." He took a breath. "Please, Peigi?"

Liam hung up just as he saw Corrato Ricci shuffle out the bank door. A biker in a fringed leather vest held the door open for him. Corrato/Aedan was carrying the small shopping bag he'd taken in with him. There was definitely something in it.

Liam held his breath until Aedan was in the van, the door closed. "Any problem?"

"No problem." Aedan spoke with an old man's voice, though not Corrato's. He could only mimic voices he'd heard.

As he pulled out of the parking lot, Liam glanced at Aedan. He was himself again. "What'd you get?"

"Weird."

"Weird?" Liam looked at him, then the road.

"A jumbo crossword book." He pulled it out of the bag, reading it as if he was selling them.

"A crossword puzzle book?" Liam checked his rearview mirror and moved over into the turn lane to merge north onto Route One.

"An old one. Look, the pages are faded." Aedan fanned the book, creating a slight breeze on Liam's face.

"Open it up."

"It's crossword puzzles," Aedan announced, opening to the first page.

"Keep going." Liam knew very well Corrato hadn't gone to the trouble of getting a lockbox at a bank to store an old crossword puzzle book.

Aedan flipped the pages. "Crossword puzzle, crossword puzzle, crossword puzzle."

"They filled in?"

"Some. Not all. Some of the ink is pretty faded. It looks like it was filled out at different times."

Liam motioned with his hand. "Keep going." He looked at the book in Aedan's lap. That was Corrato's handwriting, all right. Black pen, always a black pen.

"Hmm," Aedan said.

" 'Hmm' what?"

"Hmm, as in, 'hmm, this is peculiar.' This puzzle is filled with numbers, not words." He studied a page for a second. "Letters and numbers."

"Letters and numbers," Liam repeated. "What the hell? Random numbers?"

"Don't think so. Series of numbers."

"How many in a series?"

"Let's see. It looks like he wrote them left to right, leaving a space between each series. It's definitely alphanumeric, and there's, let's see"—he counted out loud—"twenty-one characters in each group." He looked to Liam. "The topic of this crossword puzzle is household items. Mean anything to you?"

"Twenty-one characters," Liam repeated. He passed a VW Bug going 45. "Does each one start with the same number or letter?"

"Nope."

Twenty-one characters, numbers and letters, Liam thought. It couldn't be land coordinates, then. What other numbers did people record? Important phone numbers, dates, account numbers... Of course, it was a bank. Account numbers!

"The combinations don't start the same way?" Liam asked.

"Nope. But they end the same way. HC."

"H, C, H, C," Liam said. "What the hell is HC?"

"It's not HC," Aedan announced after a second. He was obviously pleased with himself. "The numbers are recorded backward. It's CH."

"How do you know?"

"I don't know. Because I'm a smart guy?"

"CH?"

"It's the country code for Switzerland. I've seen them before. Got one or two myself." He grinned at Liam. "Looks like your old guy does, too. Swiss bank account numbers. Look." He folded back a page, lifting the book so Liam could look at it for a second. "CH states that it's a Swiss account. The 10 is some kind of IBAN control digit."

"IBAN?"

"International bank account number," Aedan explained. "Not important. 00230, that's the bank clearing number for all Swiss accounts, and the last numbers and letters are his actual bank account numbers."

"I'll be damned." Liam gripped the wheel, gazing out at the barren fields on both sides of the highway. It was bitterly cold today. "I wonder if the Sunshine Boys sold the diamonds."

"Not likely, from what you've been telling me. Your girl would have had to have known something was going on. There would have been contact with outsiders: Internet, mail, phone calls, something." Aedan hesitated. "Think your girl's lying to you?"

Liam shook his head. "No way."

"You're sure? Gut sure or just sure?" Aedan asked.

"Gut sure."

"Gotta go with the gut," Aedan agreed. "Okay, so there's cash banked internationally. The brother went to jail for tax evasion. Anything he made after he got out of the joint, he certainly would have been more careful with."

Liam looked at the book again. "Is there just the one page of account numbers, or more?"

"Let's see." Aedan flipped the pages. "Things at the Zoo, blank. In the Office, blank. Birds of a Feather, completed. He had a little trouble with '*Grackle,* one that mocks but is not mocking.' Used Wite-Out." Aedan pointed with his finger.

Liam smiled to himself. He loved Aedan for his childish innocence, for his ability to see delight in every little thing, despite the fact that, like Liam, he had seen the worst of what God's world had to offer. "Any more bank accounts?"

"No. No. No." He turned the pages. "Hmm."

"Not the 'hmm' again, Aedan. Do I need to pull over?"

"Looks like dates, names, places. Was your old guy a drug dealer?"

Liam exhaled. "I don't think so, but at this point, I don't know."

"Well, nine kilos of something arrived from CO in January of 2003 and I'm thinking that's Colombia, not the Centennial State."

"Cocaine? Corrato was dealing in cocaine?" Liam mused aloud. "No way."

"A few weeks ago, you didn't think he knew anything about his brother's occupation."

"Yeah, but in 2003, Corrato was living here, running an antiques shop. He might have known about it, maybe after the fact, but he didn't participate."

"Lots of reasons to write this kind of crap down, but a guy who's doing this kind of crap, he doesn't write it down. Take my word for it. He keeps it in his head."

"So who writes down stuff like that?"

"No one." Aedan closed the book.

"Unless," Liam said, "you're starting to lose your memory and you don't want to forget the details."

"To what purpose?"

"I don't know." Liam exhaled. "To blackmail someone? But that still doesn't sound like Corrato."

Aedan cut his eyes at him. "Maybe to turn state's evidence."

Mai was watching the window when Liam came down the street and pulled into the alley beside the antiques shop. "He's here!" She darted for the door.

"Mai, we should wait here for him," Kaleigh called.

But Mai couldn't wait. She unlocked the apartment door and ran down the steps. Kaleigh followed behind her, ordering Prince to stay put in the upstairs hall.

Mai met Liam at the bottom of the landing, just inside the door. A cold wind blew in from the outside. He was holding a crossword puzzle book. "Where did you get that?" she demanded, reaching for it. "Is that my dad's? I thought you went to the bank. Did you get into the lock-box?"

Liam held the crossword puzzle book just out of Mai's reach. He was quiet for a second and then Kaleigh turned and stomped up the steps. "Fine!" she declared, obviously annoyed with Liam. The weird thing was, he hadn't spoken to her.

"I'll wait upstairs," Kaleigh said. "You think I won't find out? I know *everything*, Liam. Eventually."

Liam waited until Kaleigh had gone into the apartment and closed the door before he looked at Mai. "Have you seen this before?" He held up the book.

"I don't know. Is it my dad's? Maybe. Do you know how many crossword puzzle books he owns? You saw the house. There's probably a hundred." She hugged herself, feeling like she was on the verge of a breakdown. She didn't cry, because she was afraid she wouldn't be able to stop. "Enough with the drama. Just tell me what's going on, Liam."

"This was all that was in the box." He held up the book, which she could now tell was old. The cover was slightly dog-eared.

She stared at the book in his hand. "My father and Uncle Donato got a lockbox at a bank to store a crossword puzzle book?"

"Only your dad's name was on the box. It was leased three years ago. Corrato's been in it several times. He had to sign in each time he asked to use his key. Aedan saw the signature card."

"How did this Aedan guy see the signature card? Why would my dad put a crossword puzzle in a bank vault?" Suddenly Mai felt slightly sick to her stomach and she sank down on the bottom step. The stairway was cold and drafty, but she wasn't going anywhere until she found out what was going on.

Liam sat down beside her, set the book on his knees, and opened it. He flipped through the first few pages.

Mai recognized her father's handwriting and tears welled in her eyes. "I honestly don't remember this book, but that certainly is his writing. Look." She touched her finger to a note written in the margin. "We must have been out of milk and he jotted it down. Three years ago he was still driving. He would have gone to the grocery store for us. He could have gone to the bank and rented a lock-box."

"See these?" Liam turned to the page filled in with numbers. "This mean anything to you?"

It just seemed like a jumble of numbers, with an occasional letter. She shook her head.

"Swiss bank account numbers. And see, the pen is darker than some of the other pages. This was filled in more recently."

"My father has Swiss bank accounts?" She gazed into Liam's dark eyes, finding the idea almost beyond belief. Who was this man she had known all her life as her gentle father? Was he really a member of the mafia like Donato? It seemed beyond belief, yet not any more beyond belief than anything else that had happened in the last couple of weeks.

"I'll have to see what I can find out about these accounts. I know a guy who might be able to help me out, but it will have to wait until tomorrow. Banking hours are already over for today."

"You know a guy who can get you into a bank vault? A guy who can check federal records? A guy who has access to Swiss bank account information? Who are the hell are you, Liam?"

His face was so close to hers that she could have kissed him.

"Actually, I know a *girl* who can check federal records."

She closed her eyes for a moment. In any other situation, she might have smiled. "What does it mean? The Swiss bank accounts?"

"It means that he has money that he didn't want anyone to know about, or that Donato did." He turned the pages until he found one with the notes. "And this means that he was either involved with criminal activity...or he knew someone well who was."

She stared at her father's handwriting. He had put letters and numbers into the crossword puzzles so that if you hadn't looked closely, you might have thought he'd just done the puzzle, but after a second, it was obvious to her that he wasn't doing the puzzle. It all looked like such a mess. Dates, names. She looked up at Liam again, confused. "What is it?"

"It's Corrato's handwriting, right?"

She wanted to say no. She wanted to tell Liam it was all a mistake, or that it was Donato's writing. But this, in her heart of hearts, was what she had feared was true ever since the night her uncle was killed. Now she really couldn't go to the cops. "It's his writing," she said softly.

"These are details of criminal activity: names, places, dates. A *lot* of criminal activity."

"But this doesn't make sense. My father couldn't have been involved in crimes. I've lived with him for years. I knew where he was almost every second of the day."

"But only, what, five years? You said you moved in after his heart attack."

"Right, but I talked to him every day before that. I saw him three or four times a week. I always knew where he was and what he was doing."

"Did you know he was investigated by the FBI and met with agents in Philadelphia?"

Anger bubbled up inside Mai. She wanted to scream at Liam, call him a liar. But he wasn't lying. She could see it in his eyes. In the tightness around his mouth.

"Did my father sell drugs?" she asked in a whisper.

"I don't think so. The dates follow a pattern fitting what we know about Donato. There's nothing recorded for the years he was in prison. I don't know for sure, but I'm pretty sure your father was aware of many of his brother's activities and was keeping the information in case he ever needed it. A lot of it appears to have been written recently."

"Why would he ever need anything like this?" She stared at the book, hating it. Wishing Liam had never found it. "Tell me," she said when he didn't answer. "Please. I have to know."

His dark, sad eyes met hers. "Maybe it was insurance to keep you safe."

Chapter 26

In the early hours of Tuesday morning, when it was still black outside, Liam put a call in to a guy who worked at UBS and owed him a favor. Olli Burgin was out for the day, so Liam left a message. Olli was a good guy; Liam liked Swiss vampires. At least for the most part. Once Liam had a chance to talk to him, Olli would look into the origins of the accounts without calling any attention to them.

Liam didn't sleep the rest of the night. Instead, he lay in his bed with Mai in his arms and the rat terrier curled up at the end of the bed. He listened to the howl of the wind. He remembered lying in another bed, in another time and another place, a woman asleep in his arms, just the way Mai was now.

Roxanne had been the last woman, human or otherwise, whom he loved and she had died because she loved him. It had been the Roaring Twenties: Prohibition, legal opiate drugs, a serial killer stalking the streets of New York City. Roxanne had been a jazz singer on the Upper West Side; they'd met one night when he was stalking the stalker. She'd had the smokiest voice, and a laugh that he could hear even now, when he closed his eyes. He hadn't meant to let her get tangled up with his investigation. He hadn't meant to love her. He hadn't meant to make that tiny misstep that night. He hadn't meant to hold her lifeless, battered body in his arms.

As the sun rose, casting faint light in the bare room, Liam looked down at Mai's sleeping face and promised himself he wouldn't fall in love with her. He told himself that as long as he didn't love her, he would make no mistakes and Mai would survive this.

When full morning came, Mai and Liam showered and dressed and sat down to a breakfast of cold cereal. But even though she poured a bowl, she didn't eat. She just drank her coffee, staring at Prince, who sat by the door that led downstairs.

"You think he needs to go out?" she asked. Those were the first words she'd spoken since she woke.

"I took him out while you were in the shower." Liam ate a bite of Rice Krispies, trying not to think about the fact that he'd bought the box for Corrato.

"He's waiting for Dad."

"Probably," Liam agreed.

She pushed back from the table, leaving her bowlful of soggy Cheerios. "So what do we do today? We wait?"

"We wait," he said. "The Weasel will contact us."

"But he hasn't yet."

"He will. He's just trying to wear on us. It's how it's done."

"*It's how it's done,*" she repeated sarcastically. "Because you know *how this is done,* don't you, Liam?"

He assumed her question was rhetorical. He let her go on.

"You've done it before. Dealt with kidnappers, drug dealers, murderers. Something like that. I knew it." She slapped the kitchen table. "I knew you were too good to be true."

He pushed his bowl aside, no longer hungry. "I never

promised you anything, Mai. Except to help you. *You* came to me. *You* asked me for my help."

She surprised him with the faintest smile. "I did ask for your help. I asked you because I knew in my heart that if anyone could help us, it was you, only you. And you're right. You never promised me anything but that," she whispered. "But I hoped. A girl can hope, can't she? That there really is the right guy out there? A man you can trust?"

He forced himself to meet her gaze despite the emotions that twisted his gut. What he wouldn't have given at that moment to be standing in a cold alley alone somewhere instead of sitting in the warm kitchen with her. "You can trust me."

She exhaled slowly and glanced at the dog waiting at the door. "You think the Weasel will contact us today?"

"Probably." He got up, taking their bowls with him.

"And while we wait?" She sipped her coffee.

"While we wait..." He dumped the bowls and rinsed them. "We start sorting jewelry."

"We *sort jewelry?*"

He watched the milk turn watery as it went down the drain. Rice Krispies swirled, pooled, and were swept away. "It's better if you keep busy. It helps pass the time." He saw a flash in his head of the hours he had waited in that Paris apartment, waiting for darkness to fall, waiting to pay that visit to the Gaudet brothers. It had been some of the longest hours of his life. "You can stay up here if you'd rather. I can do it alone."

She rose from her chair, taking her cup with her. "And miss the opportunity to size rings? No way."

Downstairs in the shop, Liam opened the blinds so he could keep an eye out for anyone who approached the building. It was a cold, gray day and when he went outside midday to walk the dog, he smelled snow in the air. It didn't usually snow in early November in southern Delaware, but snow approached from the west, nonetheless.

Kaleigh was at the front door, tapping on the glass, before four. Welcoming a break from the boring task of sorting hundreds of pieces of jewelry, some worthless, some worth small fortunes, he unlocked the door and let her in. "How was the quiz in calculus?"

She wore her backpack and carried a small brown box. "Sucked. I got 110 percent. You know it's starting to snow out there?"

He locked the door behind her. "How the hell do you get 110 percent?"

"Extra credit." She walked over to where Mai sat cross-legged on the floor, her back up against the counter. The rat terrier slept beside her, curled in a ball like a cat. It was such a dark, dreary day, they'd put several lamps on the floor, running a tangle of extension cords to several different outlets.

"Expecting something good? I ran into the UPS guy on the corner. He asked me if I could bring it, since I was going this way." Kaleigh tossed the box into Mai's lap. "It was at the door. Hey, cool earrings." She dropped her backpack and crouched to pick up a pair of paste diamond chandelier earrings from the forties.

"It's for me?" Mai turned over the four-by-four-inch package, wrapped in brown paper, to read the address. "It can't be for me. No one—" She looked up at Liam.

Kaleigh looked from Mai to Liam and froze. "Shit," she said. "I'm sorry. I'm an idiot. I—"

"Give it to me, Mai."

Mai held the box tightly for a second. "It's not a bomb, is it?"

He held out his hand.

Mai got to her feet and slowly handed over the box. "Maybe I should open it."

"I don't think so." He turned it over, checking every side. It was addressed to Mai, with his street address, but there was no return address, of course.

"Should I take Mai upstairs?" Kaleigh asked, chewing on her lower lip.

"No." Mai's voice trembled. "He can open it, but I stay. It's *my* dad missing. *My* dad who created this mess."

He went to the counter, found a pair of scissors, and took his time cutting off the paper. He knew he had to open the box, but he didn't want to. The flaps of the small cardboard box were sealed with packing tape. When he opened them, the first thing he saw was a smear of blood on the crumpled paper towels inside. He glanced away for a minute.

"What is it?" Mai demanded, her voice shaky.

Kaleigh grabbed her shoulders to hold her back.

"Jesus H. Christ," Liam swore when he pushed back the paper towel. Inside was Corrato Ricci's wedding ring. Still on his finger.

Two hours later, Kaleigh remained upstairs with Mai, making her a cup of tea, while Liam took the dog outside. The thing about having a pet was that, even in a crisis, it still had to pee. Liam didn't bother with the leash. He just carried the little guy down the steps and deposited him in the grass that was slowly becoming covered with snow. There was no way the dog was going to take off; Liam was sure of it. The dog had come back to him because it expected Liam to find his master, and the Prince of Dogs wasn't going to let him out of the obligation.

Liam looked up and down the alley as he flipped up the collar of his leather jacket against the biting wind. He didn't sense any humans nearby, but how long would it be before they came if they didn't get what they were looking for?

When Liam's phone rang, he hesitated before answering

it. It was inside his coat. With Corrato's finger, which was now in a Ziploc bag. It wasn't that Liam really wanted to carry the guy's finger around with him; he just didn't want to leave it in the apartment or the shop where Mai could find it if she got it in her head that she needed to see it again.

Prince whined, looking up at Liam. The dog obviously wanted him to answer the phone.

"Okay," he muttered. Snow was beginning to sting his face. The wind had shifted and he turned his back to it. "Fine, I'll answer it."

It was a cell phone number with a New York City area code. Liam knew who it was before he answered. "You forgot to block the phone number," he pointed out to the caller.

"I intended for you to see the number," the old man on the other end of the line said. "So you could give me a call back, after you chat with your girlfriend. Disposable phones. Nearly untraceable. Wonderful technology."

"You found us through Anthony."

"Lucky break, him finding me."

"You shouldn't have done that to him."

"He shouldn't have been so stupid. He was a braggart. Had he kept his mouth shut and just chatted with me, he'd have probably learned all you wanted and I'd have been none the wiser."

Liam knew the Weasel was right; that didn't make it go down any easier. But he hadn't called to talk about Anthony. "Is this the part where you tell me that Corrato will lose more than a finger if we don't come up with the diamonds?"

The old guy chuckled, then coughed a smoker's cough. "Something like that."

Liam could just imagine the Weasel smoking a fat cigar

as he talked. "And if I tell you she...*we* don't know where they are?"

"If you told me that, I would tell you that would be a terrible shame, Corrato Ricci dying for a bunch of rocks. *My* rocks."

Liam picked up the dog. It was shivering, but he didn't want to take the phone call inside and risk Mai overhearing him. After a second's hesitation, he stuffed the rat terrier inside his coat. With the finger. "Corrato okay?"

"For now. Tough old bird." Machhione coughed again. "Got a lot of fight in him."

"What if they really don't know where the diamonds are?" Liam demanded. "What if Donato sold them years ago?"

"It's not about the money. It's about taking something that is mine. Old beef. Donato never sold them."

"How do you know?"

"Because the bastard told me so. Right before my guy held him down and I slit his throat," he growled.

"Guess your temper got the best of you. The truth of where your diamonds are might have died on the floor of that antiques store. You think of that?"

"You've got two days."

Liam knew the call was just about over. "Wait. What if we do find them? If I bring them to you, will you really let Corrato go?"

"I said it wasn't about money, but it's always about money. You bring the diamonds, you get the old man. You don't bring me the diamonds, the old man dies, slowly. Then we come for the daughter. You can get me at this number for the next two days. After that, I come find you."

Chapter 27

Liam found Mai and Kaleigh back in the shop. Someone had pulled down the blinds, but he could hear the wind. It tugged at the awning, making a flapping, groaning sound.

"You think you ought to hit the road?" he asked Kaleigh, depositing the dog on the floor.

Kaleigh and Mai both sat on the floor, the lamps around them, sorting through jewelry. Several small cardboard boxes were stacked nearby.

"Called my mom, told her the storm was really picking up and I didn't want to walk home," Kaleigh answered.

"She didn't offer to come get you?"

"And risk wrecking her new Volvo? No way. I'll just sleep in Mr. Ricci's bed." She slipped a silver filigree ring on her finger. "Mai said I could stay."

"That right?" He pulled off his jacket and tossed it over the counter.

Mai hadn't said a word. He looked at her until she looked at him. "You okay?" he asked.

"As okay as I can be, considering the fact that someone cut my father's finger off and gave it to me in a box."

Her face was pale, but she was hanging in there. She was strong, stronger than even she realized.

"He did it to make sure we understood that he meant business."

"Obviously." She pushed aside a pile of earrings and leaned back against the counter. "Where can the diamonds be, Liam?"

"What if he hid them a long time ago?" Kaleigh got up on her knees and opened a cardboard box. Prince wandered over and stuck his nose in it and sniffed.

"We've probably got enough jewelry out," Liam said, leaning on the counter, watching Kaleigh. "It's all got to be sorted, recorded."

"That's boring. I like seeing what you have in these boxes. It's like buried treasure."

Liam looked back at Mai. "How old were you when your uncle went to jail?"

"I don't know. Maybe nine."

"We have to think outside the box. If you were Donato and you knew you were going to jail, possibly for a long time, where would you hide them, where they'd be safe? Can you think of any contact you had with him just before he went to jail? Did you and your dad go to visit him? Did he come to see your dad?"

"Wow. Look at this!" Tearing away tissue paper, Kaleigh held up a silver and gilded bronze jewelry box. She looked at Mai. "Maybe your uncle gave your dad the diamonds and your dad didn't even know it."

Liam looked at Kaleigh. "That's good thinking." He squatted on the floor in front of Mai. "Think, Mai. Did anything new appear in your house around that time? 1987, 1988, 1989? Before your uncle went to jail?"

Mai pressed her hands to both sides of her head as if thinking hurt. "I don't know. I don't know. I don't want my dad to die. I don't care what he did. He's a good man. I swear he's a good man."

Prince trotted over and sat down next to Mai, looking up at her with his big brown eyes. Half-laughing, half-crying, she stroked the little dog's head.

"He's not going to die, Mai. We're going to figure this out."

"And then what?" She looked up at him, tears filling her eyes. "All those things my father wrote down, a lot of it had to do with crimes the Weasel committed or ordered committed. Find the diamonds, don't find the diamonds. We're both dead. If I was him, I wouldn't let us live."

Liam stood up and walked away, clenching his fists in frustration. She was right. This whole mission, it had been fucked since day one. Donato, Corrato, and Mai had probably been fucked since the day the Weasel got out of jail. Who was he kidding, to think he could save any of them? The day he had gone to Donato's funeral, he'd been on some kind of power trip. He felt guilty about all those kids he hadn't saved from the Gaudet brothers and somehow, in this idiot mind of his, he had thought that if he could protect Mai and the old man, he could somehow be absolved of his guilt. But there would be no absolution. There never was. Best thing he could do right now is put Mai and the dog out on the sidewalk and toss her the keys to her van. At least then the mafia wouldn't be roaming Clare Point.

But if there was no absolution, why did he do the things he did, roaming the earth, seeking evil, destroying it? If there was no hope, why did the Kahills, why did dear Kaleigh rise each morning, hoping that maybe today would be the day that God would determine them absolved of their sins? It was hope that made Liam, and Kaleigh and Fia and all of them, fight the good fight.

Which meant there was still hope that he could save Corrato and this beautiful woman sitting on the floor of his shop. It meant he had to try.

He grabbed Mai's hands. "Think," he said. She was cold and he rubbed her hands between his.

"You said you didn't see your uncle that often," Kaleigh said, sitting cross-legged, the old jewelry box on her lap. "So it must have been a big deal when you did. Maybe you just met for dinner, or—"

"Oh, my God," Mai whispered. She was staring at Kaleigh. "Oh, my God. I might know where they are." She shook her head, almost seeming dazed. "But Uncle Donato wouldn't have..." Fresh tears filled her dark eyes again. "He wouldn't have risked my life, would he? I was just a kid."

"Where are they?" Liam asked, looking into her eyes.

"It's probably crazy."

"Anything could help," he insisted, squeezing her hands. "You never know."

Mai took her hands from Liam's and reached over to take the jewelry box out of Kaleigh's lap. "He gave me a jewelry box for my seventh birthday. It's a beautiful, black lacquered box. It was Chinese, of course, not Vietnamese, but I loved it anyway. He gave me the box and a pair of tiny diamond stud earrings. I lost the earrings years ago." She met Liam's gaze again. "But I still have the box," she whispered.

"Of course. Always hide things in plain view," he said. "It's at the house?"

"They knocked it off my dresser. Remember? My jewelry was strewn all over my bedroom. They looked in the box. There's no diamonds in the jewelry box. I would have found them years ago."

The moment she said it, Liam remembered the lacquered black box. He had put it on her dresser after nearly stepping on it. "What year did he give it to you?"

"1987." She hugged the silver and bronze box to her chest. "I was seven in 1987."

Liam offered his hand to help Mai to her feet. "Kaleigh, grab the dog. We're going for a drive."

Liam, Kaleigh, Mai, and the Prince of Dogs stood in Mai's bedroom, staring at the jewelry box on her dresser. Their clothes glistened with melting snow.

"I've opened and closed that thing a million times," Mai insisted. "There's no way there can be diamonds in that box."

"Let me see it."

Mai seemed unable to move.

"You want me to get it?" Kaleigh asked her gently.

Mai shook her head. "No. I'll do it. I was just thinking that if those diamonds aren't there, my dad—"

"They're there, Mai." Liam said it with such certainty that even he believed it.

Kaleigh and Liam watched as Mai crossed the short distance to the dresser and picked up the box. She dumped the contents on top and turned to offer the jewelry box to Liam.

Liam grabbed it, set it on the dresser, and pulled a lamp closer so he could get a better look. Outside, he could hear the wind roaring and told himself that that was what made him nervous.

The storm outside was what was making his pulse beat too fast. The box was perhaps ten inches long, six wide, and six tall. It was some sort of wood painted in black lacquer, with leaves and butterflies painted in pinks and oranges and reds. The top opened to reveal a red velvet tray with a place for rings on one side, and on the other side, a tray for additional small pieces. He pulled out the tray, felt beneath the lining, and set it aside. He ran his fingers along the inside of the box.

Mai peered over his shoulder. "See what I mean? There's no place to hide diamonds."

Kaleigh, leaning over his other shoulder, reached out and closed her thumb and forefinger around the edge of one wall of the box. "It's just one piece. No hollow wall. What about the bottom?"

Liam placed the box back on the dresser and squatted so that he was eye level with it. Prince approached again, as if he needed to examine the box more closely, too.

Liam ran his finger along the front. On the bottom, there were two drawers. Each had a knob, but the outlines of the drawers were merely carved into the wood and painted over; they were obviously fake drawers, an illusion created for decorative reasons. There was no break in the wood.

"Fake drawers," Mai explained. "This one handle comes off all the time." She reached out, pulled it, and it popped off. "I just superglue it back on." She shoved it back in again.

Liam flipped the box upside down, then right side up. Still studying it, he reached under the pant leg of his jeans and took a knife from its holster. It wasn't his ceremonial knife; he wasn't permitted to carry that except when he was sent out to do the High Council's bidding. But it was a good knife and he kept it well-sharpened.

"Guns. Knives. You're a scary guy," Mai said, only half-kidding.

Kaleigh frowned, shaking her head. "He's really not all that scary; he just wants us to think so," she said in a pseudo-whisper behind his back.

Liam drew the knife along the indentation of the drawers, cutting through the paint. "Come on," he murmured. "There's got to be a drawer here." He dug deeper with the tip of the knife.

Mai looked at Kaleigh. "I don't think there's a drawer," she said, sounding defeated again.

"There's got to be a drawer," Liam insisted. He had

truly believed the diamonds would be here. He had thought he would find them and save the day. Save the girl. But there was no fake drawer. No diamonds.

"Break the damned thing!" Mai cried angrily. Reaching past Liam, she grabbed the box from his hand and slammed it as hard as she could on the hardwood floor.

At the sound of the shattering box, Prince yipped and sprinted for the door.

The thin wood splintered, leaving nothing but a pile of red velvet and black lacquer. "See? No diamonds," Mai said, tears running down her cheeks.

Kaleigh stood beside Mai, staring at the mess at their feet. She was wearing a pink knit hat with a pom-pom on top that moved with her. Slowly, she squatted and picked up one of the drawer pulls. "How big are these diamonds?"

"Not big. Around a carat each." Liam started to sheath his knife.

"Gimme that thing." Kaleigh opened and closed her hand. When Liam didn't respond at once, she flashed him a look that surprised him. It was one of authority. Authority he dared not challenge.

"Be careful," he warned. "You could—"

Kaleigh put the drawer pull on the dresser and, holding the flat side of the blade, hit it hard with the handle of the knife. The wood shattered and diamonds shot across the dresser.

"Oh, God! Oh, God!" Mai screamed, shaking her hands, then covering her face. "It's the diamonds!" She spun in a circle. "I can't believe it's really the diamonds."

As astounded as Mai, Liam picked up the other drawer pull from the ruined box on the floor and handed it to Kaleigh.

"You want to do it?" the teen asked, offering the knife to Liam.

"No. I think you deserve the satisfaction."

Kaleigh broke open the other drawer pull and Mai threw herself into Liam's arms. "Please tell me you can make this work. Please tell me you can save my father. Please, Liam. I don't care about the other stuff." She gazed into his eyes, wiping her nose with the back of her hand. "You know what I mean. I don't care."

Meanwhile, Kaleigh scooped up the diamonds, dropping them into the velvet tray they had left on top of the dresser.

Liam pulled Mai close to him, his heart pounding. "I can do this, Mai." He was so overcome by emotion that he could barely speak. He told himself it wasn't real, this ache he felt for the human in his arms, but it was real, all right. Painfully real.

"Now what do we do?" Kaleigh asked cheerfully, checking behind the lamp for wayward diamonds.

"First things first. We're taking you home. Then I'll contact the Weasel."

"Taking me home?" Kaleigh picked up the tray of diamonds. "I'm not going home."

Liam stared at the jewels; there was barely more than a thimbleful. It was hard to believe they were worth so much money, let alone human lives.

"You're going home." Liam walked into Mai's bathroom and came out with a medicine bottle from an old antibiotic prescription. "You're going home and then I'm making a phone call to Brooklyn."

"You have a number?" Mai asked.

"He called me. The Weasel." He took the lid off the bottle, took the tray of diamonds, and began to carefully dump them into the bottle.

"And you didn't tell me?"

"I didn't want you to be upset." He screwed the lid on tightly and added the bottle to the pocket already holding

Corrato's finger. "Let's go," he barked, suddenly anxious to get this over with. He wouldn't be able to sleep until he got rid of the damn diamonds, until Corrato was safe. "Kaleigh, get the dog." He walked out of the bedroom, flipping the light switch off as he stepped into the hall.

Kaleigh and Mai followed him.

"I can't believe you're making me go home, Liam McCathal," Kaleigh argued, cradling Prince in her arms. "I swear, you're going to owe me for this one."

Liam took the steps two at a time. "Put it on my tab."

Chapter 28

Mai stood in the doorway of Liam's bedroom, watching him reassemble the pistol that lay in pieces on his bed. It was late afternoon, but not dark yet. He was meeting the Weasel at four, in the park in the middle of town. There, he would exchange the diamonds for her father.

Mai held her father's dog to her chest and stroked his sleek, silky-soft back. She hated guns. They scared her. To her knowledge, growing up, there had never been one in their house. But maybe that wasn't true. Right now, it seemed as if her whole childhood had been a lie. She clung to the idea that her father hadn't known about any of the incidences he had recorded in that crossword puzzle book. She told herself he'd written it all down long after the fact, maybe just in the last few months. But she didn't really believe it. She knew he had known about some of that stuff, even if he'd never actually participated. So maybe her childhood hadn't been a lie, but it had certainly been a life based on deception. Corrato Ricci was not the man she had believed he was.

Even knowing that, she still loved him. No matter what he had done beyond the walls of their home, he had never been anything but good to her. She knew he loved her and she still wanted him safe in her arms, reunited with his little dog.

Mai watched Liam. "You said this was going to be a peaceful exchange. You're doing it in the park. Anyone could drive by. See you. See them. I don't understand why you need that if you're not expecting any trouble."

"I'm not *expecting* any trouble. The Weasel just wants his diamonds back. But just because I'm not expecting any trouble doesn't mean I shouldn't be prepared for it."

"I wish you would let me go. I feel awful, allowing you to put yourself at risk this way." She walked into his room, still cuddling the dog. "I've been thinking—I should make the exchange."

Prince whined and she set him on the floor. He seemed to sense something important was about to take place. Instead of sitting, or jumping up on the bed, he began to pace, his nails clicking on the hardwood floor.

"There's no way I'm letting you go, Mai."

"But this isn't your problem. And...and it might be safer for everyone if I go. If I take the diamonds. They're not going to hurt me because I'm not physically a threat."

She took a deep breath, painfully afraid of what was coming. What had been coming since the day they met. No matter what happened, whatever she and Liam had found together would soon be over. She could feel it in the air...in her heart. "You should let me do this and then we'll just go home, *Babbo* and I."

"You're not going." The gun reassembled, he pushed an ammunition clip into it and chambered a round. It made an ominous click.

She flinched at the sound. "I'm scared, Liam."

"No need to be scared." He got off the bed, pushed the gun into the rear waistband of his jeans, and gave her a quick kiss on the cheek. "I'm going to get your dad. You're going to stay here. If anything goes wrong, if your father and I don't come back in a reasonable amount of time, you call the number I left on the table. That's

Aedan's number. Just tell him I told you to call him and that you need to get out of here."

Their conversation was becoming surreal. Was this really happening? "Get out of here?"

"You don't need to worry. Nothing bad is going to happen. Promise." He slipped on his leather jacket. "I should go."

"It's still early. You're not supposed to be there for an hour." She heard the panic in her voice. "I don't want you to go." She bit down on her lower lip. She wouldn't tell him again that she loved him. What was the point? She'd said it. He knew it. It would only make the inevitable harder. Maybe for both of them.

"Come here." He opened his arms.

She fought tears as she wrapped her arms around his waist and laid her head on his chest. She could feel the heat of his body through his shirt; she could feel his heart beating steadily. She also felt the handle of the pistol he'd hidden under his coat. "There's no way I can thank you for what you've done." She lifted her head, opening her eyes to look into his.

He shifted his gaze to something distant in the room. "I need to go, Mai. I'll be back in a little more than an hour." He wiped a tear from her cheek with his thumb and kissed her hard on the mouth.

Mai clung to him, fearing this would be their last kiss. She took his mouth hungrily, never wanting it to end.

He pushed her arms down. "I have to go," he said firmly. "I want to get there before they do. Get my bearings." He hesitated. "This is what I do, Mai. I'll be fine."

She hugged herself, feeling more lost and forlorn than she had ever felt as a child. "I'll be right here," she told him. "I'll be waiting." She followed him out of the room, down the hall to the door.

"Lock it behind me," he said.

And then he was gone.

*   *   *

Liam felt a nervous energy as he went down the steps. He shook out his hands. This was a familiar feeling, one that went through him every time he went out on assignment for the sept. Despite the possible impending danger, it felt good. *This*, he could handle: the adrenaline rush of apprehension, the risk of threat to himself and others. This was far easier than dealing with the feelings that coursed through him every time he took Mai into his arms...every time she smiled at him.

Once this was over, once the diamonds had been returned to the Weasel and Corrato was safe, Liam decided he was going to go before the Council and demand to be heard. He was going to demand that he be granted his hearing. Immediately. And he wasn't going to take no for an answer. He was tired of their bullshit, of the stalling. If they weren't going to give him his job back, then he had a right to know.

What would he do, if that was their decision? He didn't know. The punishment would last a hundred years. This lifetime and the next. Maybe he'd become a mercenary for other vampires. It wasn't permitted, but there were ways around being officially sanctioned, if the operation was for a good cause. As in the human world, some things in the vampire world didn't fit neatly into square boxes. There would always be garbage that needed tending to.

But that would never happen. He had the highest kill count, the highest success rate in the sept. They'd be idiots not to let him go back to work. And it wasn't as if the Gaudet brothers hadn't deserved to die....

Liam took his time navigating the snowy street. They'd gotten about ten inches, and though the county snowplows had come through the day after the storm, there wasn't much activity in the town, even two days later. The Kahill vampires were all nestled in their cute little bungalows, drinking hot chocolate and playing Scrabble, enjoying the freedom the winter brought them. Without human tourists around, they were all relaxed. Almost carefree. At least as carefree as any vampire could be.

The park was about half the size of a city block. Arriving, he drove the perimeter. He and the Weasel had agreed to meet at the fountain near the southeast corner of the park. It could be seen easily from the road, especially this time of year when the greenery had died back. There were benches around the fountain, which had been drained for the winter and covered with tarps.

Liam decided to park on a street running perpendicular to the street where he assumed the Weasel would park. The guy was old. He wouldn't want to walk far, especially in the snow.

Liam was just getting out of his car when his phone rang. "Shit," he muttered. If it was the Weasel, if he wanted to change the meet—

It was his mother. He ignored the call.

She called again.

Then a third time.

"Ma, I'm busy," he said into the phone, halting on the sidewalk in front of Elly and Mac Hill's house. Someone had built a snowman. With fangs made from twigs. "That's why I didn't pick up."

"You should have called me. You promised to call me and tell me what happened at the Council meeting."

He watched a female cardinal flutter from one icy elm branch to another in the Hills' front yard. "You know very well my case hasn't been heard. Your spies keep you up-to-date. I figured I didn't need to."

"I don't like hearing news about my son from other people. Your brother calls me."

He rubbed his temple. "Ma, I can't do this now." Hearing a car, he stepped behind the Hills' pickup, parked on the street. He recognized the vehicle. He continued down the sidewalk. "Can I get back to you?"

"You won't."

He exhaled, suddenly feeling tired. Worn out right to his bones. "I will, Ma," he said gently. "In a couple of hours."

"See that you do."

Liam hadn't taken ten steps when the phone rang again. "Ma!" he snapped. "I said I can't talk."

"I'm sorry. Expecting a call, sonny?"

It was the Weasel. He knew the raspy voice.

It took Liam a split second to change gears and refocus. "Is there a problem?"

"No problem," the Weasel said. "I just wanted to make sure you had the girl with you. The daughter."

"No. No, that wasn't part of the agreement. There's no need for her to get involved. She never knew anything about her father's dealings with you."

"His dealings?"

"You know what I mean." Liam eyed the fountain and the surrounding area. He saw no unfamiliar cars. Nothing was not as it should be.

"I want the girl there. With you. Just so you don't get any crazy ideas in your head about keeping my merchandise."

Liam heard mumbling in the background, then a different voice on the phone. It was an old man, but not the Weasel this time. It was Corrato.

"Liam, that you?" Corrato said in a faint voice.

"Corrato. You okay? I'll be waiting for you. You understand? I'll be here."

"You'll be there." Corrato's voice cracked. "Take care of Mai. Don't let anything—"

"That's enough." The Weasel came back on the line. "Four o'clock, at the fountain. With the girl."

Liam stood staring at the phone for a second and then turned to walk back to the van. He didn't like this, but honestly, he was surprised the Weasel hadn't said to begin with that Mai had to be present for the exchange. The bastard knew very well that Corrato's daughter was as important to him as he was to her.

Fifteen minutes later, he was back at the park, this time with Mai. She wore a puffy yellow ski jacket and multicolored knit gloves. They didn't talk on the way. There was nothing to say.

He pulled in front of the Hills' house again and they got out.

"No, you have to stay," Mai said, when Prince tried to hop out. She grabbed him and sat him on the passenger seat. He tried to jump out again and she had to hold him back with one hand and close the door quickly, pulling her hand out at the last second.

Prince began to bark.

She walked to the rear of the van and looked back. The farther she got from the van, the louder Prince barked.

"Shut him up," Liam ordered, glancing around. They didn't need a vampire audience when this went down.

"I can't." She went back to the van window. "Prince, hush."

Liam watched from the sidewalk as the rat terrier put its paws on the window and barked wildly. "Jesus, Mary, and Joseph," he swore. He unlocked the door, using the remote on the key. "We'll have to take him with us."

Mai opened the door, grabbed the dog, and hurried after Liam. "Sorry," she murmured, tucking him under her arm. "He won't be any trouble. I swear it."

"We should have left him at the apartment." Liam pulled on his thin leather gloves.

"But my dad will want him." She didn't look at him when she spoke. "I don't expect you to understand."

They walked in silence for a few steps. "You stay behind me. You understand? They let your father out of the car, you don't go running through the snow toward him. This isn't a movie." He hadn't meant it to come out so harshly, but maybe it was just as well. Maybe it would make the good-byes a little easier.

"I'm not stupid, Liam."

It was on the tip of his tongue to tell her he knew she wasn't stupid. In fact, she was pretty damn smart. It was one of the things he liked about her. He kept his mouth shut.

They didn't have to wait long for the white panel van to appear on the street. Liam stood at one of the benches and watched the vehicle park. He reached into the waistband of his jeans to check the position of his pistol. He could feel Mai standing behind him, close to the fountain. He could hear her breathing.

The snow around them gave the whole place the surreal look of a postcard. *The beautiful village of Clare Point in winter—wish you were here.* It didn't seem like a spot that might erupt in gunfire at any moment, a street where ugly red stains could suddenly dye the snow crimson...where a sweet girl, a savvy senior citizen, and a nervy little rat terrier could end up dead in the blink of an eye.

There was an old man in a black wool overcoat and bowler hat in the passenger seat. He was a thinner, much older version of the photos Liam had seen online. The Weasel's face was nothing memorable; he was just another elderly Italian man. The driver was fairly young, a big guy with a flattop haircut.

The Weasel waited for the driver to get out of the van and open the door for him. The Weasel got out slowly. He had a cane.

The driver then opened the back door of the paneled van. From this vantage point, Liam couldn't tell how many were inside. Just as the driver reached in to help someone—Corrato, Liam assumed—he spotted movement to his left. He turned his head to see Jim Kahill dressed in a hat and coat, walking his greyhound.

Shit, Liam thought. He glanced at the van, then back at Jim. *Turn around,* he telepathed. *I'll explain later.*

But Jim and the dog kept walking right toward them, as if he hadn't heard him.

Liam returned his attention to the Weasel, who was now walking toward them. He was maybe forty feet away, taking his time walking down the sidewalk that led to the fountain that someone had shoveled. Corrato appeared from behind the van and Liam heard Mai inhale sharply. But she didn't move.

Prince growled. Mai hushed him.

The driver had his arm around Corrato. The old man, his left hand heavily bandaged, was walking under his own power, but barely. Even at this distance, Liam could see bruises on his face.

"Why'd you have to do that?" Liam demanded, unable to help himself. He motioned toward Corrato, speaking to the Weasel. "You didn't have to hit him."

"He wasn't cooperating. At first." The Weasel's eyes were such a pale blue that they almost looked white.

Liam felt his muscles tense and his fangs vibrate ever so gently. Anytime he was in the presence of evil, this happened. It was a natural thing to him, wanting to kill bastards like the Weasel. And it didn't matter that he had the Glock; his instinct was still to attack. To bite. To rip out the enemy's jugular, to savor the taste of hot blood, and let him bleed to death in the snow.

Liam flexed his fingers, willing his heart rate to slow. Jim and the dog were walking right toward them. There was nothing he could do to stop them at this point; he would have to just let them pass.

The Weasel stopped on the sidewalk, watching the man and his dog walk by. Liam met the mob boss's gaze. If Jim noticed anything strange going on, he didn't say anything. But how Jim could *not* notice, Liam didn't understand.

The Weasel and his men didn't know that no strangers came to Clare Point this time of year. They didn't know they were the only humans in town besides Mai and her father. But Jim knew.

"You got 'em?" the Weasel asked when Jim was a short distance away.

Liam held the old man's gaze as he reached into his pocket and pulled out the prescription bottle with the diamonds in it. Corrato and the driver had almost reached them.

The Weasel held out a gloved hand.

Liam held the plastic bottle tightly in his hand. "Let him go to his daughter first."

The Weasel hesitated for a second, then turned to his driver and nodded. The driver let go of Corrato's arm and Corrato made an exaggerated motion, jerking his arm away. He tottered toward Liam. Mai stayed put, as she'd been told.

The dog began to bark.

"I left my crossword puzzles in the van," Corrato said as he walked past Liam. "Four of 'em."

The old man was babbling. Liam just wished he would hurry the hell up. He didn't like Mai out here, vulnerable like this. Whatever happened to Corrato here, he'd brought it on himself, but Mai was innocent.

Liam heard her make a sound, something between a sob and a cry of relief. He ignored her; he ignored Corrato as he hobbled past him. He focused on the two in front of him.

"I'm glad we could do this in a civilized manner," Liam said, slowly offering the little bottle. "In the end."

The Weasel accepted it, hooked his cane over his wrist, opened the bottle, and dumped it into his gloved hand. He counted. There were twenty-two. Liam knew because he had counted them. The old man nodded, carefully pouring them back into the bottle, replaced the lid, and turned to leave.

It was over. It was done. Mai was safe; Corrato would live to have to explain to his daughter the things he had done and why.

Behind him, Liam heard Mai's voice, the dog barking. He felt the weight of the Glock in his waistband. The snow glimmered in the last rays of sunshine of the day. Out of the corner of his eye, he saw Jim, still walking away. As the Weasel walked past his driver, his voice was so soft, had it not been for Liam's superior hearing, he'd never have heard the whispered words.

"Kill them all."

Chapter 29

"**M**ai! Get down," Liam shouted, reaching for his Glock.

The driver drew a nine-millimeter pistol from under his coat, but not before Liam was able to squeeze off the first shot, then a second.

Everything seemed to happen at the same instant after that. The driver's left shoulder exploded with blood and gore. Mai screamed and Corrato gave a grunt as she pushed him into the snow. The Prince of Dogs shot forward, streaking past Liam.

Liam fired twice more. The Weasel had abandoned his cane and was running at a pretty good clip. Prince darted around the driver and went after the Weasel.

Liam dodged left, afraid the driver would shoot Mai or her father, trying to shoot him. Liam pulled the trigger, again hitting the driver in the left shoulder, but this time it was enough to drop the goon to his knees.

The Weasel was more than halfway to the van by then. Prince dove at his feet, snapping, and the old guy shouted with pain, trying to shake off the dog. He went down on one knee in the snow, the dog snapped at his hand, and the pill bottle tumbled to the ground.

That was when Liam saw the other guys pouring out of the back of the paneled van. Four of them.

Corrato had been trying to warn Liam. He hadn't left four *crossword puzzles* behind in the van. He'd left four *hit men.*

Shit and double shit. Liam had one pistol, only seventeen available shots, and he'd already pulled off at least six, maybe seven. In the confusion, he hadn't counted.

The four guys running at him fired and the ground exploded around Liam, snow and mud flying in the air. Bits of cement flew from the lip of the fountain."Get behind the fountain!" Liam barked.

He kicked the gun from the fallen driver's hand and went down on one knee, trying to use the driver's body to protect himself. The men from the van fired anyway, and Liam felt the impact of the multiple bullets as the driver was hit in the back and pitched forward.

This was bad. It was very bad. Vampires depended on surprise attacks, not guns. They were better with their fangs than with bullets.

As Liam tried to hold up the driver's body, now lifeless, he spotted Jim and Sugar running toward him. As he ran, the dog on the leash morphed from a greyhound into Arlan Kahill. And Jim wasn't Jim at all, but Aedan.

Liam would have smiled, had the situation not been so grim.

The line of men moved forward and Aedan and Arlan darted across the snow, around behind the men with the guns, moving faster than the humans could see.

"Prince!" Corrato cried hoarsely from behind Liam.

"Babbo! No! Stay down!"

Shoving the dead guy to the ground, Liam pedaled backward. Mai and Corrato were both lying facedown in the snow. He squeezed the trigger, hitting a guy square in the middle of his chest.

Aedan struck the one closest to him, tackling him like a

three-hundred-pound linebacker. He had him down in an instant, ripping out his throat with his fangs. The victim screamed in agony. In shock. With a flying leap, Arlan descended on another and the game was fair again.

The only guy still standing stopped and then began to back up, staring, in horror, at what had befallen his comrades. Arlan and Aedan were snarling and grunting as they sank their fangs again and again into their victims.

Liam heard the van start up. The Weasel had reached it. Running toward the road again, Liam took aim and fired at the guy still firing at him. It was a clean shot and the punk flew backward under the impact. Liam couldn't let the Weasel get away. If he did, Mai and her father would never be safe. Someday, when they least expected it, another van would pull up and then not even a tough little dog and a pride of vampires could save them.

The van pulled away from the curb, slid on the icy road, and shot forward.

Liam was torn between running after the Weasel and going to Mai. But there was no way he was going to catch up with the van, not now. "Mai, you okay?" he shouted over his shoulder. Then to Arlan and Aedan, "Enough!"

Aedan stood up, backed off, and wiped his mouth with his coat sleeve. Arlan did the same.

"Mai!"

"I'm . . . we're okay!"

Reaching the guy who had tried to run, Liam kicked away the gun that had fallen in the snow. Not that it mattered. He was already dead.

Prince ran a circle around them both, then darted in the direction of Arlan and Aedan. He plopped himself down in the snow and studied one and then the other carefully.

Panting hard, Liam walked back toward Mai. In the distance, he heard a police siren. People were beginning to come out of their houses to see what the commotion was.

He spotted Peigi's car as she slammed on her brakes and threw open the car door.

Liam walked slowly toward Mai and her father.

"Oh, God, who...who are they?" she moaned.

"Who?" he panted.

Mai sat up in the snow, still holding her father in her arms, trying to see past Liam. Her face was covered in wet snow, her eyes glazed with shock. "Those men. They came from nowhere. The ones who helped you."

"It's okay," he soothed, still trying to catch his breath. He tucked his gun back in the waistband of his jeans. He helped them both to their feet and walked them around to the other side of the fountain, blocking her view of the bloody carnage in the snow.

Corrato didn't seem interested in the dead men or how they had gotten that way. "Where's Prince?" he asked. "Anyone seen my dog?"

On the other side of the fountain, Liam took Mai's arm. "Mai, this is vital. When you were on the ground, when there was gunfire, did your father see anything?"

Her lips were pressed tightly together. She shook her head. She was shaking all over.

"What do *you* think you saw?" he asked, afraid of the answer. If she had seen too much, her memory would have to be erased. It wasn't difficult to do, but he would hate to do it if he didn't have to. The thought of marring her beautiful neck, of leaving it anything but pristine, actually brought him physical discomfort. He had refrained from biting her for three weeks, the short three weeks he had known her. He didn't want to have to do it now.

She glanced in the direction of the dead men, though she could no longer see them. "I...I don't know." She seemed afraid, but not of him. "It all happened so quickly. Did... did they have knives? There was so much blood. Who are they? Government agents?" She gazed earnestly at them. "Do those men work with you? *For* you?"

So she hadn't seen the morph, or the attack with fangs. Somehow, thank God, she had missed it in the fray. That was good. It was excellent. Liam hugged her with one arm. His other was bleeding. He had been hit, though when, he couldn't say.

"You're hurt," Mai murmured.

"I'm fine."

"My dog." Corrato turned slowly in a circle in the snow, holding his bandaged hand against his body. "Prince!"

The dog came flying around the fountain. Corrato bent down and Prince practically flew into his arms.

Mai stared at her father and the dog for a second. "I'm so glad you're alive, *Babbo,* but why?" she said, her words becoming more forceful as she went on. "We found the crossword book in the bank lockbox. Why did you do it? Why did you get involved in those terrible things?"

"Mai," Liam said gently. "Maybe this isn't the time."

"I have to know." She practically shouted her last words. This was a side of her Liam had never seen before.

Corrato regarded her for a moment. "I didn't kill any-one, if that's what you think," he said, sounding remark-ably cognizant, considering everything he'd been through over the last few days. He hugged his dog. "I didn't *do* much. A few things here and there, mostly launder money."

Tears filled her eyes. "But why?"

"Why? How do you think I could afford the house, the cars, your private high school, then college tuition? I was only an electrician, Mai. You deserved better than I could give you." His lower lip trembled. "Maybe if I could have given your mother those things, she wouldn't have left us."

She closed her eyes. "Oh, *Babbo.*"

"Hey, you guys! You okay?"

Liam looked up to see Kaleigh running toward them. "Arlan said I couldn't come 'til it was over. He made me wait in his truck." She reached Mai and threw her arms around her. "Thank God you're okay. I was so scared when I heard the gunfire." She glanced at Liam and made a face. "Eww, you're bleeding."

Realizing what she'd just said—before the part about him bleeding—Liam grabbed Kaleigh's arm. *Wait a minute. Arlan made you stay in the truck?* he telepathed. *You sent Arlan and Aedan here?*

Kaleigh gave him her best "you're an idiot" face. *I couldn't let you go up against them alone. What if they tried to double-cross you? Which obviously they did.*

"But how the hell did you know when or where we were going to make the exchange?" Liam demanded, looking at Mai, not even realizing he had spoken out loud.

"I didn't tell her," Mai said. "I would never have put her in danger that way."

I'm telepathic, you dummy.

Liam met Kaleigh's gaze again. *You were able to read my thoughts from a distance?*

From my house! Cool, huh? Kaleigh grinned.

He started to open his mouth, then closed it. He'd address this with Kaleigh later. Right now, he had to get these two out of here, before the entire sept descended on them. "Arlan's truck close by?"

Kaleigh nodded.

He put one arm around Mai and the other around Corrato. "Get them back to the apartment. Let no one in. The Weasel got away."

"Oh my God!" Kaleigh covered her mouth with her hand. "What are you going to do? He'll come after them!"

He took a deep breath, thinking about all the incriminating evidence back at his place written inside the pages of the crossword puzzle book. And there was no telling how much more Corrato knew.

Mai gazed into Liam's eyes.

"It's okay," he assured her, kissing her wet cheek. "I have an idea how to end this. How to guarantee you'll be safe forever. And I know the person who can do it."

As Kaleigh led Mai and Corrato away, he walked around the fountain, through the snow, past the dead bodies, and dialed Fia. People called his name, but he ignored them. Fia answered just as he picked up the prescription bottle out of the snow.

Late that night, Liam stood on the curb in front of his shop. Kaleigh stood beside him, holding the rat terrier. Fia waited in the car, but she kept it running. She couldn't tell him where she was taking them, of course, but he trusted her.

"We have to go, Liam," Fia said gently.

He leaned in the window. "You've got the diamonds?" he whispered.

"All twenty-one of them. They'll eventually be returned to the original insurer."

"And the Swiss bank accounts?"

"Already seized. But turning in that money will go a long way. That was probably Corrato's ticket into the witness protection program as much as the information he has for us." She offered a grim smile. She knew how hard this was for him, to let Mai go like this, to just let her disappear. She also knew not to bring it up. "Talk to you soon?"

Liam nodded, stepping back from the window. "Mr. Ricci." He offered his hand.

"I told you. Call me Corrato." He looked down at the snowy sidewalk. "Or whatever my new name will be." He looked up again. "I didn't mean to make such a mess of my life or my daughter's." His wedding ring shone on his right hand. "I'm not a bad man. I just made some bad decisions."

Liam thought about the Gaudet brothers. "We all have, sir." He squeezed his hand. "You take care."

"Good-bye, Mr. Ricci." Kaleigh hugged him tightly, her eyes teary. "Take good care of Prince," she said, passing the dog into his arms.

"You kidding? The Prince of Dogs takes care of me."

As Corrato got into the backseat of the unmarked sedan, Kaleigh hugged Mai. "Take care of yourself. I hope Fia finds you a great life."

Mai smiled through her tears as she hugged the teen. "You take care, too, and I meant what I said. I don't care what your boyfriend says, you have the right to decide."

"Oh, that?" Kaleigh laughed, wiping at her eyes. "Old news. I told him I wasn't ready and he said okay and we went for ice cream." She shrugged. "All that teen angst for nothing." She looked at Liam. "I'll let you be alone." She gave Mai another quick hug and then backed away.

For a second Liam just stood there, his arms at his sides. He didn't know what to do, what to say.

"I have to go," Mai said. "So can we just get this over with?"

He pulled her into his arms, crushing her against him, fighting the waves of emotion that kept rising again and again, threatening to knock him down. And if he went down, he was afraid he would never get up again. "Just because I didn't say it, Mai," he whispered in her ear, "*couldn't* say it, doesn't mean I don't feel it."

She pulled back a little, looking into his eyes. "It's not about the words, Liam. It's about what's here." She laid her hand on his chest, over his heart. "And I know what's here."

And then she kissed him. It was the sweetest kiss; she barely brushed her lips to his. "I'll never forget you," she whispered.

And then she was gone.

Liam stood on the curb and watched Fia drive away, fingering the single pink diamond in his pocket. It would be his keepsake, to remind him of Mai, of how she made him feel.

When the tail lights had faded, Kaleigh stepped out of the shadows.

"So now what?" he said.

"What now?" the teen repeated. "Now you suck it up and you go back to work, and you fight the good fight."

He stared at her in the darkness. "Back to work?"

"Peigi just texted me. High Council's in session tonight. You've been cleared in the Gaudet case. You'll get your new assignment in a day or two. And she convinced them that the mess in the park today wasn't your fault. I think Fia must have put in a good word for you."

Liam was stunned. "I'm cleared of the Gaudet case? But how can that be? I...I was never interviewed."

She smiled mischievously. "Actually, you were. No one ever questioned your ability to do the job, Liam, just your emotional well-being."

"No, you're mistaken." He shook his head, still confused. His arm ached from the gunshot graze Mai had bandaged. His head ached. It was spinning. "No one interviewed me."

"*I* did." This time her smile was smug. "Several times, in fact. Those little chats we had." She waggled her finger, pointing at herself, then him, then herself again. "Interviews. Once the report is typed up, you're welcome to see it. Just check with the Council secretary."

"I'll be damned," he swore. He studied her again, but with new eyes. This was a big deal for someone her age, being put in charge of an internal investigation. "But you never asked me what happened that night. What I did."

"I already had the report from the scene. I was just jerking your chain on the whole cannibalism thing." She punched his arm playfully.

Then her face changed and he was no longer looking into the eyes of a teenager, but the eyes of a woman. A wisewoman. "I knew what you did. I saw the photos." She rested her hand on the same arm she'd just punched. "Needless to say, Liam, you can't do that again. We don't mutilate bodies. Not even the bodies of men like the Gaudets. They're still God's creatures, made in His image."

He hung his head. "I've waited for this for weeks, and now..." He looked up again, thinking of Mai. "I don't know if I can still do it."

"Sure you can. Because you might have lost the girl"— she lifted up on her tiptoes and kissed his cheek—"but you found your heart again."

Liam was still smiling when he entered his empty, dark apartment. And as he made a bowl of Rice Krispies, he wondered if it was time he got a dog.